A Viking Queen's Legacy

Alfreða Jonsdottir

A Viking Queen's Legacy
Copyright © 2020 by Alfreða Jonsdottir

Tellwell Talent
www.tellwell.ca

ISBN
978-0-2288-4186-9 (Paperback)
978-0-2288-4187-6 (eBook)

Dedicated with love to my
granddaughters, Charlotte and Emily

Glossary

Icelandic/Old Norse vocabulary:

Afi – grandfather

Amma – grandmother

Ansatt snikmorders – Norwegian for hired assassins

Dagmal – day meal/breakfast. During the 9th and 10th centuries it was common to only have two meals a day.

Berserker – "serker" means coat or shirt and "ber" means a bear in Old Norse. Berserkers were an elite Viking army who wore animal skins in place of the traditional armour. According to legend they were naked under the skins. The Picts, meaning 'the painted people' in latin, covered their bodies in blue tattoos and fought naked, with the exception of chains around their neck and waist, which held their weapon and shield. They, like the bersekers, appeared to be in a frenzy while in battle, terrifying their opponents.

Bjarnahofn – Bjorn's harbour

Bless bless – goodbye. An Icelandic expression sometimes used to say goodnight.

Broðir – brother

Elskamin – my dear

Feilan – little wolf

Fotbitr – foot biter

Frænka/Frænkamin – aunt/dear aunt

Frændi – cousin

Fylgia – spirit

Goða nott – goodnight

Goði – chieftain

Hardfisku – hard fish

Hel – hell

Hellavitas – Oh hell

Hersir – a military commander

Hugr – a person's appearance

Jæja – okay

Jarl – earl

Knarr – cargo ship

Langafi – great-grandfather

Langamma – great-grandmother

Litla – little

Longphort – an Irish term used for a Viking port or fortress

Mamma – mother

Mærajarl – powerful earl

Nattmal – evening meal

Pabbi – father

Þing – assembly led by a chieftain, earl or king

Þingvellir – parliament or place of the assembly

Staðir – place

Skol – cheers (Scandinavians use this term toasting with a drink)

Sköll – Old Norse for wolf

Skyr – a form of yogurt

Suðreys – The Vikings referred to the Hebrides, Orkneys, and all the islands in that general area as the Southern Isles.

Systir/systirmin – sister/ dear sister

Takk/Takk fyrir – Thanks/thank you

Thrall – slave

Trolltunga – troll's tongue

Turf – a thick mat of grass and plant roots. Houses were made from turf due to a lack of trees

Velkommen – welcome

Viking – pirate. It was a name given to the men who pillaged and looted the monasteries and other places. Generally they all came from Scandinavia but the ones that left from Norway were known to leave from a harbour called Vik and were said to be "viking", ie, going on a journey of piracy. They were also referred to as Northmen or Norsemen as they were thought to have originate from the northern Scandinavian countries.

Wergild/Weregild/Wergeld – man payment. Blood money paid to a family for their loss.

Gaelic Terms:

Ard-Ri hEireann – High King of Ireland

Currach – a small round boat with a frame made from wicker which was usually covered in leather and propelled by a paddle. In ancient times butter was used to make it watertight.

Dubhlinn – the ancient Gaelic term for Dublin

Tanistry – chosen one. In ancient Ireland and Scotland the oldest son was not always chosen as next in line.

Character NAMES

Aud Unn, later Aud the Deep-Minded: The lead character, whose ambition and personality influence many of the events that occur. Youngest daughter of Ketill Flat-Nose and Ygnvild Unn, widow of Olaf the White, king of Dubhlinn, and mother of Thorstein the Red, king of Northern Scotland. Clever but ambitious to a fault, she dreams of creating a dynasty of kings.

Olaf the White: King of Dubhlinn, the unfaithful husband of Aud the Deep-Minded and father to Thorstein the Red. Also very ambitious and intelligent, he engineers the Longphort of Dubhlinn, creating a safe haven for the slave trade, making him a weathy, powerful man. His ambition for more drives him into creating a partnership with four other powerful men. Together they plan to increase their power and wealth; Olaf, Ivar and Ketill pillage and plunder other lands to accumulate the means to accomplish their goals.

Ketill Flat-Nose: Starts off as a Norwegian hersir under King Harold's command, then joins Olaf's partnership. Father of Aud the Deep-Minded, Jorund Unn, Thorunn Unn, Bjorn and Helgi. Husband to Ygnvild Unn, the mother of his children. No other children are known to exist. He negotiates the marriage contract of his youngest daughter to Olaf, to solidify their partnership.

Ivar the Hated: Cousin and partner to Olaf the White and cousin to Jon the Priest. Despised by many but especially by Aud the Deep-Minded.

Kjarval, king of Ossory: Another partner to Olaf. His ambition is to take over as the High King of Tara from his aging grandfather. He marries Aud's sister Jorunn and they have many children.

Jon the Priest: Cousin to both Olaf the White and Ivar the Hated. Loyal to Olaf but leery of his cousin Ivar; his respect for Aud's intelligence is evident.

Thorstein the Red: Son of Olaf the White and Aud the Deep-Minded, he becomes the king of Northern Scotland with the aid of his *afi*, Ketill Flat-Nose and Sigurd, *jarl* of the Orkneys.

Ygnvild Unn: Wife of Ketill Flat-Nose and mother to Aud, Jorunn, Thorunn, Bjorn and Helgi. The marriage contract between her daughter Aud and Olaf the White is her brain wave.

Jorunn Unn: Daughter of Ketill Flat-Nose and Ygnvild Unn, sister to Aud, Thorunn, Bjorn and Helgi. She marries Kjarval, king of Ossory, after he becomes the High King of Tara. They have many children.

Thorunn Unn: Daughter of Ketill Flat-Nose and Ygnvild Unn, sister to Aud, Jorunn, Bjorn and Helgi. She marries Helgi the Lean while still in Norway and they move to Iceland with her two brothers.

Bjorn: Son of Ketill Flat-Nose and Ygnvild Unn, brother to Aud, Jorunn, Thorunn and Helgi. He moves to Iceland and establishes a great estate there with all the wealth collected from his Viking days. He marries a local woman in Iceland and has four children.

Helgi: Son of Ketill Flat-Nose and Ygnvild Unn, brother to Aud, Jorunn, Thorunn and Bjorn. He moves to Iceland but with only one Viking expedition under his belt he cannot build an empire in Iceland like his brother. Fortunately for him he eventually marries a wealthy Christian woman who is an only child. He becomes a staunch Christian.

Nine Sisters: honouring the spirit of the northern sea
The Eighth sister: Unn (Udr) Frothing wave

Hail, Lady of the tides
Heartbeat of the ocean against the skin of land
Keeper of the memory of time,
Keeper of the dance of months and years,
In and out, back and forth forever,
The hourglass and the spilled sands,
Hail, Lady loved by the moon-god,
Silver track on the shimmering water,
Counting shells and sea urchins,
Counting stones and waves,
Counting lines in the sand,
You who understand the language,
Behind the numbered count of time,
Help us to remember what is important,
And, even more, help us to forget.

http://www.northernpaganism.org/shrines/
ninesisters/unn/honoring-unn.html
(Used with permission from Raven Kaldera@cauldronfarm)

Prologue

Hvammur in Dalasysla, Iceland about 900 AD

Arm in arm, two tall woman walked slowly along the river's edge, then veered off towards a wooden Celtic cross near a bluff of small trees. They bowed their heads for a moment in prayer then they both made the sign of the cross and turned to face each other.

"Are you feeling better now Vigdis? We have eaten and drunk a lot these last three days, so I am not surprised your stomach was upset. Your child is objecting to all that rich food, I should think."

Vigdis cradled her stomach and as they turned to head back towards the crowd of people she suddenly realized just how many were at this celebration. "Good lord! Look at all those people, it looks like the whole country is here for Olaf's wedding!"

The tall woman chuckled softly as she patted the young woman's hand. "No *elskamin*, only the important ones are here."

Vigdis understood exactly what she meant by that comment; all her life her *amma* had always stressed the importance of being connected to only the powerful and the wealthy, especially the families with the lineage that had a direct line to a royal family. She had married one of those important men, and now lived far from home in the north, on a large estate. There was no arguing with this strong-minded woman she was walking with, but she desperately wanted to tell her that she was homesick for Hvammur, the only home she had known in this country until her marriage.

Her happy memories of living on this estate filled her mind, but she was determined to make the most of her union. Maybe once she gave birth to this child she was carrying it would be different. Although generous, her man was not the kindest or the most thoughtful; he was ambitious and determined to make his estate the largest in the northern region. He was unlike Jon, the man that had raised her, the man she had called *afi*, who was the most thoughtful and kind man she knew. His only ambition was to make their lives—hers, along with her sisters and their brother Olaf's—comfortable, safe and happy. She knew that her *amma's* life had not always been easy before she married Jon, so for her sake she must be strong and make the most of her marriage. She had not seen her *amma* since his funeral. Instead of confiding her innermost feeling and her intense loneliness for Hvammur to this matriarch, she simply asked about the man she called *afi*. "Do you still miss *afi* Jon?"

"More than you will ever know. He was my husband for many years, but he was also my very best friend. He would have loved to have been here to see Olaf married to such a well-connected woman." She chuckled with this comment. "Funny how he always teased me about my need to marry you all off to such important and powerful men. Now Olaf being the youngest grandchild is the last to marry and I searched everywhere, as you know, to find the right match for our Olaf—Feilan, our little wolf, as you girls used to call him. My god how he loved to chase you and your sisters when he was but a young boy; he would growl like a wolf as if ready to attack." She chuckled out loud with the memory. "My extended search worked. I had to reach out all the way to the Hebrides, to my old friend Einar. There he found the right woman for our Olaf, Alfdis Konalsdottir, who is well connected and has a large dowry. Now that you are all married and settled with the right ones I can leave this life in peace."

"*Amma*, don't frighten me, you will be here for a long time yet."

"Maybe, maybe, but I am tired and ready to join Jon—I miss him so. Now enough of this maudlin talk, I have an announcement to make."

They walked back towards the enormous tent set up over all the feasting tables, only to be stopped by a young boy pulling on the tall woman's cloak, demanding her attention. "Now who can this be?" She turned in wonderment for his benefit, knowing full well just who that young voice belonged to.

"*Langamma,* it's me Hoskuld. Look what Olaf just gave me, my very own sword!", he declared with extreme pride.

She bent down stiffly and ruffled his hair. "That is because you deserve it, *elskamin.* Your Uncle Olaf tells me that you are growing up so fast and that he thinks you are very mature for your age. He has promised me that he will foster you as if you were his own son. I am confident that he will take good care of both you and your *mamma,* his beloved sister, now that your *pabbi* has left to go *viking.*"

"I miss *pabbi* very much!"

"Oh my dear boy—of course you do!" Straightening up slowly with her hand on her back, she said, "*Jæja*—give me your hand, young man and escort me to the head table. I have a very important announcement to make and I will need you to be by my side."

Together they walked hand in hand to the head table set facing all the others. Turning to young Hoskuld, she asked for his sword and banged the hilt on the table, then asked for silence, all the time holding onto his hand. He looked up at her with pride and a devotion beyond his young years.

"Thank you one and all for coming here to witness Olaf's marriage. Now that he is settled with the right woman I am asking all of you present here today to witness my legacy to my young grandson, Olaf son of Thorstein. I leave him this estate; all my lands, all the buildings, including all my loose wealth, which includes Thorstein's sword Fotbitr; all the grains; fish dried and pickled; all the animals; the many ells of cloth; and my trunks of silver and gold. My intention is to give him everything I own—today! All of you girls are well placed so you have no need of any more wealth. That is why two years ago, after *afi* Jon's funeral, I split up most of my jewels among you, so there would be no arguments when I was gone. I am announcing this to all of you and not just to my family—you are all my witnesses! I want no confusion after I have left this life and no arguments! Thank you once again for attending our joyous occasion but I am off to bed. I am tired after so much celebrating. *Goða nott—bless bless.*"

She bent over young Hoskuld and handed his prized possession back to him, thanking him for lending her such a valuable object. She kissed the top of his head, blessed him then said goodnight. Everyone watched as this tall, dignified woman walked away towards her stately *turf* house, to go to her bed. From the back she looked rather stout, but her hair was still beautiful and intricately braided showing her wealth and status. The ones that knew and loved her could see that she was more than just tired; she looked old, very old.

The next morning when she did not show for her morning *skyr* Olaf went to look for her. He knocked at the door of her sleeping room several times while calling out her name. Getting no response he slowly opened the heavy, intricately carved door and there she was, sitting up on her bed with the pillows still tucked behind her back. Her eyes were open but he could see that the life had gone from them. Looking around the room before he went to her, he noticed that her night candle had burned itself down to nothing. Olaf immediately realized that she must have died as soon as she got into her bed the night before. He lovingly closed her eyes then went back to the main room and asked his sisters to prepare her body. He quickly organized a funeral before all the wedding guests could leave.

His wedding celebrations were over, it was time to honour her, for them all to recall her acceptance of the "frothing waves" that had flowed through her long life, bringing good times and bad. Now was the time to tell her story, about both her pagan life and her Christian existence; but just how favourable were the gods? Olaf knew that there would be a full moon tonight and even though he had been baptised a Christian, he was surrounded by pagans and knew that this was a very good sign to all. Whether some believed that the moon was God's creation or that it was actually the goddess Unn's lover, Mani the moon god, was unimportant. He firmly believed that they were all present ready to embrace her *fylgia* and take her home to rest. Before any god, Christian or pagan, or any goddess that may be lingering nearby could take her soul, the family and friends must first gather together to say their farewells to this great lady. She had been their matriarch and their very own "keeper of the memory of time." She was gone but would never be forgotten; they would make sure that her story lived on for future generations.

Part I

Late spring about 853 AD

Ambition is putting a ladder against the sky.
Anonymous

Chapter I

Romsdal, Norway

The grey murky mist rolled in with the frothing waves and crashed against the steep granite cliff wall, spewing its angry mists heavenwards. Standing on the uppermost ledge known by the locals as the Trolltunga, or the Troll's Tongue, a cloaked stranger stood as still as a statue, studying each swell that slammed against the overhang. The mysterious figure, although appearing to be absorbed by the raging sea, stood and quietly whispered to the goddess Unn. *"Goddess of the frothing waves, I call on you to protect me from the sleeping giant who I know lives here, please do not let these violent waves wake him up. Remember my mother who is your biggest advocate and staunch supporter, who makes daily sacrifices to you."* As darkness descended, the cloaked figure turned and walked slowly away, only to return at the same time the next day and the next and the next.

As each day passed by the cloaked stranger returned and stood watch, as still as a statue, on the same spot on the sleeping Trolltunga. The regular rhythm of the frothing waves, like the constant pulse of a mother's heartbeat, continued to calm the giant instead of waking him. The goddess was looking over this still figure.

Although the troll remained deep in his winter slumber, the days were starting to change as the bright spring sun gradually warmed up the cold grey granite. This unexpected heat could change everything. The Trolltunga cracked and moaned as it steadily absorbed the sun's rays. This particular day was exceptionally warm, with only a few clouds scattered in the bright blueness of the sky. The vast horizon appeared to go on forever; it was possible to see for miles. Suddenly the cloaked stranger moved forward, stepping dangerously close to the edge of the precipice, and studied the view through the light mists that continued to rise upwards from the crashing waves. A dark spot appeared on the shimmering sky, which soon revealed itself to be a longship. Trailing close behind were several more ships, all with dragon heads. A fleet of six longships with their typical red and white sails and bright yellow banners sailed towards Trolltunga.

As the ships slowly wound their way closer to the mountain, the statue became animated; it jumped up and down, waved its arms wildly with vibrant excitement. The intensity of the motion knocked back the hood of the cloak to reveal that the statue was in fact a young woman with golden hair, such beautiful long hair, which the wind soon blew into a frenzy of knots. A pole appeared out of nowhere from her cloak, with a yellow silk banner. The very same banner and colour fluttered on the approaching ships' masts, all showing the identical symbol of Thor's hammer embroidered in red. As she lifted her banner it made a cracking sound in the gale force winds. She waved it back and forth sending a definite message of welcome. Then ever so faintly a female voice could be heard as the swift breeze carried it out to sea to greet the arrival of the long awaited ships.

"*Pabbi*! You have arrived at last! Freya has mapped out your destiny as before and allowed you to return safely home once more. Praise be to Freya, praise be to Unn the goddess of the frothing waves that carried your ships home, praise be to all the gods! You are home!"

The gods continued to watch over this enigmatic figure as her greeting increased in volume. Even her jumping up and down did not appear to wake the giant troll from its deep slumber. As soon as the lead ship entered the mouth of the fjord, she lifted her skirts and ran like a deer through the forest, using the pole with the yellow banner to whip aside any low-hanging branches. It was a long run to the village, but she had recently discovered a shortcut through this forest and before long her tangled hair was laced with stray leaves. As she neared the village by the harbour she heard the horn blow again. It would be her father warning her that he was very near to the dock, but then, so was she. Determined as ever to beat him, this time she felt sure she could do so because of the shortcut she had discovered. As she ran up to the dock her heavy breathing alerted the gathering crowd and they parted to allow her through. They were not surprised to see this young woman panting and running with great speed towards it; in fact, they expected to see her. This race to the dock was nothing new to any and they had all heard the same horn announcing the ships arrival.

The young runner was Aud Unn, the youngest daughter of their chieftain, Ketill Flat-Nose, who would be in the lead ship. She had finally beat him! The pleasure of winning felt magnificent; she savoured the moment as she eased her pace even more and sauntered slowly through her people, smiling to herself as she could see that her father's longship was not quite there. Her father would never let her win just for the sake of winning. She knew that she would have to earn it, and earn it she did. She had won at last!

As she waited and tried to catch her breath her two older sisters joined her, Jorunn Unn and Thorgerd Unn, along with their mother Yngvild Unn. They had two older brothers, Bjorn and Helgi. Bjorn, the oldest, had been roaming around Russia and pillaging for several years now with the same band of Vikings from Sweden. He had arrived home earlier during the first full spring moon, with his recent treasures to add to his already extensive fortune. *Pabbi* had promised he would arrive with that same full moon as normal, but this year he was later than usual. Bjorn arrived at the dock to greet their father with the family and was standing arm-in-arm with their mother. Helgi, the next oldest, had left the year before with another group of Vikings who were from Norway. They planned on making their fortunes somewhere in the Far East or Africa. No one knew for sure where he was but they did expect him home later this year, if not by the first spring moon of the next year. Aud Unn felt a nudge as her mother sidled up to her and whispered into her ear.

"I fear for you alone on Trolltunga. Every day I made sacrifices to Unn herself, goddess of the waves, to keep you from harm. Why your father approves of it is beyond me. You may think yourself brave but that giant troll is only sleeping and can easily be stirred awake by one of those violent waves that crash against his throat. The gods have been watching over you—thankfully!"

Then she stepped back and exclaimed, "Just look at you! Why do you persist in leaving all that hair loose? Your display of ignorance towards the gods can only get you in trouble. After greeting your father, go directly to the longhouse and tidy your face and hair—you look sweaty and unruly—and this time get Elsa to braid it for you! You know that the gods consider loose hair a sign of weakness; when hair is joined together into a braid it shows strength of character. Being stubborn, which you continue to be, does not represent strength. Your father may not care about your hair, because of your childish race, but I care what you look like. Tidy hair will show the people that you have a strong mind and the intricate braids will symbolize the wealth and power of your family. Remember always, you are a jarl's daughter—so look the part!"

Headstrong, the young woman just looked straight ahead, ignoring her mother's cares and concerns. Her mother mumbled to herself as she walked away to rejoin her son. "At least your older sisters listen to me! They never distress me as you do!"

"You are right mamma—pabbi will not care. Why can you not understand the bond we have? To show that you are jealous of your own daughter shows your own weakness, does it not mamma? Besides, if pabbi is not afraid of the giant troll why should I fear him?" She wanted to shout this out to her mother's receding back but bit her tongue, for she loved and respected her mother almost as much as her father, maybe even feared her wrath more than his. Also, deep down Aud feared the sleeping giant as much as her mother did.

Once the lead ship was secured to the dock and the gangway was launched, without wasting time Ketill Flat-Nose walked across it to greet his family, leaving his crew to secure his ship. He hugged his wife first, then his daughters. He approached Aud Unn last. "I finally beat you *pabbi*!" His youngest daughter couldn't resist; she was inordinately proud of her accomplishment. "Aud Unn, I have been expecting this loss for some time. You must have a new strategy, which we will discuss later. Well done!" her father replied.

Last he turned to his son Bjorn; while pounding his back, they stood for several seconds forehead to forehead—a traditional Scandinavian greeting. "Welcome home son, we have much to talk about." The crowd parted as Ketill and Yngvild walked side by side with Bjorn following them and the girls trailing behind. They all knew their place in the family hierarchy. Tonight there would be a magnificent feast for their father and his crew. Aud Unn knew that she would not get to see much of him at first but she was anxious to ask him why he was so late. There must be a story of adventure and intrigue there, so she was itching to have her father to herself. Her sisters never cared much about his adventure stories, not like she did; they only cared about the treasures he brought home. This booty would be put on display that very evening, when his crew would receive their fair share.

"Life is not fair! I wish I was born a man so I could go out on my own adventure, make my own fortune. Instead I have to learn to cook, weave, knit and sew and how to make a man happy. Pabbi will be more interested in talking to Bjorn first—not to me. At least as a man, even though I would have been the youngest son, I would have been included." Aud Unn pouted as she dragged her feet to the longhouse. That long run down the mountain had tired her out more than she thought possible, plus the disappointment and the disparaging words from her mother had dragged her down. *"Why can't mamma be as proud of me as pabbi is?"*

Once they passed through the carved main door Aud Unn went off directly to wash her face and tidy her hair as directed by her mother. Ketill and Yngvil Unn sat themselves down on their high seats as soon as they had entered, which indicated that the celebrations would now begin. The beer, wine and mead were poured immediately; soon the people were talking all at once and the noise became deafening. Ketill would have a few horns of beer first then he would quiet them all down and give his thanks to the gods. Only then would he start to tell his people some of his adventures. "There is plenty of time before the stories start—I always have to wait" mumbled Aud Unn as she slipped into the room she shared with her sisters.

She threw her cloak on her bed and called out for her maid, Elsa, giving her orders to fetch some warm water for her to wash, then to fetch her comb and a fresh tunic. Tonight she would have Elsa braid her golden locks just to please her mother. Normally, she avoided braiding her hair because it felt too heavy and constricting; if only her mother could understand her need to be free. This youngest daughter was also rather spoiled and maybe a little too proud of her thick blond hair with its natural curl and chose to let it hang loose in order to show it off. *"Tomorrow mamma I will have it washed with lye soap and leave it loose like I prefer."* When it was freshly washed it shone as bright as the sun and people could not help but admire its luminous glow.

Defiant as ever she got up to leave her room as soon as she heard the familiar call to gather. Ketill's slave had effectively got the crowd's attention when he struck the gong a second time; everyone stopped talking as their chieftain rose to speak. First Ketill nodded his approval to his slave who remained standing beside the vibrating gong. This gong, a large flat circular bronze disk, was a treasure he had brought home from the Far East when he was roaming as a Viking in that part of the world. He treasured this gong and found it to be a useful tool to silence the masses or to call them to gather.

He held his arms out to everyone as he scanned the crowd; when it became totally quiet, then and only then did he address them. "Welcome! My good men, I know you all feel the same as I do—it is good to be home! Our journeys this past winter were tough but eventful. We were successful in tracking down many of King Harold's enemies and in a few days we will prepare to sail to Hordaland so we can report to our king. I am sure that he will be grateful to all of you. Tomorrow will be the first full day back and as usual I will make myself available—all day—to hear any disputes from my people, so pass this on to your families and neighbours."

"It is too late in the day to make a sacrifice to the gods so we will hold the ceremony before the *Þing* in the morning then afterwards there will be another feast, this time for all the village. I am thankful to be home with all my crew intact and to be back with my family. In the morning I will give my blessings and gratitude to Odin, Thor and Freya with a sacrifice. After the village feast tomorrow night my bard will glorify our journey. Now drink up, enjoy the feast that my good wife and her *thralls* have prepared for you. Enjoy."

Aud Unn slipped into the hall while her father was still speaking. He gave her a nod which made her feel special; he had noticed her. Threading her way through the mass of people she sat down beside her old friend Einar instead of joining the family.

"Why do you not join your sisters, Aud Unn?"

"They annoy me with their greed, Einar. It is always about what father has brought them."

"Isn't it more important to show your father respect by joining the family?"

As she reached for a chunk of meat she replied to Einar's comment. "Yes of course, you are right as always. I will later, but right now I am starving and the food is here and you are here. I need to speak about Johann, your brother and my intended. As you know he promised me that he would be back after the winter away raiding with my brother Helgi and their Viking friends. Every day I miss him and it is only with you that I can speak freely of him."

"I understand, Aud Unn. I too look forward to my brother's return."

With a pout on her lips she confided her inner thoughts to her oldest friend. "It is so unfair that I am a female and cannot go on adventures like my brothers. I would have gladly joined Helgi and Johann on their exciting journey. As you know, my father has never approved of your brother as a match for me, and now that he is back I am concerned that he may have found someone else. Johann was and always will be my first choice; he is the man I want to live my life with. I have left sacrifices to the gods and asked that he come home safely and with much wealth so he can claim my hand in marriage. Tell me, what else can I do, Einar?"

"There is nothing else you can do, Aud Unn, other than to keep your faith in Freya's destinies for you and for Johann. Hopefully she has both of your life journeys intertwined. I too pray to our gods that Johann is still alive, for all our sakes, and that your father has no one else in mind for you."

"*Takk*. You always make me feel better, old friend. Now tell me if this rumour I overheard is true—that you will be joining my father's troops after the seeding is completed this year."

Einar just nodded his head as he drew a long draught of beer from his horn.

Smiling her approval, the pout disappeared from her lips. "Soon you too will desert me and I will be left here with all the women, *thralls* and all the old men and children! Life is truly unfair, but I do understand what an honour it is for you to join my father's army."

Aud Unn rose up to join her family while still chewing on a meat bone dripping with grease. Einar chuckled as he nudged her with his elbow, "You really should have been born a man!"

Chapter 2

The next morning a cow was brought forward as a sacrifice to the gods. It stood stoically as if it understood the honour that was about to be bestowed upon it. Ketill, a farmer first, wasted no time and ordered the slave to slash its throat before the poor animal could sense its impending death. With the help of the other slaves, the ropes were tied around its hind legs, and together they struggled to hang it high enough up the tree. A container was quickly positioned under it to gather the dripping blood, the sacrificial gold of the local pagans. As it flowed into the bucket Ketill made his usual incantations to the gods. After their *jarl* had given his thanks and the sacrificial cow had bled out, the slaves removed the heavy container, which was filled to the brim with the cow's blood. Then with much difficulty they dropped the massive animal onto a cart below. It took several slaves to push the heavy load to a specially prepared pit, where it would be skinned, butchered and roasted all day in order to feed the mass of people later that evening.

While the slaves pushed the prized cargo away Ketill gathered his people and went into the longhouse where he settled himself on the high seat alongside his wife. He honoured her by allowing her a say at the *Þing*—not just because she had a good mind and often gave him sensible advice, but also because she was always here while he was not. In all likelihood she would have knowledge of some, or maybe even all of the complaints that would be presented today, from several sources. This made his wife a valuable asset. Both Bjorn and Helgi, being men, were allowed to sit with them, while the daughters, female and unmarried, sat elsewhere. Her parents felt that it was not their place to attend a Þing until they could sit beside their own man—and then only if he allowed it. Children were well-loved here and were normally allowed to run about freely, but during an assembly none could come in because their boisterous natures would disrupt the discussions. All parents understood this and accepted the ruling.

An exception was made for Aud Unn as a young girl when she revealed her interest in their laws and proved beyond a doubt her understanding of them. As a compromise, a wattle screen was placed behind the high seats and behind it was where she now settled herself, unseen by any local who approached her father and mother with their complaint. Even though they all knew she was there, no one ever complained. Here she could relax on some skins in privacy, sip some wine or mead and nibble on some flat bread and cheese while listening to them as they governed their people—handing out advice or settling disputes. She had never broken her promise to them to remain as quiet as a mouse.

Once her father was settled, he raised his hand to the law speaker who then stood up and recited their charter—verbatim. Their culture had no written language; everything was handed down orally. The law speaker, a very valuable asset to any chieftain, *jarl* or king, would have been chosen for his ability of total recall and even then would have been trained for years in order for him to be able to accurately communicate their body of laws verbally. It would be a long day, she thought to herself, but then she appreciated all the perplexing details of governing—unlike her two older sisters, who found it all so boring. Being female could be so frustrating at times, but she felt strongly about attending these assemblies so she appreciated her parent's concession to her demands.

After many discussions her father was finally able to rest until the feast. Later, he stood at the main door and as his people entered he greeted them personally, making a mark on each forehead with some of the blood gathered from the sacrificial cow. With this action he honoured his people as he bestowed the blessings of their gods on each one. The bulk of the blood had been sent to the cookhouse where it would be made into blood sausage. Nothing was wasted. Once marked with the blood, the people found their regular spots as they gathered together in the great hall for the spring feast. Ketill's personal greetings made for many loyal followers. This style of leadership he had learned from his own father, Bjorn Buna, who had made his fortune and lived a long life by being fair and honest. Tomorrow Aud Unn would finally be able to speak with her father alone, although part of her dreaded it in case he had found her a husband other than Johann Thorvaldsson, Einar's brother and her chosen man. Last night Bjorn got to stay up and talk with his father alone and according to her mother they had much to drink and much to talk about.

The very next morning after the village feast Aud Unn was summoned by her father. He asked that they walk about the village as they talked. She knew that this would not be conducive to good conversation as there would be many interruptions but she agreed; anything to have her father alone. She found him standing outside the longhouse talking with his law speaker. She slipped her arm through his as she gathered her skirt up with the other, making ready for their walk. Flipping her freshly washed hair as she looked up adoringly at her father, she then turned and greeted the other man with a respectful tone in her voice. "Good morning Magnus. May the gods give you good health and a long life."

The law speaker acknowledged her greetings then left them alone.

"I finally have you all to myself *pabbi*; now tell me why you were so late this year."

"Well as usual it was because of a skirmish with some Norwegian rebels that have been outlawed by King Harold's campaign to take over all of Norway. As his *hersir* it is my duty to find these outlaws, to give them chase, to capture them or even kill them if they resist. If not possible to capture them or rid ourselves of these rebels, then it is crucial that we report to King Harold on their probable locations and their identities so other convoys of ships can track them down"

"Was it dangerous?"

"No—no—not this time. Actually the end result was that it was an eye-opener for me. We came across these outlaws while we traveled towards the Orkneys in the north of Scotland. Once we spied them we gave them chase but later gave up; they had too big a lead on us. We sailed back to the Orkney Islands, which of course was our original destination, to make repairs to our ships before our return to Norway. While there I hoped to discover any information about this fleet of longships. I had my suspicions that that was where they had been all along and we had just missed them, which later proved to be true. Just think how close we were to catching them there—if we were just a few hours earlier! Alas we did not—if it was to be our destiny to have caught them there we would have ended up in a battle and it turns out that would not have been a good thing. In life, my daughter, you will discover that there are turning points and our destinies can be affected by a few hours delay—sometimes it is good and sometimes bad."

"I don't understand, *pabbi*."

"Listen to my story and you will. A few days later those same Viking ships managed to slip back into the Orkneys without us knowing. It turned out as I had suspected, that these outlawed ships do have a safe haven there plus the protection of the people including *Jarl* Sigurd himself. You have heard of his brother, the famous Rognvaldur "*mærajarl*" Eysteinsson, who is King Harold's favorite man. When the king made this legend the *jarl* of both North and South More in Norway, Rognvald gave up his leadership of the Orkneys to his brother Sigurd, who, as it turns out, is a much easier man to deal with and much less greedy."

"Everyone in Norway knows of the famous Rognvald the Powerful, *pabbi*. But why is his brother, Sigurd, giving his support to these rebels?"

"Patience daughter, I will get to that. Sigurd broached the subject of talks with this rebel who had slipped in undetected by our guards and not surprisingly, he turned out to be the leader of the ships that we had just given chase to. Because it was Sigurd himself who asked I did agree to talk with this rebel leader, who was none other than the famous Olafur Ingjaldsson, better known as Olaf the White, the king of Dubhlinn. Olaf explained his position, clearly and honestly, saying that he was in partnership with an Irish king called Kjarval, king of Ossory, and is actively looking for another partner.

Remember, I have explained to you before about Ireland. This country has many kings, like Norway used to be before King Harold. Some of these Irish kings or chieftains want the Norse out of their country, whereas some are happy that they are there and they partner with them to help maintain control of their own regions. Apparently this Irish king, Kjarval, not only wants to protect his holdings, he wants to become the High King of Ireland, the king of Tara. Olaf had agreed to help bring this about and that was why he was in the Orkneys, trying to convince Sigurd to become his new partner. Sigurd explained his position on this deal; he said that he had made a half-partnership with Olaf by promising him a safe haven whenever he was in the northern islands of Scotland, especially the Orkneys.

He stated that he was simply not interested in sailing that far away to other countries anymore, but Olaf still required a partner who was willing to pillage in other far-off lands with him. Not only does he need to fill his own coffers, he needs to raise the funds required to make a man like King Kjarval the High King of Tara. To accomplish this feat it will take a great army of men; this great army will need to be fed and eventually paid. And trust me, Olaf is not doing this from the kindness of his heart. Once Kjarval is the king of Tara, he will have access to a great power. He will have a partner who will bestow honour and respect on his position as king of Dubhlinn."

"Are you interested, *pabbi,* and if so why would you be? I thought you were working for King Harold?"

"It all depends on my meeting with our great King Harold Fair-Hair. As Olaf explained he is actively looking for a man to build a stronger partnership with, not only to maintain his power in Dubhlinn but to also help his other partner, this King Kjarval, become more than he is now. Like *Jarl* Sigurd, this Irish king will not leave his land and go *viking* with him but this new partner he seeks must be willing to go on raids in England and France, where there is much wealth to pillage. He felt that this new partner's power should also lay in the northern regions as it would give them another escape route besides Sigurd's offer of asylum. He claimed that he had heard much about me, that he knew I was Harold's *hersir* and that I had secured control of the Hebrides and the Shetland Islands in his name. He did not know about the Isle of Man as that is not common knowledge yet, but he did suggest that I should keep the islands for myself."

Aud Unn was aghast at such a plan. "*Pabbi*! Would you do such a thing?"

"As I said before, it all depends on how King Harold greets me in a few days. Olaf said that he had heard that there was much discontent amongst Harold's men and even Sigurd encouraged me to join forces with this Dubhlinn king. I stayed with the *Jarl* longer than I had planned only because I wanted to get to know him better, to try to understand why he was going against King Harold of Norway and his own brother Rognvald. I also needed to learn more about this outlaw, this warrior-king of Dubhlinn. Plus a couple of our ships needed repairs before we could head home, so I had a good excuse to remain longer than planned. Now you must never speak of this to anyone. Do you understand?"

"Of course *pabbi*. This news may be shocking to me but never doubt my loyalty to you."

"If King Harold hears that I had private words with Olaf under Sigurd's protection he will distrust my motives, as well as Sigurd's. My strategy right now is not to tell Harold where this Norwegian outlaw is or what protection Sigurd has promised him. I have much to negotiate with our king of Norway first but I am hearing many distressful stories of his broken promises and not just from *Jarl* Sigurd."

Just then Ingi the blacksmith walked up to Ketill. "Come to my shop, my lord, as I have made a beautiful sword that you would be proud to own. Aud Unn, join us; I know you too will appreciate the beauty and craftsmanship."

They followed him to his place of operation, where the central fire was giving off a great heat. He opened a chest and lifted up a sword and handed it to his leader as if it were a cherished treasure. In truth any sword is a venerated treasure; only the very wealthy can afford such a weapon. The axe and spears, although quite effective, were the only choices available to most warriors, along with small knives which would be used in close hand-to-hand battles.

"This blade is double-edged as a good quality sword should be, and is the length of a man's arm so you can hold it with just one hand while still holding onto your shield. As you can see, it comes to a fine sharp point which will kill a man immediately. It has taken me many moons to make this beautiful prize. Now tell me, what do you think? And would you care to buy this from me?"

Aud's father accepted it as if it were indeed a treasure. He went into a warrior's stance, pretending he held a shield as he whipped the air with his moves. Then he examined it thoroughly. "The inlay on the pommel is quite incredible, Ingi."

"It took me much time to cut the fine channels to create this pattern in the iron pommel. Then I hammered fine silver and gold wire into them to create this herringbone pattern. The black iron makes the design stand out. The pommel and this upper guard were fashioned out of one piece of metal so there is no fear of it ever breaking apart. The tang was hot peened and polished with whale oil until it now looks like a black gemstone instead of just iron."

"The blade is magnificent with all the typical Nordic designs and there looks to be runes carved into it. How did you make it feel so light? Is it solid iron like the hilt?"

Aud Unn ran her hand over it as her father held it up to her.

"No—not iron. Iron blades are heavy and they do not last long. They rust faster from the exposure to our salty seas. My slave from Francia is a very talented blacksmith and has melded strips of different metals together, not just for the pattern but for strength. It is stronger and lighter than pure iron will ever be; it is a warrior's weapon and not just for ceremony or for looks. Look at the runes—you can see that I have named it *Fotbitr*—a fearful sword-name for a worthy warrior. By giving it a name, the sword will gain much power and recognition for its owner. Also there is my name in runes on the other side of the blade. With a famous man such as yourself carrying one of my swords, I hope to make a name for myself and become as well known as Ulfberht from Francia."

"What is your price for this superior object?"

"A half-mark of gold. I do believe it will be a valuable addition to your arsenal of weapons, my Lord, and something valuable to hand down to one of your sons or maybe even to one of your daughter's sons."

"I agree Ingi, let us shake on it. *Takk*. Take it to the longhouse this evening and I will see that you are paid."

They each spit into their hand before shaking; the deal was sealed. "*Takk fyrir Jarl* Ketill. As you know, Gisli son of Thorvold's work with leather is outstanding and he will make the perfect sheath for this sword. Do I have your permission to take it to him first in order for him to make proper measurements?"

"Of course."

Aud Unn followed her father out of the hot house, fanning herself with her hand once out in the fresh air. "That place it much too hot for me. How does Ingi survive in such heat, *pabbi*?"

"We all get used to our surroundings, *elskamin*. But that is indeed a treasure I will be proud to carry. Now tell me all your news."

"*Pabbi*, nothing changes here. I still anxiously wait for Johann son of Thorvald's return to fulfil his promise to marry me."

"You know that this marriage does not have my approval and may never have my approval. He is just a lowly farmer and you deserve to be married to a *jarl* or even to a king, Aud Unn. Remember your place, you are a *jarl's* daughter."

"What if he returns home a wealthy man and is able to buy a *jarldom, pabbi*?"

"That will never happen, especially after raiding for only one winter. It will take many raids and many years to achieve power and wealth such as you speak of."

Part of her did not want to know if he had someone in mind for her, but the part that needed to know won out. "What then, *pabbi*—what are your plans for me?"

"Right at this moment I do not have any plans for your future; there is time, you are still young. My own future may not be as stable as I previously thought. As I said before I am becoming more and more distressed hearing about King Harold's broken promises. You have to be one of his inner circle of friends to gain any wealth or power and I always thought that I was part of that group. Now I am not so sure. Sigurd warned me that a few very powerful men, including his own brother, are trying to take the control away from the rest of us. If this is the truth of the situation here in Norway, King Harold could easily reduce my station and I know from past experiences that he is capable of anything. Once upon a time I had great respect for this man but one must never build a life on dreams—flimsy dreams at that—always be prepared for the worst. You and I are much too smart for that *elksamin*—so do not let your heart rule your decisions—ever! That includes your decision about Johann!"

"Yes *pabbi,* I do understand what you say, but it is easier said than done. Johann is all I have ever wanted—I love him and he loves me!"

"You are still young and the young always follow their hearts rather than their heads."

They returned to the longhouse where they shared some mead while they continued their discussions. Aud Unn was relieved that no other name was ever brought up for a marriage proposal.

Ketill did not stay long at his village; it was time for him and his men to report to King Harold in Hordaland. Aud Unn's friend Einar was excited to be asked to join them on this trip, which meant that he would get out of the seeding process. Her happiness for her friend as well as her disappointment that he had left her behind was evident as she mumbled to herself while she watched them all leave. *"Just old men, women, children and thralls left to talk with—what a boring life I lead!"* She walked very slowly back to the longhouse where she tried very hard to concentrate on her many womanly duties, weaving being her least favorite. It was so repetitive and she always managed to mess up the pattern. Whenever she went to her weaving her mother miraculously appeared and hovered over her! "Why can't one of the slaves just do it *mamma*? Why do I need to know this boring craft?"

"This boring craft, as you call it, brings in much wealth to our household. Never disparage these activities; once you are a lady of your own longhouse you will not only need to teach your own slaves all the crafts required to run a large estate but be knowledgeable enough to catch their mistakes—just like I am finding all of yours!"

"Mamma, I am sorry. I know that I am such a disappointment to you but I really do realize how important it all is; it's just that I am so bored and worried for Johann and Helgi."

"Concentrate on this *elskamin*; believe it or not it will help you to forget your worries. I too had to learn; you have no idea how many days and nights I have worried for your father's life, how many sacrifices I have made to the gods in his name and for my children. Your stressful days and worries have yet to begin. Try singing to yourself while you work. You love to sing."

"Yes of course *mamma*, you are right as usual."

"Daughter of mine, I have much experience while you have years ahead of you to live and learn."

She set her sights on her weaving while quietly humming a tune and with this song in her head she finally managed to concentrate on this new pattern. Before she knew it the call for the *nattmal* broke through her thoughts. The best part was that the day had passed by quickly and she had put in a good day of labour. *"As usual—mamma was right!"*

Chapter 3

T he morning quiet was shattered by a horn blowing—warning the village of approaching ships. Some of the villagers including Aud Unn gathered by the waterfront to see if they were friend or foe. She immediately recognized the banner and shouted out to her mother, then ran onto the wooden dock.

"*Mamma*—it is Helgi's ship! They have returned much earlier than expected!"

Her mother and sisters rushed out of the longhouse to join her on the dock as Aud Unn struggled to contain her excitement, telling herself *"Johann will soon be here. Einar will be so disappointed that he is not here to greet his brother. I do hope all is well? I wonder why they have returned so early in the year."*

More people started to gather once they realized the ship was a friendly one. Aud Unn was hopping from group to group, excitedly exclaiming that Johann and Helgi were coming home. Then she saw Helgi and only Helgi standing in the ship with a few other men. "Where is Johann?" she shouted out to him. He just waved at her but said nothing. Fear gripped her heart. *"Freya—what have you done? I prayed so hard to you and to Goddess Unn to keep his destiny in safe hands. I made many sacrifices to both of you! Why have you let me down?"* Her heart was racing too fast by the time Helgi finally came ashore. She ran to him, hugging him tightly, and whispered into his ear. "Where is Johann, Helgi? Please tell me he is safe."

"I am so sorry Aud Unn—Johann is in Valhalla drinking and carousing with Odin."

His devastating news shocked her to her core but somehow she managed to get her words out. "How—how did—this happen? I prayed—so hard—to keep him safe. What happened? How is this possible?" Suddenly all her repressed sobs exploded from her as reality hit. Johann was no more!

Helgi held her tight as he whispered into her ear. "Shhh, *systirmin*. I will explain it all later. Hold your head high. You must not show such weakness to our people."

Thankfully for the family, her sorrow choked her; no more words were forthcoming from this talkative younger sister. Instead of listening to her brother's advice, she hung her head, allowing her mop of hair to cover her tearful face while clinging to her brother's arm as he greeted his mother and his other sisters. Aud Unn had not tied her hair back as her mother would have preferred—now it had become an effective mask, but her mother never missed the silent emotions of her children. Her deep distress was very evident, but being a wise woman Yngvild Unn knew enough to remain quiet for the moment and not draw attention to her. Once inside the longhouse Aud Unn flipped her hair back and demanded to know what had happened. "Do not put me off any longer brother, I must know what happened!"

Her mother stepped forward and wrapped her in protective arms. This show of motherly love broke her strength and she sobbed wildly into her mother's shoulder. Helgi shushed his sister once again; he could not handle all the crying, and claimed he needed to sit down, demanding a horn of mead before he could explain. Through her sobs she shouted at him, "Helgi! You are being too cruel!"

"Ok—ok—*systir*—here goes. Last fall we raided in a country called Spain, in a beautiful city named Seville which we took over in only a few of days. This city has so many riches; at first, life was incredible there but unfortunately that was short-lived. We only managed to hold it for one full moon. The people there are very religious, but different from Christians. They believe in the same one God as the Christians, but their saviour is not Jesus. It is someone called Mohammed and they call themselves Moslems; their religion is called Islam. They pray many times a day to something called Mecca. They are a very strange lot of people, so different from us, with much darker skin and hair than we have. The men dress like women in flowing gowns made of colourful silks, or made of plain silks in white or black. They wrap their heads in cloth and call them turbans. The women are beautiful, but they cover their whole bodies including their face according to their religious laws, also in silks of many different colours. But their food—*jæja*—such wonderful food! Strange fruits and vegetables—and their spices, I have never seen or heard of any of them before! If only we could have held on!"

"Johann—what about Johann?" Aud Unn cried out to him but Helgi held his hand up to her.

"Have patience—let me explain! *Hellavitas, mamma*—tell her!" Ygnvild Unn held her daughter tight and cooed loving words into her ear. This seemed to work.

"After we took their city the men fled, but soon gathered together a great army and later chased us all out. We had to run for our lives— sadly Johann did not make it. He fought valiantly—he even saved my life as well as other lives. He deserves to be in Valhalla with Odin. These men had strange looking swords with a curved blade—incredible swords which were extremely sharp. Killer swords! They were very accomplished with this weapon and some even wielded it while riding a horse. Their horses are many hands tall, not like our miniature ones here; they mowed us down as if we were nothing. And these men rode as if they were part of this animal—I have never seen an army like it. Very powerful and very dangerous—we did not stand a chance. We were lucky to escape at all. Some arrived by land and some in ships—many ships—plus they had a great many fighting men. It was a well-planned attack! Fortunately our ships were hidden in a different harbour and were faster than theirs. We flew over the sea and escaped to North Africa to a place called Morocco where we received safe harbour. This town was well known to all sailors to be a good hiding place."

Aud Unn struggled with her sorrow—howling at times with the pain of it all—while her mother and sisters hovered by her side, trying to get her to sip some wine. Helgi continued his story, not knowing what else to do with such pain.

"We spent last winter in Morocco where some of our ships still remain. Most of us wanted to return home so we left the others behind. We had to sneak past Spain where that great army was—and in all likelihood still is, strongly defending its coastline. We were very lucky to get through. Fortunately our ships are much lighter and faster than theirs. I never want to return there—even with all its riches. Those people are very powerful, united as one under their strange beliefs— their doctrine is too different for me to understand. When we first arrived in Seville we kidnapped many women and children, and at the same time freed a couple of Christian priests. They had been kidnapped by the Moors and made into eunuchs to guard all their women, who are kept hidden away in a part of the castle they called a harem. What a treasure trove it was! This harem was filled with dozens of women of all ages. We let the old ones go free, but they just wanted to stay in the harem since it was the only home they had ever known. They even had the nerve to spit at us, too. Imagine that! As for the others we just wanted to get them to Dubhlinn's trading centre where we would be well-paid for such beauty. Fortunately we had kept them under guard on our ships, which we had kept hidden away in a secluded bay away from their harbour in the city of Seville. That was our defense strategy just in case of an attack and it proved to be a good plan in the end.

Since we had hidden our ships so well, we managed to escape safely with our lives as well as the lives of all our slaves. Our ships are built for speed and can outrun most other vessels that are built to hold more. Their ships were heavy, and rely mainly on the wind—sometimes even to get out of the harbour. Their hulls are taller and much wider than ours, and their weight makes them more difficult to row. Like madmen we rowed our narrow ships out to sea, then set sail. Fortunately for us they could not catch us; we even managed to outrun their deadly arrows. They have incredible bows that can shoot arrows much farther than ours, but still we managed to widen the gap between them and us. Our gods must have been looking over us—how else could we have escaped from such a terrorizing army?"

To change the subject, Jorunn Unn asked Helgi to describe the city of Morocco. Helgi was only too happy to talk about something other than their escape. "Morocco was safe enough but the weather was suffocating—much too hot for most of us and much too crowded and not the right place to sell our slaves. Rats were everywhere and sickness was rampant; most of us wanted to leave, but knew it would be better to spend the winter there. We sailed out early this spring and when we finally reached our destination in Ireland, the slaves were traded for much silver. A man called Olaf has made himself the king of Dubhlinn and has transformed its black-water bay into a great, safe harbour and into a very important trading centre. One great advantage is that the harbour has very deep water, so all types of ships can dock there. There were ships there from all over the known world."

Olaf, the king of Dubhlinn—that name caught Aud Unn's attention. "*Pabbi* was just telling me about this man called Olaf."

Her comment surprised Helgi; not wanting to be outdone by his father, he told her all he knew about this warrior-king. "Olaf is the son of a Norwegian warlord, and although born in Ireland he is considered to be a Norwegian outlaw by our king of Norway. This Olaf is a king to be reckoned with and has a great future, providing our king does not catch up with him. Olaf's father Ingald Helgasson has left much devastation along the shores of Norway with his constant raids and I do believe Olaf himself is guilty of raiding the Norwegian coasts. Harold Fair-Hair has sworn an oath of revenge on all his family. Enough stories! Mother—I am tired and hungry. My men need to be fed and watered with more mead and beer."

"It is under control, Helgi." Nevertheless, his mother rose to look after her son while the other two continued to soothe their young sister.

Helgi was never able to deal with either silence or a crying women, so he continued to talk while sipping his mead. "Both of the priests we had kidnapped were very learned men. The younger one was a countryman of ours but born in Ireland, called Jon. They had both been made into eunuchs in order to guard the women in the harem. The other one, much older, had the English version of the same name, John. This older priest, Father John, had much knowledge of our language and customs. He explained this Christian religion to me so well, that he convinced me to get baptized."

Usually very attentive Aud Unn missed the new strange word *eunuch* but did not miss his admission of baptism and choked out a sob. "How could you?"

"Easy. After all, their god is just another god. Why not embrace theirs as well as ours? It is only to our advantage to accept him. No big deal—all you have to do is make an occasional prayer—give a few silver coins to their church and the Christian world opens up to you. It makes perfect sense to me—trading with them as a Christian is so much easier now. It was a pragmatic decision, one I do not regret."

With that answer Aud Unn rose and fled to her room, throwing herself upon her bed and howling for Johann.

Helgi shouted at her fleeing back. "That is why women do not make good leaders. They are much too emotional."

Chapter 4

ince Bjorn and Einar had left with Ketill, Helgi was useful to have around. His mother and sisters rejoiced in his company, despite his Christian conversion. Even Aud Unn came to accept it; he still seemed like the same Helgi she had known all her life. At first, she felt someone had to take the blame for Johann's death, and it just seemed easier to blame her brother for talking him into going raiding. Eventually she came around to accept that it was not his fault; it was no one's fault. After all, Johann had made his own decision to go. Freya had already mapped out his destiny—to die young and to be a hero—so now she must celebrate his short life, and the fact that he was in Valhalla celebrating a hero's life every day with Odin. Even though she had forgiven Helgi, the pain of her loss lingered, which put a cloud of sorrow over everyone. Her mother started to realize just how much in love her youngest daughter really had been, so she talked with her constantly about Johann, knowing that this was necessary for her: to be able to hear his name and to be able to talk of him, in order to heal.

To his mother's delight Helgi took over the seeding process, while giving them all much of his time. He continued to tell them tales about the foreign lands where they had pillaged, filling their minds with both horrors and delights. He had brought each of them some amazing silk fabrics and silk threads that kept them all busy sewing up new colourful smocks to wear under their wool tunics, while he told his tales. Despite Aud Unn's continued mourning, there was much laughing, with plenty to drink and eat. Their mother saw to it that they were fully sated with both food and wine or mead to help Aud Unn forget about her young man, but deep down she was thankful that her youngest daughter no longer had any commitments to him. Although she spoke with a deep respect of him—often—with Aud Unn, he had been a man with no future or any wealth. Her husband would also be much pleased that their daughter was absolved from her untimely commitment. As a mother she was very relieved that they would not have to deal with her disappointment or her anger towards them, as Johann son of Thorvald could never have been accepted as their son-in-law—this union was always an impossibility!

Time passed, the sun warmed the earth, the seeds in the fields started to sprout new growth, and Aud Unn's grief slowly ebbed and flowed with the changing weather. Still Helgi told story after story, often repeating the same ones; they never tired of them. During one of his tales they heard the horn blow, warning everyone of an approaching ship or ships. Helgi grabbed his axe and went to see if there was any danger; the sisters trailed behind him, but it soon became apparent that no danger awaited them. It was only their father, as they had hoped it would be. Now Aud Unn and Helgi had to face Einar with the news about the death of his brother. Surprisingly Einar took it much better than Aud Unn had; maybe it was because he was a man and a man is not supposed to show such emotions. "It was to be expected if he went off to foreign lands. That is the risk we all take."

Helgi agreed with his remark. "Now can you not see, sister—this is how a real leader, a real man, thinks! You keep insisting that you should have been born a man—well *systirmin*, one must accept that danger is always lurking around the corner, or behind any man or woman for that matter. Einar, we are sorry for your loss but as you know, when one of us dies we all take his share to divide it up between the remaining survivors. However, just before your brother died he made me promise to give you a special gold arm band. As I owe your brother my life, I have it safely stowed in my chest and will give it to you later tonight."

Ketill approached his daughter and gave her a big hug. "My daughter, life is not meant to be easy. You must learn to live with loss like the rest of us. I too have some disappointing news, which we will discuss later tonight. Freya has brought Helgi back early, for which I am thankful. Now we can make our plans together as a family." This exclamation from her father sounded ominous. Aud Unn gave her father her bravest smile as she linked his arm and walked with him into the longhouse.

Later, after the *nattmal*, Ketill gathered his family together in privacy. "I have had long discussions with King Harold Fair-Hair. As predicted by Sigurd of the Orkneys, this king of ours has reneged on another promise. Originally I was named *Jarl* of Romsdal and Rognvald was made *Jarl* of both North More and South More. Now he has taken my title away from me only to give it to Rognvald the Powerful. He has made him *Jarl* of both Mores and now also of Romsdal. He said he did this after a drunken feast where Rognvald claimed that Romsdal lies between South More and North More and was really a part of his land. King Harold says that he cannot take back his promise to this man. Rognvald is much too powerful, and he cannot control all of Norway without this man's huge army. Either that or he is afraid of all his power—yet he is not afraid to break his word to me."

"This move proved to me that I was no longer a valued servant of his kingdom. Romsdal is—or was—my homeland. He promised me that there were other regions where I could be made a *jarl* but I no longer trust his word. So I left him thinking that I would contemplate any offer he will make, but I was lying through my teeth—just as he has done. We can both play this game of lies. He thinks that I conquered the Shetlands and the Hebrides in his name; I did not tell him about the Isle of Man. Now I plan to return and keep them all for myself. We must prepare to leave this place before Rognvald comes to claim it; I do not want him to have to force me to leave. You can all come with me, and decide whether you want to go elsewhere from the Hebrides or stay there with me. It is your choice; there is no safe haven anywhere in Norway for any of us anymore."

Bjorn spoke up first. "I have heard much about this new land called Iceland. They say that there is still much land to claim, so I will go directly there."

Helgi piped in next. "I too have heard much about this land and so far King Harold has avoided it, so I think it will be the safest place to settle. The original settlers named it Iceland purposely to keep people like King Harold away—or so I have been told. Yet it is the land of the gods! We can all go there, *pabbi*. There is enough land for all of us."

"I have no intention of living out my life in a 'fishing camp'—but it looks like we have all reached a decision. Tomorrow we will feast, then we prepare to leave."

Bjorn was not happy with his father's comment. "Why would you call it a fishing camp, *pabbi*? Many people have settled there now and the news that has come back is that it is a good place to settle."

"That may be true son for parts of the country but my own *langafi* went there by accident many, many years ago. He told me this when I was but a young boy, that life there was tough even though the fish were plentiful. At that time for whatever reason the fish had moved further out to sea, far away from the shores of his land. They had to go much further out to find anything. While they were pulling their nets a storm blew in and took them off course. They ended up where you plan to move, to this place you now call Iceland. Then it did not even have a name but they set up camp and fished for a time because they had no choice. They had to make some repairs to their ship and the trees were not strong and tall like ours here in Norway, but apparently they were able to use some driftwood. He told such stories about the fish; they were very large and very abundant, according to him, but not a place to live. The rivers were well stocked with salmon, nor did they did have to go far out in the sea to find large schools of fish. They either dried, smoked or put them in brine, then came home. He survived to tell his story."

"Was there any settlement then?" Bjorn was curious about this place.

"Well, not that he could see, but he did say that they came across a small group of Irishmen with the tops of their heads shaved, that had set up a religious colony on the island. He found it very strange, weird even, that a group of men would want to live in isolation without any women, so they just ignored them and got on with their fishing. Once their ship was seaworthy they just wanted to get back home to their women and children."

Bjorn was adamant. "Well we are going there because I have heard nothing but good about the country; there is much land to be had and with all my wealth I can set up a fine estate there, which would be impossible to do here."

"And so you should, son. It will be a great adventure! Just remember that our door is always open if it does not go well. You can always find a home in the Hebrides. I have chosen these islands as my base because there are many islands to choose from. The locals call them the Inner islands and the Outer islands, and there is land enough there for all of you, if you should choose to leave Iceland."

Both sons thanked their father for his understanding and for his generosity.

Ketill then gathered his crew and gave them the option to either follow him, follow his sons, or to stay in their village as before. He thought it only fair to give them choices. He talked to Ingi the blacksmith, hoping he would follow him, but Ingi chose to stay, saying that this was his home and the shop was his life. All leaders need a good blacksmith so he felt quite safe to stay behind. Ketill respected his decision not to leave his homeland, but many others chose to follow him.

The next morning Helgi the Lean approached Ketill to ask for his daughter Thorunn Unn who was present. She nodded her agreement, so Ketill agreed to his terms and later that night at the feast he announced their union. The very next day another feast was held to celebrate their marriage, but there was no time to waste in case Rognvald and his crew should appear unannounced. They planned to leave before the midday sun on the day after the wedding feast. His two sons, along with their sister Thorunn Unn and their new brother-in-law, and all their families, immediately began to pack up their ships, ready to sail northwards in the direction of this new land called Iceland. Meanwhile, Ketill's crew packed his ships, making them ready to sail west with his wife and two remaining daughters, while he walked through the village saying his final goodbyes to the ones who chose to remain.

Chapter 5

The Orkney Islands

Aud Unn and Jorunn Unn stood on each side of their father as they sailed up the fjord towards the open sea; following behind them were their two brothers and all their ships. Trolltunga jutted out from the ominous granite cliff as they sailed past the mountain where the troll lived and remained sleeping. Aud Unn could see just how dangerous that ledge really was from their view in the longship. No wonder her mother made sacrifices to her chosen goddess, Unn, who held the spirit of the Northern seas along with her eight sisters.

"You were either very brave or very stupid, Aud Unn, to stand on that tongue like you always did—waiting for *pabbi*." Jorunn Unn's opinion cut through her thoughts. She knew that she was well loved by her older sister, but Jorunn Unn could never control that sharp tongue of hers.

"She was brave of course," their father interjected, "Never stupid. Now that she has finally won the race, we need never return to this land of our births. Norway will never be the same under the rule of this king, Harold Fair-Hair. He has proven himself to be ambitious at any cost and his greed will defeat him in the end."

Aud Unn cut her father's words off by shouting and waving frantically. "Look everyone—wave goodbye—the ships heading to Iceland have started to turn towards the north. Will we ever see our brothers and sister again, *pabbi*?"

"Possibly never again, I am sad to say—but Iceland is their destiny—not ours."

The Orkneys would be their first destination and Ketill and his crew made landfall there a few days later, where they were well received by Sigurd, the brother of Rognvald. This man Rognvald, *jarl* of both Mores and now Romsdal, had become the sworn enemy of Ketill Flat-Nose, but his brother Sigurd was to become his closest friend and mentor. The *Jarl* of the Orkneys formally met them with his banners flying in the wind. As they were walking off the gangplank with Ketill in the lead, the *jarl's* booming voice greeted them. Because of his booming voice he had received the nickname of Sigurd the Mighty. "Welcome back Ketill, I see you have brought your family with you this time. I welcome you all to the Westness in Rousay. My people of the Orkneys greet you with open doors and open hearts and I invite you to stay as long as you like in my home. I call it *Skaillstaðir*." It was the largest longhouse Ketill's family had ever seen.

Ketill and Sigurd had much to discuss; not only about the recent unjust treatment from King Harold Fair-Hair, but also about this new alliance with Olaf. Before he left Norway Ketill had decided that he would join Olaf the White's partnership while he was still healthy enough to travel to other countries to loot and pillage with him. Before finalizing this partnership, he had a plan to present to Olaf which would make his place in this complex agreement more secure. Sigurd would be just the man to get the word to this king of Dubhlinn. It was Yngvild Unn who actually came up with the idea of a match between Aud Unn and Olaf, and they had discussed it thoroughly during the voyage, but only when they were alone and away from both of their daughters' perceptive hearing. The timing was perfect; Ketill saw the strength of such a match. He thought his wife was brilliant for coming up with it, but he questioned whether their daughter was ready; they might need to sell her on such a union. Surely she would see the sense of it, as she would become a queen. He always knew that she was special and would make a worthy consort for any man, and now in his sights he had a very powerful one—the warrior-king himself. But would this man consider his daughter a worthy catch? Although beautiful and intelligent she was still a young and inexperienced girl.

Sigurd and Ketill talked long into the night and made many plans—but first things first! He needed to return to the Hebrides and the Shetlands with his ships and men to secure the lands in his name, as well as settle all the people who followed him onto these new lands. The Isle of Man would have to wait for a while as it was that much further away. He would send his new man with a few ships to inform them of this change, after securing the other two. After acclimatizing his people and putting the right man in control of each place he would then talk to Olaf about their partnership, hopefully in person. A marriage between Olaf and Aud Unn would give him more stability in their partnership and he wanted to secure Olaf's agreement before he had to convince his daughter to accept. He felt more confident now that Johann, the love of her life, was gone; but would she be ready to bend to his will? He knew that the youngest was the most strong-willed of all his children.

Within this immense complex the *jarl* with the booming voice entertained Ketill's family in high style while Ketill went on to claim his islands. There was no time to be wasted, it was vital that the people of his islands understand that he would be their new leader, not King Harold of Norway. He had long since decided which trusted man to put in charge of each of his newly acquired holdings to control and govern while he was away. Yngvil Unn and their daughters would remain with Sigurd for over a month before he would able to return.

Shortly after Ketill had left, Sigurd commissioned his most trusted man to take a couple of longships, fully manned, to Dubhlinn. Those ships returned a few weeks later followed by more ships. Olaf the king of Dubhlinn had arrived and was well received by Sigurd. Yngvild Unn and her two daughters joined the *jarl* in the receiving line while all around them there was much commotion and excitement running throughout the whole village. Olaf was obviously well known and well respected here by all. Ketill's family took note of all this while anxiously awaiting their introductions to this warrior-king.

The first man off the ship was the king himself. He was tall and extremely fair—so fair, in fact, that his hair was almost white. "Hmmm, no wonder he is called Olaf the White," muttered Yngvild Unn to her daughters. He was also very handsome and decked out like a proper king.

Sigurd pounded his back as they touched foreheads in the traditional Nordic greeting, like a father and son would give each other. *"They must be very fond of each other,"* thought Aud Unn. "Come King Olaf, meet the wife and daughters of Ketill Bjornsson, the famous *hersir*, Ketill Flat-Nose!"

After the formal introductions everyone walked back to the longhouse together where drinks and food were being made ready. Aud Unn could not take her eyes off this man. Just being near him aroused an intensity of emotions she thought were buried and would remain submerged deep into her soul after the loss of her beloved Johann. This reaction to a man whom she had just met frightened and intrigued her at the same time. *"Have I forgotten the love of my life already? What kind of feckless woman am I?"* Another thing that surprised and unnerved her was that she appeared to be tongue-tied in his presence, which was so unlike her. Fortunately her mother and sister had no problems speaking with him, but they asked such silly questions—like "Do you have children?" "Are you married?" Aud Unn was getting frustrated with them and with herself. *"He is going to think I am an imbecile, unable to speak. Normally I have so much to say to anyone. What is wrong with me! They should be asking questions about his conquests— do they not realize that he is a great warrior-king and not just an ordinary man?!"* Startled out of her pathos she heard her name spoken. "I—I—I—beg your pardon my lord, I did not hear your question. I must confess to have been daydreaming."

"Ahhh—I can see that, you are a deep thinker. Sigurd tells me that you are very interested in our laws and the rights of our people. Why would a young person, a woman at that, be so interested?"

He had struck a nerve and suddenly the words flowed from her mouth. The curse of attraction appeared to be broken—for the time being at least. "To be honest some of my best friends are ordinary people, ordinary farmers and some have ambitions to be more than they are. It is important that laws are in place to protect their rights as they work to fulfill their goals. Don't you think?" She was thinking of her Johann.

"Now then—are you saying that our laws are only for our leaders? I think we protect the ordinary man as well. What do you think about people who take control through force?"

"The laws are there to protect all—even slaves—I do realize that!" Aud Unn retorted. "Everyone has a say but sometimes I think that ordinary people are dominated by the powerful families and some can make it difficult for them to move forward. There should be many ways for them to achieve their goals and that is why I admire my father so much. He is very open to his people improving their way of life. As for force, that is something we people of the North understand and live by. But once we achieve a goal, even if we win using force, we must be fair to the people that follow us. As you know, Norway has a king—a very ambitious king—who is driving his own people away by not being fair with them. All that does is create revengeful, angry people and inevitably more wars than necessary. What do you think, King Olaf? You have become a great warrior-king, but do you have ambitions to be more?"

"Of course I do! But I have no intention of becoming like King Harold of Norway! His greed forced my family off their land in Norway many years ago. My father and I feel justified in harassing his coastland and by doing so we have become his mortal enemies." Looking her straight in the eyes and laughing, he said, "His anger with us does not frighten me and I will not stop plundering his coasts! As for my ambitions, with Odin's wise direction, with Freya's destiny for me— hopefully her designs for me are aligned with my plans—and with Thor's protection, I can do as you believe I should. I intend to keep good people with me on my journeys and I promise you that I look after them well."

Jorunn Unn cut in, "Aud Unn wishes she were a man and could go to battle. We cannot fight our destinies now, can we?"

Olaf turned and smiled at her. "Maybe not, but I do like that she wants to be more than she is and not just a woman to be married off. What about you, Jorunn Unn? Do you just want to find a husband and have many children? Is that all you desire?"

"No, of course not. I want a man with much wealth and power—someone like yourself, King Olaf. My sister does have some merit in what she says—I will give her that."

Olaf roared with laughter. "I think I will like having Ketill and his family as part of this alliance. What do you think, *Jarl* Sigurd?"

Sigurd agreed wholeheartedly.

Chapter 6

Ketill sailed into the Orkney harbour with his horn blowing, announcing his return. Such excitement ran through the village, Aud Unn felt an intense pride well up inside her. She could see that her father had much respect here too, and this gave her much hope for the future away from the Norway they once knew and loved.

After the *nattmal* Ketill settled in for a long night's discussion with Sigurd and Olaf. Their privacy was assured as they dismissed the women by bidding them all a good night. The women settled into their own quarters knowing the men would be discussing their alliance, but the girls noticed that their mother had a look of consternation on her face as she asked her two daughters to sing for her. This made them wonder what she knew that they did not.

While the sisters sang to their mother, the men discussed their partnership and made their promises to each other. A deal was struck but before Ketill finalized it he said he had an offer to make to Olaf first. "Olaf, King of Dubhlinn, as a sign of solidarity I offer you my daughter Aud Unn's hand in marriage. My wife and I firmly believe that the two of you together will make a strong union and this match will guarantee that you and I will be honourable and just in our dealings with each other. Do you accept?"

"If I do not accept does that mean you will not partner with me Ketill?"

"You already have my agreement—there is no doubt of a partnership happening—but this union would certainly seal the deal. There is much honour in families, don't you agree?"

"As it happens I do agree and I accept. But I have come to know your daughter—will she accept?"

Laughing, Ketill admitted to Olaf. "When Yngvild Unn and I first agreed that this was a good idea we were worried that she might resist because she recently lost someone she loved but our daughter is a smart woman and knows that her future depends on a good marriage. Since arriving earlier today I have already witnessed how she talks with you and have seen the respect and admiration in her eyes. Now I do not believe there will be any question that she will not agree."

"Good, I do think she will make a worthy opponent though, and it may prove to be an interesting union."

"I give you fair warning, my youngest daughter is quite special. Ygnvild Unn has anointed all our daughters with the name of *Unn* after the goddess of the frothing waves, just as she was anointed by her mother. But I firmly believe that somehow Aud has been blessed by all of the nine sisters and not just the one. She has not only been gifted with intelligence, but also with wisdom and compassion and a deep understanding of the rule of law."

"Warning taken. *Takk.*" Ketill and Olaf shook hands and touched forehead to forehead, sealing the deal.

"One question Olaf, if you do not mind? I am quite familiar with your father's paternal ancestors, and with your great-grandfather Guðroðr Halfdarnarson, the king of Vestfold, but I am unsure of your father's maternal ancestry."

"My father's mother was Thora Sigurdsdottir; her father was Sigurd Snake-in-the-eye Ragnarsson, the son of the famous Ragnar Lothbrok and Princess Aslaug, his consort."

"I did hear rumours of this but it was from an unreliable source. Now that you have confirmed this ancestry I will be very proud to repeat it. Family history is very important to me; I view family trees as a tapestry and one thread is not enough to create a wall hanging. The different threads from established, well-respected lines, woven tightly together, create a story and a history worthy to pass on to our children. If there is no history, no knowledge of where we come from, then it is too weak to survive and it will quickly fall apart. Now if we have many known threads, what I mean by this is that we can go back many generations, woven together they build not only a beautiful tapestry but a very strong one that will endure everything, even wars. *Takk.* Tomorrow Yngvild Unn and I will present this marriage contract to our daughter and then we will have much to celebrate."

Olaf agreed. "I have one request only—that this union occurs in the presence of the three partners in this room. With *Jarl* Sigurd's blessings, of course, as we are his guests."

"I am honoured that you will marry this man's daughter in my home."

Olaf went over to each man and spit into the palm of his right hand with each handshake, sealing their partnership and now this marriage contract. Ketill and Sigurd followed his lead and did the same with each other. "Now with your daughter as my soon-to-be queen we can begin this family tapestry you so eloquently described, Ketill. In the meantime the three of us can move forward and make plans for creating much wealth together."

Yngvil Unn's smile beamed throughout the *dagmal* the next morning, all the while whispering with her husband. Jorunn Unn was more in tune with her mother's emotions since the youngest sister had eyes only for the white-haired king. Typical Jorunn Unn, she could not contain her thoughts so she whispered something to her younger sister. "Have you noticed how different *mamma* is from last night? Something has happened to make her this happy, what do you think?"

"I never noticed, but now that you mention it, you are right! She does appear to be smiling all the time. We will ask her after the meal." They did not have to wait long; after the meal ended Ketill asked his daughters to meet in their room. Both sisters looked at each other in wonder. What had happened during the night to wipe out the anxiety her mother had displayed the night before? It had to be good news, so they were anxious to talk to their parents.

Ketill made his presentation to two very surprised daughters. Aud Unn was stunned into silence while her older sister could not contain her frustration. "Why Aud Unn, *pabbi*, I am the older one?"

"Yes you are, but I think Aud Unn will make a stronger union with Olaf than you can. Her knowledge of the law and her stubbornness will give her the emotional strength that a woman married to such a man would need. Do not worry, I will find you a husband with as much power as Olaf has—maybe even more. Tell me your answer, Aud Unn."

She managed to find her tongue. "What if I refuse, *pabbi*?"

"Be sensible now—you will be Queen of Dubhlinn! Did you ever think you would become a queen, daughter?"

"No, of course not. I only ever thought of marrying Johann and we both know he was never to be a king. Recently though, I dared to dream of this possibility, as I have come to respect this man, Olaf. I do believe he regards my opinion, even in the matter of the law and in justice to the common man. He certainly asks enough questions about it, don't you think Jorunn Unn?"

Her sister's jealousy got the better of her. "Yes and how boring your discussions are too!"

Ketill stood up and went to his older daughter. He took her hands in his and looked into her eyes smiling at her, "I see that you do understand why my choice was not you." Looking back into his eyes she could see that her father really did care for her and this stopped her from making any further harsh comments. Then he turned to his wife and asked for wine to make a toast to this marriage contract. "It is agreed then—Aud Unn! Let us toast to this powerful union—a match that could start a family dynasty!"

"Yes *pabbi*—a family dynasty it will be and Dubhlinn will be an excellent start to this legacy!"

He raised his glass to her once more. "Olaf would like the wedding to be celebrated here so you can join him in Dubhlinn right away along with the rest of us. While you women organize this celebration Olaf, Sigurd and I have to make plans to find the wealth we require to raise a great army for this Kjarval, to make him the High King of Tara, the king of all Ireland. This may be one man's dream that is too big to complete, but now that we have made an oath to each other we must find a way to make it happen."

Chapter 7

Torrential rains came down with a fury, while the winds whipped about the guests, throwing them off balance as they approached Sigurd's great hall. Despite the weather, this marriage feast would not to be missed by anyone. These rain-soaked guests, whether locals or out-of-town visitors staying with friends and family, had no choice but to brave this tempest, unlike Sigurd's house guests. They all remained warm and dry since the wedding celebrations were to be held in his longhouse where they were all safe from the storm's fury. Unaware of Aud Unn's proximity to the entrance, each person arrived wet and shaken. They complained to each other about the violent winds and heavy rain, saying the gods had cursed this wedding. These negative comments soon dissolved into a silent vacuum once the drinks started to flow and were soon forgotten, except by Aud Unn, who had overheard them all. She was very suspicious of any bad omens and feared that this was a premonition of unlucky things to come. Anxiously waiting for her father to escort her through the great hall to her husband-to-be, this fear of the unknown absorbed her soul before she even had a chance to walk towards her future. *"Is this to be an ill-fated union?"* she pondered to herself as she considered what sacrifices would be sufficient to overcome this warning.

She had chosen to stand behind the wattle screen to wait for her father and in doing so became an accidental witness to all these complaints about the weather. Disheartened by this ominous talk of bad luck she decided to return to her room to wait for their walk to the front of the great hall. Tradition demanded that the father or guardian walk the bride into the room where he would surrender his rule over her only to hand it to another man. But then she stopped and returned to the screen to search for Olaf. She could not resist this need to sneak a last peek at her warrior-king before retreating, and there he was, sitting on the high seat next to Sigurd. They were whispering about something when he looked up and stared right at her. It was if he sensed her presence and winked directly at her. She could feel her face flush red hot as a jolt of desire flowed through her body, then she fled to her room. *"Damn—damn these feelings! Freya please help me control these desires—they are not queenly!"*

Soon enough her father came for her, and despite her jumbled emotions Aud Unn looked the part of the queen she was soon to become as she walked beside her father. Her proud family were not the only ones who admired her imposing stateliness; it was obvious that the King of Dubhlinn did too. Between her mother and sister they had wound her golden locks into the most intricate braids, with amber beads cleverly tucked in amongst them in a very precise pattern. Once her father handed her over to Olaf, poor Aud Unn once again became the shy tongue-tied young woman, silenced by the anxious anticipation of what was expected of her. Whenever he was nearby he provoked such sensations of desire in her—it scared her senseless. *"These emotions are so different to what I felt for Johann. Was I ever really in love with him or is it simply because Olaf is the great warrior-king and that is all I am in love with? Or is it just lust?"*

Despite the storm, the wedding was a magnificent celebration considering they had such little time to bring it all together. Sigurd and Ketill spared no expense and all the well-placed people of the Orkneys were invited. Aud Unn had a piece of blue silk from her brother Helgi that was made into a beautiful dress, but the crowning glories were her braids and the headdress with a brim that was ringed with precious stones, a suitable crown for a newly appointed queen.

This costly headdress was a loan from *Jarl* Sigurd; his wife, Grelaud of Caithness, had worn it at their wedding. They had had one son, Guttorm, but then Grelaud sadly died in childbirth with their second child. The jarl never got over her death and so far had not remarried. His only son remained in Norway with his brother Rognvald. He had been sent there for fostering as a young boy, but had decided to remain there and fight by his uncle's side. He claimed that he had no intention of living on such a small island when he had such possibilities fighting with his uncle for Harold, the King of Norway. Deep down Sigurd seethed with anger; he felt that his own brother had taken his son away from him and this was the very reason he now opposed his brother and went into this alliance with Olaf and Ketill.

Olaf and Aud Unn stood facing each other, she with the tall headdress and intricate braids, along with Olaf's complex braids and his white fur-lined cloak. Together they represented wealth, status, and more importantly, power. Their union was sealed by the pagan ritual of handfasting with *Jarl* Sigurd officating. While holding their right hands together they made their promises in front of all, reciting the words spoken first by the *jarl*. Rather than use the local *goði* he had insisted that he oversee this union as a courtesy to his new partners. He directed each one individually to recite his words, and they each repeated after him to honour and respect each other and their families, past, present and future. Only Aud Unn had to promise to obey and to be faithful; no such promise was forthcoming from the King of Dubhlinn. Hands still clasped together, the pagan *jarl* continued his message of marriage while Aud Unn wondered to herself if this last promise she had to make was really fair. *"Shouldn't Olaf swear fealty as well?"*

After the ceremony the newly married couple had the privilege of sitting on the high seats facing all the guests, with Sigurd on one side beside Olaf, while her father, mother and sister sat on her other side. This left her seated beside Olaf. Terrified that she would make a fool of herself if she even so much as looked at Olaf, Aud Unn concentrated instead on her food and drink while speaking only with her family.

After finishing her first goblet of wine her heart slowed down to a normal beat and she finally felt brave enough to address her husband. When there was finally a break in the conversation between Olaf and *Jarl* Sigurd she got up the nerve to ask her question.

"What is the protocol, husband? Do I continue to address you as King Olaf?"

"Olaf will do dear wife, but if you are referring to me while talking to a third party then refer to me as King Olaf."

He covered her hand with his. *"Dear wife? And touching me—he certainly knows how to muddle with my head! "* "Tell me about your Dubhlinn town. What does the name mean and what is it like?"

"That is a good question, it makes me happy that you are interested in your new home. Dubhlinn is a Gaelic name and means 'black pool' because of the colour of the water. The Norsemen call it Dyflin but I have decided to adopt the Irish version of Dubhlinn. Why? Because it makes my town appear more inclusive to the local people. The Norse still struggle with this change that I have made but I was born there and grew up speaking Gaelic. Although I remain a pagan I like to think that I understand them better than my kinsmen do. It is not only important, I personally think it is crucial to include some of the Irish culture into the city. It makes them more comfortable having us Northmen in their midst, especially since we own the majority of the business enterprises there. I do encourage any Irishman, if he has enough wealth, to enter our business world. Mostly they are the butchers, bakers and innkeepers, but we value their input to our Longphort Council, which is made up entirely of us Northmen. There is one Irishman who is becoming very wealthy and is gaining much power. We are very impressed by him and may soon invite him to join our council. Now my queen, do you think I have made a wise decision?"

"I do, my lord. Do you allow them the freedom to practice their own religion as well?"

"But of course! All I ask of them is that they do not force me or any of my kinsmen to convert to theirs and so far it seems to be working."

"You really are a wise man; Odin would be proud of you."

The evening came to a close much too quickly for Aud Unn. Her sister Jorunn Unn and their mother walked with her to the bedroom that was prepared especially for the newly wedded couple. There they helped her prepare for the night's sleep—if there was to be any sleep? First they removed the precious headdress, which they packed carefully into its own trunk, specially made for it. A linen shift lay neatly folded upon the skins that covered their bed and Aud Unn quickly reached for the nightdress as she slipped behind a screen to change. Once attired for the night Aud Unn sat down in front of a small table, where her sister uncoiled her intricate braids and retrieved the amber beads and laid them on the table. Then her mother took over and combed her hair as she gave her marital advice. She was sure that they could both hear her heart thumping—it was so loud it roared in her ears. Once her hair was combed so that it shone like newly spun gold, her mother poured her some wine and then they left her alone. She was not alone for long—Olaf walked in soon after and set the bar of wood across the door.

"We do not want any interruptions now, do we? Finally—I have you all to myself!" Aud Unn could feel the blush sweep up her neck and onto her face; she hung her head not daring to look into his eyes. He lifted her head with a gentle nudge and slowly kissed her eyes, then her nose and finally her lips. Weak with desire she stood up and wrapped her arms around his neck, kissing him back with a vigour she did not know she had. Fire spread throughout her body. Once Olaf got free from her long kiss, he unfolded her arms from his neck, moving them around his waist. Surprised by her intensity he looked directly into her eyes and said, "I respect your innocence—your modesty—your purity. Your blush tells me that you are a virgin and have little or no experience with men. I promise to be a gentle and kind lover. You truly are a beautiful, passionate woman, Aud Unn Ketillsdottir. My Queen!"

Holding her hand in his he coaxed her to walk towards the bed. What he soon realized was that she needed no persuasion to follow him. Her wine was not touched until much later when they toasted to each other. Naked, Olaf walked over to the table and poured himself some wine, then walked back to their bed with the two vessels. Not knowing where to look, she quickly sat up high in the bed and pulled the bed cover up to her neck. Unashamed by his exposed masculinity, he stood by her and made a toast while handing her the untouched cup of wine. "May Freya, the Völva, continue to fill you with such passion and encourage you to always seek pleasure with our union. Freya, the goddess of fate has brought us together for a reason—now may she, as well as your goddess Unn, bless you with the fertility required to produce a male heir. I do believe I shall enjoy having you as my wife and queen, Aud Unn."

She responded, "I do believe I shall enjoy having you as my husband and king. *Skol.*"

He ran his fingers through her long silky hair as they clinked their wine vessels together. "You have been blessed with both beauty and intelligence."

Olaf and Aud Unn did not appear in public until the next evening at the *nattmal*. It was obvious to all that the night had gone well as her radiant face spoke volumes, which induced much joking and cheering as the couple walked in together. Confident now of her place in life, all the bad omens filed away, she walked beside her husband with the graciousness and self-assurance becoming to the young Queen of Dubhlinn. Intoxicated with her new husband, she had already forgotten that he had not promised to obey and to be faithful.

Chapter 8

Dubhlinn

The men made their ships ready for sailing and within a couple of days Olaf and Ketill were saying their farewells and giving their thanks to Sigurd the Mighty for his bountiful hospitality. His mighty voice boomed with warmth, inviting them all to return soon. A tent was erected on Ketill's ship, where beds were fastened to the deck for the women to sleep and to protect them from the elements. The rain had continued unabated since the day of their union and the wind taxed the skills of the men sailing the ships. Although decent sailors themselves, the women were thankful for the protection of the tents, for the beds to keep their feet off the sodden deck, and for each other's company. They recited sagas, sang songs and in between, Aud Unn's mother and sister battered her with questions about Olaf. Now a married woman, she was filled with a confidence she had never experienced before and was able to talk quite freely with them. She was happy with her new life as a wife and a queen. The trip would only take a few days but Aud Unn, separated from her husband, was already missing him and was anxious to see what kind of living quarters a queen such as herself would have in Ireland. This charismatic warrior-king had bewitched her and she longed to be held in his arms once again.

As they sailed southwards they finally left the bad weather behind them. The women gladly left their tent to stand at the stern with their father to enjoy the fair weather. Olaf was in the lead ship and Aud Unn was thrilled to be following close behind her warrior-king. Before the women knew it they were sailing into Dubhlinn, a major trading centre and Olaf's domain. The longphort before them presented an imposing image of his realm with the many different types of ships docked to it. Behind this splendid harbour were many buildings, mostly warehouses, denoting a city and not just a village like Aud Unn, her mother and sister were used to. Gasps of wonder escaped their lips as they sailed closer in to Olaf's private docking area inside the complex harbour.

"Olaf built all this—he told me all about the work he did to create and expand this important trading centre."

Jorunn Unn, unable to control her sharp tongue sarcastically responded to this comment made by Aud Unn. "Now, now, dear sister, are you not overly proud of this husband of yours?"

"So what if I am!" snapped Aud Unn.

Their mother cut in. "Enough, she has every right to be proud. Just wait until you are married—and married to a man you love—you will be just the same."

"Humph! I should be so lucky!" Jorunn Unn turned her back to them both and faced the harbour. Her mother winked at Aud Unn and smiled. They both knew she would shake off this petulant attitude very quickly and return to her jovial self; she never held a grudge for long.

Once docked and on solid land again, Olaf walked over to their group. "Welcome to my domain and your new home, my queen. The cart here is for all our trunks and soon another more grand carriage will appear to carry you ladies off to my longhouse. Ahha—I can see him now. The man driving those horses is my cousin Jon; he is a Christian and a priest who is celibate, so I have no worries about him looking after all you ladies." Laughing, he continued, "You will be safe in his hands. Once there he will show you to your room where each of you will get a personal maid who will prepare you a bath. Jon will see to that as well. You can rest until your baths are ready and after that your cases should have caught up with you. Then you can dress for the *nattmal* where I will introduce you to everyone."

Jon pulled up beside him and jumped off the cart to give his cousin a big hug. Although as tall as Olaf, this man looked more like a boy than a man, and had flaming red hair. "Welcome home Olaf. I have missed you and I see you have brought company."

"Yes Jon, let me introduce you to my new queen and wife, Aud Unn. She is the youngest daughter of Ketill Flat-Nose, and this is her mother Yngvild Unn and her older sister Jorunn Unn. My cousin here is a newly ordained priest and is eager to change the world. Do not anticipate any conversions among these ladies, they are staunch pagans, like myself, so do not get any ideas of even trying to convert them. Understood?"

"You do not frighten me, King Olaf. But I must say that I am very pleased to meet you, Queen Aud Unn. What kind of spell did you spin to capture our warrior-king, whom I thought would remained unmarried forever?" He bowed slightly to her and kissed her hand. This action surprised her so much Olaf felt it was necessary to explain his method of greeting ladies.

"I can see that you are not familiar with the Christian ways but you will get used to it. Jon, can you find them each a room with a private bed. Aud Unn, of course will join me in mine; arrange a maid for each of them, as well as baths."

"Of course my lord and master," he said, bowing in an exaggerated way and smiling at the same time as he made his statement.

"Only you can get away with such sarcasm—but do be careful! Do not test my patience dear cousin." Olaf then turned his back to them and walked away.

Watching after his cousin, Jon proceeded to greet the other two just as he had greeted Aud Unn. They were prepared for this odd greeting now and their giggles showed their enjoyment while he kissed each hand. Next he helped each lady to board the coach, seating Aud Unn next to him on his bench and the other two on the bench behind. Then he fussed with blankets while covering their legs. "Once we are moving you will feel the coolness of the air but these woolen covers will protect you from the elements." He pointed out the warehouses as they rode off and described the logic to the town planning. You could tell that he was proud of his cousin, the king of Dubhlinn.

Chapter 9

The great hall was the largest Aud Unn, her mother and sister had ever seen, but everyone referred to it simply as the feasting hall. A great fire trough built with local stones ran down the middle with a work table at each end. Long continuous tables with benches on each side ran parallel to this fire. The head table was at the top end of the feasting hall overlooking the central fire and the long tables. Great wooden columns ran down the sides of the longhouse and behind them, built-in benches lined the walls. These elaborately carved columns were the supports for the great beams that held up the heavy roof. If more tables were required they could be set up between the columns in front of the built-in wall benches and tonight there was an obvious need as the great hall was overflowing with curious people wanting to get a look at the great warrior-king's new bride.

Some of the kitchen *thrall*s were busy cooking different meats over the large open fire while others were tending to all the iron cauldrons suspended from the great central beam over the flames. Wooden boards with handles were stacked on the worktables at each end of the fire, ready for the *thrall*s to serve the food.

Once everyone was seated and had a drink in hand Olaf and his queen appeared from the front end of the great hall. They seated themselves at the head table along with Aud Unn's family and a select few on Olaf's side, which included his cousin Jon, the priest. After their goblets were filled with wine Olaf stood to greet the guests and introduced his bride and her family. There was much hooting and hollering in greeting the newcomers. *Skols* and *velkommens* echoed throughout the hall and as they bounced of the ceiling and walls they melded into one continuous salutation. Aud Unn had never seen or heard the likes of such a greeting. *"So this is what it will be like as a queen,"* she thought to herself. *"I could get used to this adoration—but will it last?"* The omens on her wedding day that had been shoved to the far reaches of her mind suddenly returned out of nowhere to haunt her.

One of the honoured guests arrived a few minutes after the introductions, making a grand entrance as he limped in and sat down in the empty chair on Olaf's side. He turned out to be another cousin; Ivar was his name. Unlike his friendlier cousin Jon, he scowled at her when she greeted him with a smile. At first she felt pity for him; she couldn't help but notice that he walked like a cripple, whether from birth or from a battle she had yet to find out. This one had hair the colour of a raven and had a look about him that gave Aud Unn the chills. By the end of the evening any compassion she had originally felt for him fled from her heart; she decided there and then to trust her instinct and to stay clear of this one. Besides meeting the dangerous-looking Ivar, in Aud Unn's mind the evening was a resounding success, but the bad omens were once more lodged in her mind.

At the *dagmal* the next morning, Olaf appeared overly attentive to his queen. *"Did he sense my unease with his cousin Ivar? They were whispering to each other a lot at the feast the night before."* Once again her instincts screamed a warning to her that there was something not quite right with all this attention, and she was right—he did not appear in their room to sleep for the next few days. Although he appeared each morning for the *dagmal* and each evening for the *nattmal,* she slept alone and was left wondering each night, *"Where is he?"* When she asked he claimed to be discussing strategies with his cousin Ivar but her curiosity and desires ate her up with anxiety. *"He is playing with me,"* she thought. Then everything seemed to right itself and she wondered if she was overthinking her gut reactions. He never explained any further why he was absent, even though she did try to work up the courage to ask again. She felt like a coward for not demanding to know where he went, but the bad omens on their day of union stopped her. She feared his answer as she knew him to be straightforward and honest. Instead she made a sacrifice to the goddess Unn, hoping this would rid her of these haunted memories.

He rewarded her patience with a private tour of his town of Dubhlinn. While walking together Aud Unn noticed that the people in the streets stopped what they were doing and either bowed their heads or curtsied. *"Hmmmm, they are acknowledging our status; this is something I could get used to,"* she thought to herself. First he took her to his pride and joy, the harbourfront where many ships were always docked.

As they walked back through the longphort, a massive fortress, he explained his design and how it was established. "This is the strength of my town, and since you believe so strongly in treating people fairly I think you will agree with how I have set it all up. Many of these warehouses are privately owned by ambitious businessmen; some I own. For example, there are warehouses that hold grains, some are for cloth, some for slaves, some are for fish and there are many others, smaller or larger. The small ones are mainly to hold luxury items like bolts of exotic silks, and threads made from silk, cotton, linen, gold or silver. Then there are warehouses for nuts, candles, beads, ivory, etc., many valuable items only the rich can afford. When the ships come in they have to pay port taxes, which come into my coffers. Whatever they carry, these businessmen bid on what they want or need. I have men who manage my warehouses and they bid for me and run the companies for me. That makes me rich so I am happy. They are well paid so they have a good life. Everyone benefits! I organized a council of twelve men to oversee any problems and they all have a chance to run for this council; everyone involved in the longphort gets a chance to vote for the man they want. How fair is that?"

"I am very impressed by all this, my lord."

"I named them The Longphort Council and because it has been so successful I do not fear leaving my town to go raiding or to do battle elsewhere. They see to the safety of all my citizens because they have made much wealth themselves and have a vested interest in keeping the town safe and under my leadership."

"I do believe you are as clever as Odin himself. This is all so interesting, *takk fyrir* for such an enlightening tour."

"Come, let us stop at the inn just ahead." A very large white building with black crossbeams loomed ahead, with a sign hanging over the door of a black swan. Although she could not read the words "Eala Dubh," she recognized that they were in Gaelic and asked what they meant.

"You are correct; it is in Gaelic and it means 'Black Swan'. You can see how smart it is to use such a sign, you do not have to know how to read; the picture tells it all. He is a very clever businessman."

Olaf walked behind Aud Unn as they made ready to enter the inn when suddenly a man came roaring out of the door, almost knocking her over in his haste to leave the premises. When he looked up he glared at her with such anger, then she saw the recognition in his eyes and what flashed between them could only be interpreted as pure hate. That glaring look faded as quickly as it had appeared when he looked past her to Olaf. It was none other than Ivar the Hated himself. Jon had jokingly confessed to his dreadful nickname shortly after that introductory meal. *"The hated, how appropriate,"* she thought to herself.

"Oh pardon me, my Queen, my haste has made me a very clumsy man. King Olaf, I am very pleased to have bumped into you, literally." To Aud Unn he was obviously trying to be funny to cover something up. "I must speak with you right away in private." He took Olaf's arm and led him a short distance away but they kept their backs to her, preventing their words from flowing towards her. She could not hear what was said but she suspected that they were conversing in Gaelic. Feeling rather awkward standing alone by the front door of the inn, she turned towards a pot of flowers at the entrance as if to inspect them. Olaf was soon at her side and took her elbow to direct her through the door.

Once they had entered a man rushed up to them and bowed his head, greeting his king. Olaf was the first to speak. "Caoimhin O'Dubhthaigh, proprietor of this wonderful inn, may I present to you my new wife and queen, Aud Unn Ketillsdottir."

"It is a great honour to meet you, my queen. My wife is an amazing cook and has just prepared a pie made with pheasants; can I entice you both to stay for some wine and a taste of her delicious pie?"

"Unfortunately my good man we cannot stay, as something has come up; another time we would be honoured. But send a pie to the feasting hall for our *nattmal* tonight. I will pay for it of course, as I do know what a glorious cook your wife is."

"Please, it is my gift and my pleasure to send it to you."

"Thank you, Caoimhin, but before I leave could I have a quick word with you?"

"Of course sire." Olaf walked off with the proprietor, leaving Aud Unn alone once again. Although she could barely hear what they were saying she recognized the odd word of Gaelic and knew she would not understand even if she could hear. Fortunately there was a dog sniffing at her feet so she knelt down to pet it for something to do and to take her mind off their interaction. A woman whom she assumed was the innkeeper's wife sent a small child over.

"I am sorry m'lady, my dog loves everyone and is only trying to say hello." He knelt down to pet the dog as well, so she tried to engage this young boy in conversation even though her vocabulary was limited. Olaf was not long, but before he turned to leave she couldn't help but notice that some coins were passed over to the innkeeper. Before she knew it they were on their way back to the great hall.

Her curiosity about Ivar got the better of her; she had to ask, "Was there a problem, my lord?"

"No—not really. Well maybe? Just a small one." Olaf hesitated. "The innkeeper had a few harsh words with Ivar over some private matter and I think Ivar misunderstood what he meant. You do not know Ivar at all but I have to admit he has a bit of a temper and once again I have had to sort it all out." He chuckled as if it was a joke. "I do think he was rather surprised, even embarrassed, when we turned up. What do you say?"

"Temper, good God your cousin is a horrible man— can you not see this?" Aud Unn kept this thought to herself as she did not want to ruin her day but realized Olaf was expecting a response from her. "I did not notice his embarrassment, just his anger, m'lord." Despite running into Ivar it was the best day ever for her but she was beginning to understand Ivar's constant anger; he was jealous of her and resented any attention Olaf gave her. He had had Olaf to himself while raiding different countries and womanizing, for most of their adult life, then suddenly Olaf came home from a voyage a married man. Things were

beginning to make sense to her now. *"I must be on the alert and observe his reactions whenever we are all together,"* she decided.

Later that evening she enjoyed her delicious meal of pheasant pie with Olaf, especially since he continued to explain the functions and purpose of the council. Ivar did not show for the *nattmal* that evening, which made it even better since she had Olaf all to herself. *"He can sulk all he wants, I like it when he is not present!"* The more she discovered and got to know Olaf's exciting town, the more she felt a part of his life. She suddenly had a vision of what her life could be like. *"I have learned much today. I do believe that the power I desire can be attained by surrounding myself with powerful, ambitious men—and women! To think I once thought it would be better to be a man and go off on a Viking raid and fight to attain wealth. What a child I was! My power comes from this man I married, a king, no less. My mamma and pabbi were right all along, even though I was trained to defend myself; as a woman, my power lies in marriage to the right man. I must never forget this."*

Many days later this king called Kjarval appeared, and since he was expected, a huge feast had been prepared in his honour. Aud Unn and her sister and mother were duly impressed with this Irish king; he went out of his way to include them in conversation at the feast. Later that night Olaf warned her that there would be much feasting at night while the Irish king was visiting them. During the day they would be either in meetings with Ivar and her father discussing how to raise an army or they would all be at his camp to inspect the men that they managed to recruit each day. He warned her that the women would have to learn to entertain themselves during the day since the men would be totally absorbed in their own private conversations. Aud Unn did not mind at all since it meant that she would see less of Ivar, even though during these days he appeared to be more charming and entertained her mother and sister with ease. This unknown side to him confused her as she watched them fall under his spell. *"Am I wrong about this man?"* Despite all this joviality she was soon at loose ends. Her mother and sister managed to keep occupied with sewing and chatting to each other, which she found quite boring. To defeat this new anxiety that seemed to take over she decided to go for a walk and explore the surrounding area. She invited her sister and mother to join her. They refused to leave the great hall; the rain was constant and cold and they preferred to remain near the fire. Aud Unn decided to get some fresh air regardless, so she set off with only her maid Una in tow.

The rain had appeared to let up as they walked about but before they realized it, it came down hard once again, so Una directed her to a church where they could rest and wait for the rain to lessen. Although small in size she found the church very welcoming; she spent some time touching the religious effigies, and flipping through the huge Bible on the altar. When Una told her the rain had stopped once again, she covered her hair with her hood, ready to walk back to the great hall, when suddenly a clergyman showed up. It was none other than Olaf's cousin Jon the Priest. He was delighted to see her there and asked if he could show her around and explain everything to her. In no hurry to leave she lowered her hood to expose her long flowing hair, as he directed her back towards the altar.

The first thing he pointed out was the Bible, which he called the written word of God. "This Bible contains many books written by many different people and their experiences with God. The scriptures and sacred texts explain God's relationship with us ordinary people." Then he showed her a psalter, a book of psalms, which he explained was a book of poems and sacred songs. "This psalter is one of many books in the Bible and only the wealthy can afford to purchase such a treasure. They use it mainly to teach their children to read; as you probably know, only the upper classes can read."

"Why does one need to know how to read?" she inquired defensively, not willing to admit that she could not read.

Jon sensed her guarded reaction and guessed rightfully why. "Aud Unn, the ability to write and the ability to decipher these words are very powerful tools. I could teach you if you ever decide it would be beneficial to you to understand the written word. It would give you much power over the common man and maybe even over your king. Even if you decide not to learn, just to look through these two books and see all the art that has gone into making them, that is an education in itself.

Much of the artwork is symbolic to the scriptures and they tell their own version of the story. So words are not always necessary."

"I recently discovered that some places of business use such a system to identify what they sell. Olaf introduced me to an Irish innkeeper who owns The Black Swan. That sign of his is very clever, don't you think?"

"It is a smart way to let people know what is inside, but he did not invent that method of advertising his business. People have been making signs for their buildings since the beginning of time, many only using pictures, no words. Like I said earlier, the artwork in our Bible and psalter is symbolic and they tell their own story, as do many of our signs."

"Also, Olaf may not want me to learn the written word. He does not trust it, I think?"

"You are partly right! He does not trust the word of God, who for me is the one and only God—he trusts only his gods. What you don't know is that Olaf fully understands the written word and knows how to use it to his advantage." Jon quickly changed the subject. "How about you Aud Unn? Who is your god or goddess?"

"Unn is our goddess. Our mother chose her for us and that is why my mother, myself, and my sisters each have her name attached to ours. She is one of the nine sisters born to Ran and Ægir, who are the god and goddess of the seas. Also these nine sisters are the joint mothers of the god Heimdel. Together they live below the sea and watch over the world's cycles. Each sister's name defines a characteristic of the sea; we know Unn as the goddess of the frothing waves, but together the nine sisters rule over all the waters that cover our earth. and are the goddesses of peace and fertility."

"That is quite a beautiful story, Aud Unn."

"Ahhhh—I understand now—it is only a story to you. Your religion would never allow a woman such power. Am I not right?"

"Maybe—maybe not! I think you are too quick to judge us Christians. The Bible is also comprised of stories, with stories of women as well. There are several books in the Bible named after a woman; the Book of Ruth, for example. Some of the stories in our Bible portray a message that helps us to understand life and become better people, like the Book of Proverbs. It also contains many stories of miracles performed by

Jesus Christ our Lord and Saviour as well as by his disciples. Besides miracles there are stories of love, death, violence; even floods, droughts, and starvation. It is very complex and can be difficult to understand for the ordinary person. That is why it is better for a trained priest to interpret these stories. The Bible is a fascinating collection of works and I would love to read some to you. They will absorb you—body and soul—I guarantee it! Better still, I will teach you to read so you can at least read the Book of Psalms yourself."

"Hmmm—it sounds too difficult, but maybe I will listen to some of your stories, Jon. You were kind enough to listen to mine today and I have many more. Maybe if we listen to each other we will both learn something?"

"Agreed!"

"Does this Bible of yours have stories of evil people as well?"

"Of course—it speaks of the devil—even has a name for him—Satan. He was once one of God's angels but rebelled against him, so he fell out of favour and was sent from heaven to earth. He lives here amongst us and works his evil deeds through unbelievers. Ones with a strong faith are the only ones well prepared to resist him; they are the ones who will join God in Heaven when they die and the rest join Satan in Hell."

"You have a *Hel*, we also believe in *Hel*. Amazing!"

"Yes I know. You seem to forget that I was once a pagan like yourself." Taking her arm gently he pointed to his ear, "I cannot hear the rain, it has either has stopped or is gentle enough to walk in. Unfortunately Queen Aud Unn, I must be elsewhere." Giving her his arm, "I would be honoured if you would allow me to accompany you back to the great hall, since it is on my way?"

Aud Unn felt an immediate companionship with this young man. *"Maybe—just maybe—I will take him up on his offer? If I do so will he think I want to become a Christian? I will need to be strong and resist his charms. These cousins have a powerful pull over my heart—except for Ivar of course. I see only evil in this man, he must be a son of Satan."* While these thoughts tumbled through her mind she covered her hair once again, then slipped her arm through his as they walked back towards the great hall, leaving Una, her maid, to trail behind them.

So absorbed in each other's ideas, they had both forgotten she was even there. It was only later that Aud Unn thought about what they had discussed and wondered if Una would report their conversations to her lover, the king himself. She had begun to suspect that she was one of his many women since Una was unable to look her in the eye whenever she asked about Olaf.

"Tell me, Jon, where does Olaf disappear to?"

"What do you mean?"

"We were not here long before he stopped coming to our bed for a week. I saw him during the day and when I asked him where he went at night he simply said that he had things to do, strategies to discuss with Ivar. Does he have another woman?"

"Olaf has many women and always has had. These two cousins of mine are well-known womanizers. But remember this, he made you his wife and queen so you are very important to him. Please do not push him, do not ruin what you have now, I beg of you."

"I suspected there were others. Maybe once we have a child he will change?"

"Just be happy, Aud Unn."

"Another thing, Jon, tell me about your cousin Ivar. Was he born a cripple? He frightens me."

"Ahhh, Ivar is different, I agree. He and Olaf are very close and together they have harried the shores of many countries, including Norway, and through these raids they have amassed much wealth. No, Ivar was not born a cripple. During one of their land attacks he was almost killed but Olaf saved his life. His leg was almost sliced off and it was difficult to heal, hence one leg is shorter than the other. Don't let his limp fool you; he can move as fast as a deer. Because Olaf saved his life Ivar is his devoted follower. His steadfast loyalty to our warrior-king is unfaltering."

"What makes him so fearful to people is his ancestry. His grandfather was none other than the infamous Ivar the Boneless, who was indeed born a cripple, and his brother was Olaf's grandfather Sigurd Snake-in-the eye. Both were sons of Ragnar Lothbrok; his genealogy is well known in all the northern countries. His saga you must have heard many times over; we northern peoples have all grown up with Ragnar's saga.

The Irish named Ivar, this crippled son of Ragnar's, Ivar the Boneless or Ivar the Hated, because he was so hated by most. They claim that he founded the Ui Ivar dynasty here in Ireland. So yes, my cousin Ivar is also nicknamed the Hated here because of who his grandfather was. He plays on this reputation to put the fear of God into us all, but he does not intimidate me. Both Olaf and Ivar are older than I but I have known them most of my life."

"Well he does disturb me! Oh my—here comes the rain again! We must hurry—the gong for the *nattmal* will soon be struck. Since King Kjarval is our honoured guest I must make myself beautiful. I have to make my husband proud of his queen. No?"

"Then I will leave you here with your maid to see you back to the hall and I will see you later tonight, since I have been invited to the feast."

"Of course! Una, I had forgotten you were even here. Come along now." The two women rushed towards the king's longhouse after saying their goodbyes to Jon the Priest.

Chapter 10

When Olaf and Aud Unn walked into the feasting hall that evening and took their place at the centre of the head table, Aud Unn noticed that her sister Jorunn Unn was seated between the Irish king and Ivar on Olaf's side of the table. She whispered to her father who sat on her left and asked him why this was. "King Kjarval requested her company. I think he likes how she looks and wants to get to know her. His wife has hidden herself away in a convent and the rumour is that he is looking for a new one. Jorunn Unn could do well here; he is quite a catch."

"Hmmm, very interesting *pabbi*, but isn't he much older than her?"

"Maybe, but he is a king and could possibly become the High King of Ireland. If he does he will then become a very desirable husband for all available women, no matter what his age is."

The feasting went on into the early hours of the morning and Jorunn Unn and the Irish king seemed to get on very well together. Even Ivar engaged with their conversations. Aud Unn set this abnormal scene in her head thinking to herself, "*I must ask my sister what she thinks of this man.*" The next morning, very few appeared at the *dagmal*. Olaf, Ivar, Ketill and Kjarval were in secret meetings once again and could not be disturbed. The women huddled together at the table, not really hungry as they had all drunk too much wine the night before. Jorunn

Unn could not resist telling them all about this Irish king, who she said was much attracted to her. One could tell that she was enamored with him, but they soon made their excuses and disappeared back to their own rooms. This was the one time that Aud Unn was grateful that Olaf was ignoring her. She needed her rest and privacy today to recover from her headache. She decided to ask about Ivar another time.

That night there was another feast and the seating pattern remained the same as the night before. Before the feast began Olaf announced that he would be joining King Kjarval on his journey back to his castle the next day, and that his queen and her family were invited to come too. Things were looking good for Jorunn Unn.

Aud Unn drank little wine that evening and decided to make it an early night, which turned out to be another night's sleep without her husband beside her. The next morning the lady's maids packed their trunks, as the maids claimed they were to be gone for a month. Apparently the maids knew more than the ladies did; according to them they were to be the guests of King Kjarval while the rest of the men went raiding the coasts of England and France. The battle for the title of the king of Tara had obviously begun. The amassing of wealth required to raise a huge force in Ireland was the start of their campaign, that much Aud Unn knew. Aud Unn did not know what to make of this silence on Olaf's part and decided that she must approach him about it. She felt it was her right as his queen to know more than her maid Una did.

The trip to Kjarval's castle did not take very long, as it was just a few hours away. By that evening they were ensconced into their own rooms, where they changed for the *nattmal*. His castle was a large building made of stones cut into bricks and layered until they reached a great height. There were two floors, which was something Aud Unn and her family had never seen before. They were used to large buildings, certainly, but they were always made of wood and stretched over one floor. Their rooms were on the second storey, with floors made of long planks of wood covered with hooked rugs made with colourful yarns, which did not quite cover all the gaps between the planks. Through them she could see to the floor below. They were cheerful large rooms, each with its own stone fireplace and with small windows that looked over green pastures filled with cattle. The windows actually had leaded glass to see through, although they were cloudy with many bubbles in them. There were shutters as well that one could close at night to shield them from the cold draughts. The bed was a four-poster and had heavy curtains that could be closed to further block any draughts.

Olaf watched Aud Unn as she stared out through the window; she appeared to be totally focused on the view outside. "One day I will build you a stone castle with a moat around it and with a great bridge to cross over. I have seen many such castles in England and France, with bigger glass windows than these and covered by drapes of beautiful cloth. The only downside of these stone castles is that they are much colder than our wooden ones. The dampness seeps through everything."

His words crept through her thoughts and brought her back to reality. "Olaf, why do you keep me in the dark about your plans? Una, the maid, knows more than I do."

"That is because I slept with her last night. If I had spent the night with you, you would have known before everyone."

"Ahhh—I see."

"No, I do not think that you do see Aud Unn. You may be my queen but I have an appetite for women that cannot be filled by just one. Do you understand now?"

"Yes, I think I do understand now." With that response, he offered her his arm and they walked out of the room and down the stairs to join everyone in the great dining hall, as King Kjarval called it. Aud Unn put on a brave face during the meal, smiling at everyone, nodding as if she was really listening to their conversations, but her heart was breaking in two. This marriage and so-called queenship was not turning out to be the beautiful dream she thought that it would become. Her attraction to him was still very strong and she wondered how was she to survive this life she had accepted so readily, if she was to share his love with other women? Then she remembered her recent conversation with Jon. *"Yes, that is what we must do—we must have a child together—and it must be a boy child. Then Olaf will choose me over the others."*

That night he came to her bed and she wondered if it was because he felt some guilt about what he had confessed to her. She set that thought aside and quietly begged the goddess Unn to do her part; after all she and her sisters were the goddesses of fertility.*" I have been blessed by you, Unn, so create your magic even if you have to ask your sisters for help to make this happen! We must have a child, a son!"* Olaf was a great lover and never failed to make her feel wonderful and well-loved, but the problem was that she wanted him to love her and only her. *"I must learn to control this jealousy; it could take over and then he may totally ignore me. Worse still, he may find another wife!"*

Afterwards, Olaf told her stories of previous raids with Ivar and she began to form a better idea of the dangers they would face to amass the booty they needed to build this army for King Kjarval. She savoured this intimacy once again and wished it could always be like this. Later the next day he left with her father to meet Ivar, who was waiting at the harbour with all their men and ships ready to raid England and France. King Kjarval remained behind, but she would be on her own with only her sister, mother and their maids. She could walk the grounds for fresh air with her maid, but she felt nothing for Una now that she knew for sure that she had Olaf's ear as well. If only her good friend Jon could be here, life in the Irish king's castle would be so much better.

Jorunn Unn was no longer good company; she spent all her time with Kjarval, forcing either their mother or Aud Unn to be in attendance to act as chaperone. She was dazzled by this man and all his wealth and authority. She hung onto every word he spoke while, Aud Unn and her mother chatted with each other whenever they were together. Their mother was looking quite content with it all and whispered words of hope to Aud Unn for a match between them.

"But he has a wife, *mamma*," she whispered back to her.

"So what? His first wife is enclosed in a nunnery and he does not want her as a wife. Because his church will annul his marriage, this will make him free and clear of any obligation to this woman. How easy is that?"

Aud Unn finally broke down and talked to her mother about her anxieties. "Oh *mamma,* I have to confess my distress with Olaf, he tells me that he sleeps with other women. I am beginning to think that all men are selfish and wayward. Was *pabbi* like this?"

"I never asked what he did while away from us all, but whenever he was home he was true to me only. I love and respect your *pabbi* and he knows it and values my devotion to him."

"Lucky you!"

"Just be thankful—you have a good life. You are a queen and one day soon you will have a child to fill your life with joy and love. Hopefully it will be soon and it will be a son. Just remember these words of wisdom, *elskamin*, 'Bedroom short time—live together long time.' A very wise woman once told me this and I think they have given me the strength to overcome any doubts I have had in my marriage."

"Who was this wise woman, *mamma*, and what exactly do those words mean?"

She smiled lovingly at her daughter as she stroked her face.

"My mother. She explained to me that 'bedroom' symbolized sex. When you are young and first married obviously it means everything, especially if you have a duty to produce that male heir. To many men a bedroom is only ever about sex, as you have discovered. To 'live together long time' represents understanding, a good relationship whether it is an arranged union or a mutually agreed union. It is about honour, respect, trust, even love—yes, even love. But it is more about eventually becoming good friends."

"Like you and *pabbi*?"

"Yes, like me and *pabbi*. It can be the same for you and Olaf, but that is up to you. Only you can make it work better, and I suppose that means accepting his other women. I know this is difficult for you, you are still so young, but we arranged this marriage because it meant a crown for you and your future child. It also made a stronger partnership for your father. Olaf will watch your father's back because of you and vice versa. We have become connected because of this union but it is also a business arrangement. Remember that!"

"I do understand *mamma*, and only recently fully understood my role and how important it really is. But Olaf has this way of making me feel so special and I just cannot get over my jealousy of all the other women in his life. Once I have that boy child, maybe I can relax and just enjoy my station as a queen. Am I abnormal because I want him to be with me all the time?"

"Oh daughter of mine, you are truly one of Goddess Unn's chosen. She has blessed you with desires and intelligence most women never possess or would never understand if they did. Use them, but use them wisely and always with your sight on the future. You will not endure as Olaf's consort if your king does not want to confide in you. Inside information, knowledge of what is going on, keeping his confidence in you are just some of the things you must focus on. Together they will give you the power you will need to retain your position of strength. Trust your mother, I know what I am talking about."

"You are the smartest woman I know, *mamma!*"

Not long after arriving at the castle their mother caught a cold that kept her in her room much of the time with chills and a slight fever. This left only Aud Unn to watch over her sister and she was soon very bored with it all. There was no one to talk to and Una was not the one she desired to spend much time with these days, but after her mother's words of wisdom she decided that she must try to be more understanding of her maid's position. Information is power and her maid sometimes knew more than she did. She would continue her sacrifices to the goddess Unn, asking that if Una conceived that she not give birth to a boy child. Aud Unn did not think she could become more thoughtful towards her if that became a reality.

Chapter II

Many days after the men had left to raid the coasts of England and France, Jon showed up at the castle. Aud Unn was surprised to see him but her delight was very obvious. "Jon, you have gladdened my heart enormously, but why are you here?"

"Olaf asked me to find some time and join you ladies for a time, to keep you entertained. He said that you liked my company and felt you would be far too lonely with him away. What a thoughtful husband, don't you think?"

"Yes, very thoughtful indeed!" was her caustic comment. "Or was he worried I may stray and find the company of another man? An Irishman maybe?"

"Do I detect a voice filled with sarcasm, Aud Unn?"

"Maybe—just maybe! To be honest, I am struggling with his need of other women, Jon."

"Hmmm, well we all have needs and mine is to hear your version of our famous pagan gods and goddesses; as you know I am somewhat familiar with most of them as I grew up with them too, but I do so enjoy your telling of them. You do remember our promise to each other—if I listen to your pagan stories you will listen to my Bible stories?"

Aud Unn laughed out loud. "Oh you do make me happy, Jon, even though you are trying to deflect my concerns—are you not? Nevertheless

I will listen to your Bible stories. I look forward to them and I am sure *mamma* and Jorunn Unn will love to listen too."

There was a small room in the castle that had one wall with a couple of shelves lined with valuable books and scrolls, and with a great fireplace in the middle. King Kjarval called it the library. It was the warmest and most comfortable room in the castle and they continued to congregate there every afternoon. Now it was all the more enjoyable as Jon enthralled them with his miraculous stories from the great Bible, while the women told both him and the king stories of battles and great deeds that involved their gods and goddesses. Fortunately Yngvild Unn was feeling much better soon after Jon had arrived, and was able to join in the conversations once again. The days flew by for all and before Aud Unn and the others realized it, the men had returned from their raids.

Not long after returning to Dubhlinn an announcement was made that Jorunn Unn was to be married to King Kjarval, on condition she become a Christian. Without hesitation she readily accepted and promised to drop the pagan Unn from her name and become known simply as Jorunn Ketillsdottir. A great wedding was planned for the next month.

In the meantime Olaf and his partners gathered together a great army that marched by foot to the High King of Tara's home castle in the neighbouring kingdom of Munster. This march would take several days and was led by Ivar and Ketill on horseback. That way they could ride up and down the columns of men who were marching on foot, speaking words of encouragement to keep the men together and on the continuous march. There were a number of carts pulled by horses and manned by one unit of men who would ride ahead to set up camps for the marching men. Ketill and Ivar understood these men; if they were well fed and had enough to drink they would stay on the march. With full bellies they would remain faithful to their cause for the short time they would be needed.

A few days later Olaf and Kjarval set sail in a longship with many men and many ships to face off with the aging king of Tara, Fearghal

Ui Nial. They met up with Ketill and Ivar and their marching army just a mile away from his castle. Kjarval, Olaf and their men marched up to the castle of the High King and confronted him with their request—that he step down in favour of his grandson, a much younger man, Kjarval Macdunghal, king of Ossory. At first the old king resisted but when he saw a much larger army led by Ivar and Ketill appear out of nowhere and surround his forces there was no question of not stepping down. He knew a battle was pointless and he conceded defeat saying, "Young Cearbhall, you would have been the king of Tara eventually but I see that you have no patience to wait for this honour. No good will come of such eagerness and greed, of that I am sure."

"You speak of greed, grandfather, but you did not have to wait as long for this crown as I have. Your inability to make a timely abdication, as your father did and his father before him, has given new meaning to the word greed."

"I am retired now; it is all yours, but mark my words young Cearbhall, no good will come from your using force to acquire this crown."

"Right, now be off with you old man, but before you go I will take your crown." With those words Kjarval turned to the mass of men and lifted the crown of Tara high in the air. A shout of approval resounded throughout the area, which made him feel quite justified in acquiring it the way he did. Now it just needed the bishop's ceremony to make him the legal High King of Tara and he wanted that done before his wedding to Jorunn. He felt quite pleased with himself; he now had the crown of all Ireland in his hands. He knew it would not give him total authority over all the minor kingdoms, but what it would give him was more wealth. These lesser kings recognized and honoured the ancient crown of Tara and would pay tribute to it.

Beside this increased wealth, Kjarval would soon have a new, young, fertile wife. Although his grandfather had referred to him as 'young Cearbhall' he was no longer a young man. He already had three grown daughters who had families of their own, so he too was a grandfather. Now all he wanted was a son of his own, and Jorunn was the woman young enough to produce many children. His daughters had all married high-ranking Northmen who had fled from their Norwegian King Harold Fair-Hair and gone to live in a far-off country called Iceland.

Any grandchildren he did have lived too far away for him to get to know them. It was vital for him to mould the right one to become the heir to his lands. Even if he had been interested in any of his grandchildren living in the far northern regions, he did not know if there any were male children. It was possible they had all had girls, or no children at all. He believed by marrying a much younger woman, he was increasing his chances of having a male heir. He truly believed that he had years ahead of him and was healthy enough to sire many more children.

Chapter 12

After Jorunn's magnificent wedding Ketill and Ygnvild Unn sailed off to the Hebrides, where they would set up their home base. Although Aud Unn did not see a lot of her older sister, Jorunn was now a higher queen than her, and by Irish royal etiquette she had to bow to her older sister; this really vexed her. Even Olaf had to pay tribute to Kjarval, which he did not seem to mind, but this just made her more indignant than ever. To further frustrate the situation Jorunn was soon with child. Aud Unn made her weekly sacrifices to Unn the goddess of fertility but so far none of the offerings had produced any results. She moaned about the lack of results from her sacrifices to Jon whenever she was in his company. *"It is better to complain to Jon than Olaf; that just makes him more frustrated to be with me,"* she had decided. One Sunday after Mass as they strolled through the church's gardens, Jon was party to her complaints once again, but this time he made a challenge to her.

"If I can prove to you that my God is more powerful than yours, would you consider converting to my religion? I know you are desperate to have a child and I truly believe—I have that much faith in my lord God—I believe that he will give you the opportunity to have a child. Are you brave enough to accept this challenge?"

Aud Unn stood and looked at him, astounded by his daring words. "Me! A Christian! Impossible, Jon—just impossible!"

"So be it! But I know a very worthy doctor who is now a strong Christian himself, and between us I truly believe he has the faith and the knowledge to help you have this coveted child. I will pray for you every day and then we will see who is stronger—your gods or my one God! You think about this offer and let me know if you dare."

Aud Unn went off to her room where she dwelt over his challenge. *"Maybe I am trying too hard and that is why Olaf leaves me alone so much?"* She knew that after Jorunn's success she was driving him crazy with her constant nattering about having a child. *"Now obviously Jon is fed up too, tired of listening to me go on and on about having a child; why else would he dare me to talk to this doctor? Maybe if I was to pass on this responsibility to Jon and his Christian doctor, maybe, just maybe I could let it go and be able to relax about not yet being pregnant. Would Olaf then come to our room more often?"*

Her father was due to arrive with the next full moon; then he, Olaf and Ivar were to sail to Scotland to harry King Constantine's coastline. Olaf and Ivar had raided in that country several times before, and the monasteries there proved to have much gold and silver. After Scotland they planned to raid Northumbria. They would be away for quite some time, so she needed to have Olaf come to her without her constant stress being so visible. *"Maybe I should take up Jon's challenge? What do I have to lose? I could become a convenient Christian just like my brother Helgi did so he could trade with them without too many complications. After all, we have many gods and this Christian god would just be one more? I could easily fool Jon, couldn't I? He is so trusting of me—I think?"*

The very next day she went to search for him but this time asked Una to wait in the vestibule, telling her that she did not plan to linger inside. In reality, she did not want Una to hear what she had to say, so she went to look for him alone and found him furiously pacing in his rectory at the back of the church.

"What is wrong Jon?"

"It is Ivar! He has killed another man with his violent temper. Even though he is my cousin he can be a vile and evil man. I talked to Olaf this morning to try and make him understand that Ivar cannot act this way in a Christian country; they do not accept this kind of behaviour. Olaf does not see it as a problem but if Ivar continues to murder and rape people the Irish will band together against them both. I tried to make him see that he will be tarnished with the same brush but with Olaf it is like talking to a stone wall when it comes to Ivar."

"What can you, a gentle kind man, do about it, Jon? They are both powerful and dangerous men. Well, Ivar is the dangerous one, but you cannot go against them."

"You do not understand, Aud Unn. Now I have to go and visit this family who are Christians and pray with them for the soul of their child. Even though he was a man, he was their child and he cannot receive the last rites because he died before I had a chance to get there. What you pagans do not understand is that these rituals are very important to us. Ivar continues to bully and terrify these people and many are not just peasants. He is stepping on the wrong toes."

"He will be leaving to raid Scotland after the next full moon, along with Olaf and my father, so hopefully if he is not seen people will forget his evil ways and just get on with their lives."

"We should be so lucky, but I have heard rumblings against him and fear there could be reprisals regardless. It is not so long ago that he raped a chieftain's maid, a man who has much power and has some ties to Kjarval. Also this maid was his favorite, if you know what I mean?" He didn't wait for her response. "If this continues even the High King will not be able to ignore his people's complaints and he could conveniently forget that he needed Olaf and Ivar's assistance to obtain that crown of his. There was another incident not too long ago, and I know Olaf paid the man off. Something to do with the innkeeper of the Black Swan."

"You know about this? I was there when Ivar almost ran me down leaving that very inn. What happened? They were speaking in Gaelic and I couldn't understand."

"I shouldn't be gossiping about this, since I heard about it third-hand, but since it was about Ivar I can believe he did such a thing. You may not know this but the innkeeper and his family are strong Christians. Some inns are little more than brothels but this establishment is a clean house. Apparently on that day Ivar had too much to drink and when a serving wench walked by him he grabbed her and fondled her in front of everyone. He thought it was very funny, but the young woman was horrified and screamed, which brought the proprietor out from the back room. It turned out that this wench was a cousin of the owner. She is a simple country girl and is living with them temporarily until she marries the farmer she has been promised to. Unfortunately her family were struggling to fulfill their marriage settlement so they came looking for help from their cousin, who they think is rich. Their cousin the innkeeper was not going to just hand over the money, otherwise all the relatives would come demanding help so he requested that she work for it. When Ivar abused his cousin, the owner of the inn banned him from returning, which threw him into a fit of temper. It is said that he threatened the owner, but I later heard that Olaf paid off the innkeeper as well as her settlement. So Olaf has made a peace offering once again for this evil man."

"I can believe this to be true as well since I witnessed coins pass from Olaf to this man. But enough about Ivar, I am here to make your day a little happier by telling you that I am seriously thinking of accepting your challenge. Does that shock you?"

"Really? Now you have made me a very happy man! I will come find you later today, after I have visited this family and hopefully put everything to rights. Olaf agreed that I could offer them *wergild* so hopefully that will be enough to appease them, but as a Christian, money is not what it is all about. This is something you will learn when you become a Christian."

"Jon—you never give up, do you?" He had a way with her that always made her laugh. "Remember, I am only just thinking about it, I am not quite convinced yet. You need to tell me more about this god of yours, and especially about this doctor."

Chapter 13

Winter had come and gone and the spring had passed, with all the seeds safely planted. Still Aud Unn was not with child, unlike her older sister who was now big with her first child. The time had come for the raids to begin in earnest, and Scotland and Northumbria were the chosen countries; soon her *pabbi* would come to Ireland. He arrived as promised during the first full moon of summer but without Aud Unn's mother. He brought some unhappy news. Since arriving back in the Hebrides her cold had returned and she had lost much weight and could not seem to get well. He claimed that he left her in good hands and was anxious to get these raids over with and return to her. He was not long in Dubhlinn before the men set off on their raids, so Aud Unn did not get to spend much time with her beloved *pabbi*.

Olaf had told her much about Iona Abbey, which was the centre of the Scottish church and claimed it held much wealth. This was to be their first destination to gather treasure, but the slaves, he said, would be the most valuable commodity. They would find them wherever they went, whether it was Scotland or England. They were only gone about two weeks, and returned with bountiful treasures and many slaves. Both Olaf and Ketill shared some of their riches with Aud Unn, which she quickly hid in a trunk that could be locked. Her father had had a long talk with her and advised her to amass and save as much wealth as possible. "You never know, *elskamin,* when a hidden treasure will be needed to save your life; so always maintain a stash hidden in several places. And never let anyone know what you have."

"Yes *pabbi—takk fyrir.* Olaf tells me that you had a meeting with one of the Kings of Scotland—he said that this king pledged to pay you a raider's tribute if you promised to stop harrying his coastlines. Is that true?"

"Yes it is. We have made a secret deal and plan to join forces with him. I don't know how Olaf does it, but it could become a very strategic alliance between us and Constantine, which also includes his two brothers. However, our spies tell us that his two brothers are vying for his crown, as is his brother-in-law Artgal. This relationship could get complicated, so I have advised Olaf to be very cautious. I will not be here all the time, and that will leave only Ivar to hold him back if King Constantine expects too much of Olaf. As you know, I don't completely trust Ivar; he normally does whatever Olaf wants but at times, left alone together, they are capable of making rash decisions. They believe that they are untouchable; they have survived many battles where there appeared to be no escape. With such an attitude it can be dangerous for them to make an effective decision when it involves so many ambitious men. I will rely on you to be mindful and always caution Olaf to be careful, to think things through before making a decision. I know he will tell you what he is planning; he always does so, does he not *elksamin?*"

"Yes *pabbi,* Olaf does discuss things with me and recently he spoke much about the siege you are planning." Aud Unn spoke with confidence.

"*Jæja*—that is good! We plan to take over a place called Dunbarton, the capital of Strathclyde. It is the high seat of Constantine's brother-in-law, Artgal, the king of Strathclyde. He wants us to assassinate this king as Constantine is quite aware of his greed and of his plans to assassinate him and his two brothers. Besides becoming Viking raiders, we are to become *ansatt snikmorders.*" He rolled his eyes and threw his hands in the air.

"Although all of us are captivated by the escalating intrigue developing in Scotland, we must be wary of all the difficulties between the brothers and brother-in-law. All this fighting between families is opening the country up to an invasion; nobody can get along with anyone. Scotland is made up of clans, which are composed of individual families that are linked through ties of blood. When they intermarry it blurs the lines. They have a hard enough time getting along with each other and they are also constantly falling out with other clans. I think the siege of Dunbarton castle is just an outlet to hide the internal strife that is destabilizing the whole country."

"The clans fight over women, land, cattle, which way the clouds fly by—anything at all!. They are such a contentious lot, they argue for the sake of arguing. Constantine also has a great army of Picts, they fight like *berserkers*; a very crazy lot of men but fierce fighters. They don't wear any clothes and their bodies are covered with blue tattoos. When in battle, they look fierce at first, but can be killed just like any other man. More easily, in fact, because their only armour is their shield and our axes can easily knock those out of their hands. Their greatest weapon is the element of surprise; they appear out of nowhere and can hide better than any army I know. Olaf has a more disciplined army, which would be a great asset to Constantine."

"If all goes the way we plan, this king could bring peace back to his country, but as I said before, we need to be cognizant of the difference between friend and foe. Before this can happen, though, I must return to the Hebrides to make sure your mother is well and then return to Dubhlinn before the harvests begin. The timing will be crucial for this siege."

His daughter slipped her arm through his as they continued their walk together in the garden. "*Pabbi*, all countries are the same. The Scottish clans don't sound any different than our Norwegian families." Smiling as she gave him a hug. "I will miss you and our conversations. Please tell *mamma* that I love her and I hope she gets well and can return with you. Jorunn would love to show off her child the next time you come and I hope to have some good news that I am with child. Jon the Priest knows another priest who is also a doctor of medicine and says he can help me."

"I don't trust doctors; do not be taken in by these so-called Christians."

"I know, I know! I think like you, *pabbi* but maybe we can be too cautious? Jon is the only other person I trust in the world besides you and Olaf. Speaking of trust, *pabbi*, since you don't really trust Ivar, how can you travel with him? He gives me the chills."

"Ivar? Oh he can look evil all right, but I do know one thing good about him and that is he will do anything for Olaf. He is extremely loyal to him and to him only. But if anything was to happen to Olaf then I would become very wary of him and you should too. You should have a plan ready to be able to flee, just in case Ivar outlives your husband."

Loneliness swamped Aud Unn after her father left. Olaf and Ivar were rarely around as they spent much time in Scotland working out their plan to seize Dunbarton for Constantine. She began to seek out Jon the Priest more than ever. One day she received a message to meet him at the church. He was finally going to introduce her to the other priest who claimed to be a doctor, so she went alone. The doctor's name was David; he simply bowed his head when they were introduced. He looked very foreign to her; he had a very large hooked nose and dark eyes with bushy eyebrows. His hair, although greying, had been very black at one time. The top of his head was shaved, and when she asked why that was Jon explained it was because he was a monk. "A monk is a priest like me, but the difference is that monks live a solitary life secluded from the people, while a priest is more active in his community."

"Funny—not long ago my father told us a story about his grandfather fishing in Iceland. His ship got blown off course and he and his men ended up there. While there they came across a small group of Irishmen who appeared to be very religious. They had made their way all the way north in leather boats just to find privacy and solitude. I never understood why they wanted such isolation and did not realize that they were called monks. Why would this friend of yours choose to live a life like that? Where is this monastery?"

"It is quite close to us and is called Baile Atha Cliath. He chose it so he could study the creation of life every day to try to understand it and then be able to cure it when it goes wrong. Like I said, he was once a doctor in his country; when he was kidnapped and brought to Dubhlinn he quickly converted to Christianity as he recognized the value of its teachings, or so he says, but the access to its libraries was the biggest reason. Right, Brother David? As a learned Christian, he can now read

Latin and before that he could read Arabic and Hebrew; he was a Jew in his other life as well as being a doctor."

He simply smiled and bowed his head once more as Jon continued to expand on Brother David's need for learning. "Our church has copies of the books of many famous writers who are or were experts in their fields. Medicine is his field and he has access to much knowledge, as well as the time to grow and study the herbs necessary to heal ordinary people. I have to give Olaf credit for obtaining copies of many valuable books for our church. Normally during a siege these books would be burned or tossed into the sea because Vikings don't read, so they don't care for what the books contain. Since Olaf understands the power of the written word he collects them for us. I know I may sound like a self-righteous Christian but I don't want to know how he gets them. This is a case where ignorance really is bliss and this attitude helps me sleep at night."

During their discussion of him Brother David continued to smile and nod his head. When he looked up and smiled at Aud Unn his eyes wrinkled with kindness. Both she and Jon were much taller and towered over him, but his gentle manner and his look of concern put any fears she had to rest. She could feel an aura of kindness surrounding him. "Brother David, I am so very pleased to meet you. My mother would love to make your acquaintance as she is very interested in the healing herbs as well. She has not been well lately, but I hope she will be strong enough to sail here with father before the harvests begin. Then maybe you can help her get well?"

"I would be honoured to meet your mother."

This was the first time Aud Unn had heard his voice and realized what a heavy accent he had. Her curiosity was piqued. "What country did you come from?"

"A place very far from here called Constantinople. You North people are such travelers, such expert sailors, you go everywhere. But you also loot and kidnap—that is why I am here—but then you are not the only ones to do this; so do men from all countries. It has proven to be such a profitable business it has become a way of life for many peoples, including my own."

He did not sound angry or bitter with his lot in life. He calmly proceeded to ask her many questions about her health and way of life, such as how often Olaf came to their bed and other things. Before Aud Unn realized it she had revealed everything about herself, including her fears and anxieties. After he had left to return to his isolation Jon walked Aud Unn back to the great hall. "How does he do that? He immediately gains your full confidence and you reveal all," she declared as she slipped her arm through his.

"That is what makes him a great doctor. It is just too bad he is not more active in the Christian community; he could draw in so many people to the church. Thankfully though, he does not hesitate to leave his seclusion to administer his healing remedies. I fear he is more of a scientist than a doctor and would never have become a priest except for the benefits that the priesthood gives him access to."

Jon's comment made Aud Unn think of her brother Helgi. *"They think the same, this priest and brother of mine. Becoming a Christian was just for the convenience of access, whether it be trade or knowledge—am I any different? I may convert only if I have a child but will I ever really believe as Jon does? Somehow I think not! Hmm—what is a scientist?"*
"A scientist? What is that?"

"This is a new word for a philosopher who studies nature or the human body. Intellectuals are calling these studies a science of nature and a physical science. I have learned much from Brother David, as you can see. So in essence a scientist asks questions, then establishes a theory and proceeds to study and research any knowledge available. They experiment with their theories and discover new ways to heal the body or to understand nature and then they write it all down to pass on their discoveries and knowledge for the next inquiring mind. We live in an incredible age, Aud Unn; with all our travels we have discovered many advanced countries. By bringing these people here, even as slaves, the Vikings have advanced our knowledge. But mind you, never admit this to Olaf, it will go to his head."

"Jon, this is all very interesting, *takk*! Yes, I will keep this conversation of scientists from Olaf. I do not fully understand all this myself, so how would I be able to explain it to him? Besides, he likes to think he is the one who knows it all, so he may well become wary of you and all your knowledge."

Jon patted her arm, acknowledging her insight into her husband's attributes as well as his limitations.

Chapter 14

Olaf and Ivar returned from Scotland excited about the upcoming siege of Dunbarton. Olaf eagerly told all to Aud Unn. "The castle sits upon a large rock called Dunbarton's Rock on the north side of the River Clyde, and another river called the Leven flows into the Clyde. We have a strategy that we think will be successful."

She was thankful that Olaf was confiding in her. "So tell me this great idea of yours, my lord."

"Simple really; we will cut off their water and food supply. The castle and the village rely solely on these two rivers for both. There is a small bridge connecting the castle to the mainland which they will raise to deny us access. We will simply build our own bridge to have ready when the time comes for us to cross over."

"Will this then prevent a great battle?"

"Correct! Less people killed means more slaves to obtain—unfortunately, many may die from starvation but they will be mainly the weak and the old—those people are of no real value to us anyways. Now, you must excuse me as my cousin Jon has requested a private audience with me."

"Of course, husband." Aud Unn escaped to her room wondering what Jon was up to, "*Maybe it is about having a child? Patience, if it is so, Olaf will soon tell me.*" Fearful of his reaction, she ordered a glass of wine brought to their room, hoping that it would quell the anxiousness she felt. He might be angry with her for confiding in a priest.

Jon had indeed requested a private audience with his cousin the king, which Olaf appeared to accept with good cheer. Jon, on the other hand, was as apprehensive as Aud Unn because it was not just about her needs. He was worried about just how well his cousin would react to his advice. The *thrall* poured them each a goblet of wine then set a basket of nuts, fruit and cheese on the table before Olaf dismissed her.

"Now cousin, what necessitates this consultation so soon after I have arrived back from Scotland?"

"Two things, my lord. First I need to know if you had that talk with Ivar. I have had some more news from two highly respected Irish chieftains. They claim that if he does not stop his harassment of their women, it may threaten your alliance with the High King himself. People are complaining directly to King Kjarval now, and may have captured his ear."

"I have spoken with Ivar and he assures me that this will stop, but I will speak to him again today. He does not see it as harassment, of that I am sure, so I will emphasize the urgency of his need to cease this action. Maybe now he will listen, as Kjarval's alliance is as important to him as it is to me. Now what is your other concern?"

"Your wife, sire."

"My wife?"

"Yes, she is so desperate to have a child and I do believe that I have found a way to make this happen."

"What? Do you plan on sleeping with my wife, cousin?"

"No my lord, how can you even think of that? Besides, I am unable to do anything as you well know."

"Ha ha, Jon, how I love to tease you. But that was cruel, I agree. Just thinking about your castration brings pain to my whole body. What a cruel and unjust thing to do to a slave. Killing them is kinder."

Jon thought that this was good time to bring up the fact that he had met Helgi, Aud Unn's brother. "My short time as a slave was not a good time for me, but it helped me find my faith in the lord God and now I am very happy where I am. The Moors can be a cruel lot, even to their own; they hide their many women away in harems away from prying eyes.

These women need protection from roving men but to ensure that the protectors cannot rape them, they make their guards into eunuchs. One of the other protectors was a priest; his name was also Jon, but he called himself Brother John. He was a monk from a monastery in England and apparently that is the English way to pronounce our common name. He converted me with his staunch faith in God and every day we prayed to be captured by one of our own to take us away from that life. His god answered our prayers; a horde of Norwegians on a *viking* journey did show up and save us. It was a miracle that convinced me of the power the Christian god wielded, but nobody, not even this powerful god could undo the butchering those Moors did to our bodies."

"You were lucky these Vikings took over that city, even if it was only for a short time."

"Yes. I recently found out that your wife's brother Helgi was part of the group that saved us when they captured Seville and took the whole harem, including us protectors, as slaves."

"Helgi Ketillsson? I did not know that he was part of the Viking group that sold you to me. When did you find this out? Why have you not told me this before?"

"I just forgot about him. He was an unknown, a relative newcomer to that Norwegian group of Vikings so he had no history. It was his first time away from Norway and we seldom spoke when together. You obviously don't remember him being part of that Viking group either! When I first met him I did not realize that he was the son of the famous Ketill Flat-Nose. The few times we spoke it was quite obvious that Helgi loved to talk and he told us a few stories, and some things about his family in Norway but I did not make the connection. It was a terrible time for me and I had banished all that happened in Seville from my mind—but something recently kindled my memory."

Jon sipped his wine and continued, "I did not want to tell you until I had a chance to confirm this with Aud Unn herself. You have to realize that at that time, these men were far from home, and many had lost their entire families to King Harold's campaign for the crown of all Norway. Many were just peasants and homesick for a land they could not return to, so some invented a family that was more powerful than their own, hoping to appear more important than they really were. Also I did not think that you would be all that interested so I left it to Aud Unn to tell you. When we spoke the other day she said that when she is with you, her attention is on you only and that she never really thinks of the rest of her family since they live so far away. But I am telling you now for a good reason."

"What is that good reason, Jon?"

"Because I liked Helgi and his stories even though I did not connect him to the famous Ketill. Also because he was part of the Viking group that saved us and brought us to Dubhlinn to sell as slaves, thus he helped save my life. I chose not tell any one of them that you were my cousin, just in case you would not save me! You did just admit to me that it would be kinder to kill a man than to castrate him so you can understand my apprehensions. That is exactly what I feared from you. Castration may have crippled my manhood but I still wanted to live. The priesthood was my calling, a safe vocation for a man such as me. I was unsure how my warrior-king cousin would accept this damaged man with such a vision, but accept me you did and I am more thankful than you will ever know. Life to me is very precious; I understand Aud Unn's desire to bring a life into the world. Humankind's desire to procreate is a very powerful force in us all, both men and women. I prayed for guidance in my search to help your wife. By helping the sister of the man who saved me, I feel like I have repaid him and the others just a little."

"Well, now tell me how you propose to help her do this, or help us both as you said. I too desire a child, and preferably a male child. Can you guarantee that?"

"Of course I cannot give such a promise but I may be able to help you both in producing a child. Through the priesthood I have met a monk who is also a doctor and his name is Brother David. He is a very knowledgeable and learned man who has studied the human body extensively in Constantinople and even here in Dubhlinn. Thanks to your raids in scriptoriums, the books you have brought back to us are enormously valuable for all the knowledge they hold within their pages. He tells me that the female body has cycles, and during part of their cycle they are more fertile than usual. If two people are trying to conceive, it is essential to spend the nights with that woman during this very fertile time. He claims he can predict Aud Unn's cycle. We both know that you are capable of producing a child, but he has made a potion for the male to become more potent as well. Will you agree to this plan, sire?"

"Recently I was just thinking that maybe I should find another wife if Aud Unn Ketillsdottir does not have a child soon. She has been driving me into a *berserker* with her nattering about having a child. But my alliance with Ketill and Kjarval are too important to me; I do not want to damage it in any way so I must keep her as my wife. Especially now that Ivar may have put it at risk, it is even more important she remains queen—at least for now! This potion, I must know what it is composed of before I risk it. Bring this monk to me tomorrow."

"He is a monk after all and likes to be secluded from people and may find your environment too overwhelming. With your permission I will bring the list of ingredients and read them to you as well as the days you should be spending with Aud Unn. Will that suffice, if he finds it too intimidating to appear before you? If not, I will surely force him to come."

"Granted."

"Thank you my king and cousin. You have my word, on my life, that it will be safe to consume."

Laughing, Jon was so relieved at Olaf's acceptance that he felt comfortable enough to make a joke with him. "Even knowing that it will not be useful to me in any way cousin, I will take a sip before you do. I am that confident that it will be safe for you to drink." As was the custom of agreements within their shared culture, they both spit into the palm of their hand before clasping them tightly. Their pact was sealed.

Olaf appeared in their room every night for the time prescribed by Brother David and drank the potion given to him each time. It gave him much energy and he decided that he must ask for it on a regular basis, as he had several women to please. Aud Unn was beside herself with joy and savoured every evening with the man she admired and respected; she felt such hope for her future as a mother.

Chapter 15

Una, her maid, was beginning to show. It was obvious to all that she was with child. Her morning sickness prevented her from leaving the great hall, forcing Aud Unn to walk on her own. Walking to Jon's church was now a daily occurrence. She was becoming quite familiar with her new surroundings, so she felt comfortable to walk about on her own. One day a cloudburst forced her into the archway of a warehouse that was on the route. Seeking protection from the heavy deluge she ran straight into a strange man, who appeared to be waiting for the storm to pass as she was. This unexpected man turned out to be none other than the most dreaded person she could have run into, Ivar!

"Well, well, well—if it isn't our beautiful queen herself."

"Ivar, I did not see you there. Excuse me, but I will just run over to Jon's church, it is very close by. Good day to you, sir."

Ivar put his arm across her shoulders, which prevented her from leaving. Then he moved closer to her, breathing hard into her face, thus forcing her to press her back against the arch. There was no escaping from his strong arm; his eyes were dark and threatening and his breath stank of wine and garlic. No longer terrified, anger flared throughout her body as she pushed him away. "How dare you accost me like you would an ordinary peasant or *thrall*!"

A loathsome smile curled his lips into a sneer. "You walk around by yourself as if you were a peasant and not a queen. You avoid me every chance you get; if I did not know better, I would think you were afraid of me. Why is that?"

"Afraid! Never—you may be our king's favorite cousin—but I am his chosen wife and your queen! Don't you ever accost me like that again! Ever! For your information I avoid you because *I don't like you, Ivar!*"

The hatred that flared in his eyes shot through her and Aud Unn realized that her burst of temper had got the better of her. She had just made a powerful enemy, an enemy known to rape and murder for the sake of it. As she rushed away, she vowed never to walk alone again. Meanwhile in her haste to get away from this now fiercely hated man, her hood brushed against his outstretched arm, falling back off her head and exposing her hair to the downpour. She did not notice in her haste, and the unexpected cloudburst quickly soaked her cloak as well as her loosely hanging hair that she was normally so proud of. Her heart was pounding in her chest with both anger and with fear, her soaked hair hung about her shoulders and some strands were plastered against her face; she realized that she would appear disturbed, broken even. As she stopped under the church door's overhang to catch her breath, her mother popped into her head. *"Mamma you are right, as always. If I had done up my hair in braids as you would have had me do, at this moment I wouldn't look quite so distressed."*

She remained standing for another moment trying hard to still her racing heart. She had intended to tell Jon about her encounter with Ivar, but as she put her hand on the door to enter the church, she realized the folly of such a complaint. He would insist on telling Olaf, not only for her sake but for the simple reason of trying to once again expose Ivar's cruel side to him. He would want to expose Ivar to a man who of course did not like to hear anything negative about this favorite cousin. Her hand over her heart, she now understood what she had to do; she would have to lie to Jon, a man she come to regard, to respect and honour. Not liking the situation, she thought to herself, *"Olaf would rather bury his head in the sand; how can he not see this side of his cousin and why did I react like I did? I don't normally lose my temper—what happened to me? Fear? Of course—who wouldn't fear such evil?"*

She entered the church looking about for any sign of Jon's presence. Relieved not to see him, she went straight to the altar to pray to the statue of Jesus, imploring him to watch over her and to forgive her small lie. She looked up at the icon of Jesus, then tried to wipe her wet hair off her face, not quite succeeding. She bowed her head in prayer once more. She no longer felt safe alone. This is how Jon found her, in prayer and dripping wet. "Aud Unn, what a lovely surprise to see such devotion to our Lord. My lord, you are soaking wet! Here, let me help you out of that cloak. I will hang it in my rectory by the fire." His words surprised her; she tried to stand up but stumbled instead. Some wet strands of her beautiful blond hair still stuck to her face exposing her distress. "My God, what happened?"

"Nothing—please, it was nothing. I tried to escape from the deluge but instead bumped into a scary old man—a stranger—it frightened me. He did me no harm—I could see that he had no intention of any harm. He was as surprised, as I was, but his ragged looks startled me. I rushed here to find you and now that you are here Jon, I feel quite safe. I have never noticed any poverty in this area before, but I assume it must exist. I promise you I will never walk here alone again, so do not worry. This has been a good cure for my arrogance. Now for my daily lesson in Christianity dear friend; it will be sure to comfort and calm me down."

"Poverty exists in every village or town, but I have never seen it come this close to the great hall before. The guards generally keep them in their own ghettos. I will speak to Olaf about this."

"No—no—please do not do that. I will be more careful in future—I promise. I will speak to him." Jon gave her a funny look and Aud Unn realized that he did not quite believe her. "*I will have to be careful what I say in future; forgive me Jon, the truth may have been better after all.*"

The Queen of Dubhlinn had indeed learned a very good lesson—to be on guard at all times around one's enemies. For the rest of the summer she never left the great hall unattended, thus she had to adjust to spending less time at Jon's church and more time on her own. She consoled herself that harvest time was fast approaching, and counted the days to *pabbi's* return, anxiously praying that her mother would appear with him. Prayer was no longer strange or foreign; it was another thing she had learned to do, besides reading the odd word in her Book of Psalms, lent to her by Jon the Priest.

One of her most fervent prayers appeared to have been answered. She suspected there would be good news to announce to all, but she must not build up too much hope, just in case she was wrong. Brother David had explained the signs of an expectant mother to Jon and he had passed them on to her, but she already knew from Jorunn and from Una what to expect. Recently each morning she had started to experience the upset stomach they both talked about and what Brother David said could be the first sign of being with child. The loss of appetite was another possible sign and lately all she could stomach was some dry flat bread. Both these signs gave her great hope, but there was also talk of an illness spreading through the village. Jon warned her to stay in the great hall away from it all, including him, in case he got infected when he visited all the sick and dying. She was more alone than ever and very bored. Olaf and Ivar were out on another raid, this time in England, leaving only her maid for company.

Handiwork such as embroidery was considered more the norm for an upper-class woman, but these days Aud Unn found it too tedious. Instead she concentrated on the rising pile of mending, which was normally the chore of her maid. Even though Una was over her morning sickness she was getting big with child and was constantly falling asleep while doing anything that involved sitting down, whereas Aud Unn had no appetite but had more energy, it appeared, than her maid did. There was no doubt in her mind that the maid's child was Olaf's, but she chose to ignore it as he would gladly tell her that it was indeed his. Part of her wanted to know the truth but until she was sure she was with child herself she would suffer the indignity, she thought to herself. *"I will show him that I can produce children too! But our child will become a king or if it's a girl, possibly a queen one day whereas Una's or the others never will!"*

Without Olaf or her *pabbi* the long days stretched into weeks, but finally Olaf returned to her. Both he and Ivar were filled with energy for the upcoming siege in Scotland. The talk was of nothing else; even Ivar seemed nicer and excited about this siege. They had many men and ships to get ready but first Aud Unn needed Olaf's personal attention. She felt confident enough to break the good news to him that she was with child. She could hardly maintain her queenly statesmanship in front of all the people for the excitement that flowed throughout her body. Once they were finally alone in their room, she blurted it out.

"Olaf, my husband and king, we are with child—finally we are with child!"

"Wonderful! Why did you not tell me in front of everyone? This is exceptional news!"

"Because I wanted you as the King of Dubhlinn to make a royal announcement instead of me, an emotional woman shouting it out to all. Also, Jon has suggested that I go into seclusion to the monastery where Brother David can take care of me; apparently there in much sickness in the village. You will not miss me because you will soon be gone on your siege in Scotland. When my father arrives, hopefully my mother will be with him and she can come to the monastery with me. Una can stay behind and stay secluded here. I won't need her for some time. Anyways, she has not been much help to me recently."

Olaf gave her a queer look. "You have it all worked out, my queen. Just in case something should happen to me on this siege, I will have a plan of escape for you and our expected child worked out with my cousin Jon. You have made me a very happy man, Aud Unn Ketillsdottir."

He hugged her with such passion; she was so delighted, she thought her heart would burst with joy. That very evening at the feast for their return Olaf announced the good news. There was much celebrating; even Ivar drank to her health. He leaned over the table to raise his goblet to her, but his eyes reflected more than his smile. His cold eyes told her that she was his enemy still and now maybe he even saw her unborn child as one, too? Her heart sank with a fear she had never experienced before—a mother's fear. *"Oh mamma—I understand now why you made so many sacrifices to the goddess Unn. My child will be everything to me and I will do anything to save him—or her—from danger."*

Not long after the feast her father arrived with her mother in tow. She was terribly sad to see how dramatically her mother had aged and as she hugged her mother's emaciated body, she whispered her good news, and promised that she would make her well again. It would prove to be a promise that she would be unable to keep.

Olaf saw to it that Ygnvild Unn was safely installed in the monastery with Aud Unn and lacked for nothing. The men left them soon after to sail off to Scotland. Brother David fussed over both of them and examined her mother thoroughly. Afterwards he came to her to tell her that her mother was suffering from a disease that she would not be able to recuperate from. Sad and terribly shocked with such news, she could not envisage a life without her mother. Although she had not seen much of her over the last few years, all she could think of was for her whole life before becoming a queen, her mother had been there for her, hovering over her, teaching her, and now she realized—loving her. "A disease? Is it like the illness spreading through our village?"

"No, nothing like that at all. It cannot be spread to other people. We do not know what causes this or what it is even called, all doctors know is that this sickness comes in many disguises and few ever survive it. The only thing we can do is make the person suffering comfortable and ease their pain. It is like a growth that devours the goodness from the body. Unfortunately, the one guarantee I can give is that her pain will only get worse, but I am pleased that she has found her way to us as I can give her potions that will mask most if not all of the pain that she suffers."

"Should I tell her?"

"It is your choice, but what little I have learned of your mother's character tells me that although very ill she is a strong woman and would prefer to know."

"I agree, but that still does not make it any easier."

Her mother was not startled by the diagnosis. "This does not surprise me, *elskamin*. I knew that I was not long for this world and that is why I did not want your father to leave me behind in the Hebrides, even though I was well looked after there too. I wanted to see my daughters and my new grandchild, and I wanted to die with some of my loved ones around me. Your father was too busy to be by my side therefore I

96

decided that the time had come for me to be close to my daughters. The thought of dying alone terrifies me more than death itself. Is that very selfish of me?"

"Of course not, *mamma,* I am happy you came to be with us in your last days. Jorunn will be here any day now with your grandson, who is an heir for King Kjarval and eventually an heir for the High Kingship of Tara. Now I too will have a grandchild for you. You have much to be proud of, *mamma*; you have already started a dynasty of queens, and now a king. I pray that I too will give birth to a future king."

"My two daughters have both given up on their gods, but I ask of you only, do not desert them just yet, and that you will honour them while I am still alive."

"*Mamma,* have no fear, I will make whatever sacrifices you need to make to Unn, your goddess of the frothing waves. I have not given her up totally; she has been an important part of my life for too many years. She will not be easy to set aside even for such a powerful god as this Christian god."

"*Takk fryrir, elskamin.* This means a lot to me."

Chapter 16

The Siege of Dunbarton, Scotland

Dunbarton village was cramped tightly together, with the newer part of the town clinging to the outside castle walls. There was not much room on top of that imposing rock for it to spread much further. Olaf, Ivar and Ketill stood at the front of their ships as they watched the people flee to the safety inside the castle. These people had had plenty of warning; the ships were seen sailing up the River Clyde long before they had arrived near their castle. They had all the time needed to bring in extra food and water. It was impossible to sneak in with such a large fleet, with the ships brimming over with the combined forces of the Irish and the powerful Northmen. All the vessels of these frightening Northmen had carved dragon heads on their bows. These carvings were there to protect them against the evils lurking in the seas as well as to create fear and intimidation in the countries they would be raiding. With their large square red-and-white sails, they were an intimidating lot for sure, and the dragonships were working their magic of terrorizing the people of Dunbarton.

The castle stood high up overlooking the sea, over two hundred feet high on a great slab of volcanic rock, and everyone inside felt safe and secure up there out of reach of this mighty force. The only bridge had been lifted, denying anyone further access to the rock. This great army was in military mode; they found a piece of flat land and set up two separate camps on either side below the rock where the castle sat. They were in no hurry, as they were not planning on going anywhere; everyone understood that this was a siege and it could take some time— it would all depend on the quantity of food and water supplies within the castle. By setting up camp on either side of the castle each with half of their force they should have sufficient men to stop any armed attempts from the Scots coming at them from either direction. So they settled in for an extended time of waiting.

There were only a couple of minor attempts at breaking through the armed men on either side of the castle. This sent a clear message to King Artgal that this siege had the approval of King Constantine himself and probably his brothers as well. He knew they were doomed but he was an unwavering Christian and prayed daily that his in-laws would see the light, since their sister was there as well.

Just over two months into the siege, the angry smug attitude of the villagers holed up in the castle began to disintegrate into fear, loathing and infighting. They were soon arguing amongst themselves over who had the most food and water and over who was not sharing. They watched as the Northmen had great cook-outs in full view of the castle, laughing and partying into the wee hours of the morning. Besides daily fishing, some small parties of men scoured the coastline hitting small farms, not to raid, only to purchase the odd cow for food. They were not in Scotland this time to take whatever they wanted without payment. Their leaders, Olaf, Ivar and Ketil, had made that very clear to the men, and that also meant that the Scottish women were also off limits. For some of the men, their only duty seemed to be to hunt or fish, while a small army of men built a dam to stop the flow of water running anywhere near the castle's pulley system, which was used to lay nets to catch fish or to haul their daily water supply. The level of the river was shrinking fast, depleting their supply of food and water.

A few ships sailed back and forth between Dubhlinn and Dunbarton, bringing in any necessary supplies. The men appeared to lack for nothing; even the large number of *thralls* that they brought with them were not there just to cook and clean, but to service the men's other needs as well. With their presence there was complete harmony among the men, but their time and daily needs were costing the partners a small fortune.

Before long, garbage from inside the castle was being thrown over the castle walls with slop buckets; the stone walls were soon covered in feces and smelled of strong urine. The people inside the castle could not afford to waste any water to flush their garbage through a pipe into the now-drying river. Even the constant rain that was often experienced in that part of Scotland could not erase the putrid smells emanating from its rancid stones. People were dying. At first, they burned their dead, but wood was limited, so they began to stack the dead in the farthest corner of the castle instead. The smell of decayed bodies just added to the already awful smell coming from within and outside of the castle.

There was a narrow spit of land at the back of the castle that sloped down to the mainland, where the bridge crossed the River Leven. This was the river where the occupants of the castle had acquired its water, with a pulley system of ropes and buckets. The dam, finally completed, now stopped the flow into this river from the River Clyde. The River Leven slowly disappeared as the water continued its route away from the castle towards the hinterland. King Artgal had raised the small bridge as soon as the ships were spotted, but these raiders were not troubled. They took their time and built a new bridge to cross over the almost-dry riverbed to the castle, as they waited patiently for the people inside to succumb to starvation. They built tall ladders as well, so men could climb up the shorter sides of the granite cliff wall. The army of men just bided their time waiting for the surrender.

The siege was into the beginning of the fourth month when a white flag appeared in one of the arrow slits high above the main door of the castle. The new bridge stood aloft at the ready, across from the original bridge standing unused on the other side. A small group of strongly built men lowered their new bridge across the gap over the River Leven. The ladders were raised; the men wasted no time in climbing up. Meanwhile Olaf took a group of men and walked over this newly built bridge towards the front entrance. They walked up to the main door, which opened slowly. King Artgal himself walked out with only two armed men, each carrying a white flag. Olaf knew the reason for surrender; they had given up because they were at death's door and King Artgal himself confirmed this.

"I know who you are doing this for King Olaf, but I must surrender as my people are starving."

Olaf had this to say, "King Artgal, your submission is a wise move, I accept your surrender. There will be food and water, but each person must bring out their own bowl, spoon and goblet to drink from. Then they must march into the River Clyde to wash themselves and their utensils before they can receive any food. If you have any clean clothes to change into that would also be a good thing to do."

Defeated, the people slowly filed across the narrow new bridge and slowly entered the River Clyde either naked or fully clothed to wash themselves, knowing they would not be given food to eat or water to drink until they had cleansed the stench from their bodies. Most managed to bring a change of clothes and the ones that did had undressed and tossed their old dirty rags onto a fire built for this very purpose near the river. The few that had not shivered in their wet clothing as they waited for food. Huge iron pots were steaming over the fires and the smells that emerged were a further torture to these poor emaciated people.

The cook warned each person to eat and drink sparingly, as too much would make them very ill. That was too difficult for this ravenous mass to understand; they just wanted food and lots of it. People who did overeat were soon running to the river to vomit; many did not make it. Quite a few had to enter the river again to clean themselves a second time. After the second cleansing those prisoners were herded near the fires to dry off as quickly as possible, then they were forced to march onto waiting ships, with many of them still damp and shivering with the cold. Regardless of whether they were wet or dry, they were to be taken to Dubhlinn as soon as possible to be sold as slaves.

King Artgal was a different story. Both Olaf and Ivar wanted to finish him off right away, but they had had several months to debate their differences with Ketill. He advised them that to assassinate him here in front of his people would not be a good idea, and he recommended that they take him as a prisoner to Dubhlinn where he could die of something unknown. They must all appear to be the saviours of these people from their supposedly wicked King Artgal. They both eventually came to accept his reasoning, so King Artgal and his wife were taken to a smaller ship with their own private tent, where they would be treated better than his own people, who were herded onto the slave ships. So much for being saviours of the people. They were now all slaves, while their king was treated with respect, or what looked like respect.

Ivar was to stay behind at Dunbarton Castle with half of the men and ships to hold the castle for King Constantine, along with half of the *thralls* to cook and clean as well as entertain the men. But first the dam was to be broken apart so that the River Leven could once again continue its natural flow.

Olaf and Ketill organized their half of the armed men for the voyage back to Dubhlinn. These were the men who had herded and filled the ships with their bounty of slaves; most of these slaves were peasants, while the rest were of royal blood. Their bloodlines were of no consequence to the three leaders, as they were supporters of King Artgal and King Constantine did not want them back in his care. With the sale of such a bounty the wealth of the three partners had easily multiplied tenfold. Realizing it would be better for them to be sold as soon as possible so that the new owners could now clothe and feed all these slaves, they wasted no time in sailing back to Dubhlinn where their fortunes awaited them.

Chapter 17

O nce in Dubhlinn the mass of people were taken off the ships and deposited into the slave warehouses where they were readied for sale—all except for King Artgal and his family. They were put into better accommodations but still under full guard. Olaf and Ketill did not stick around to watch over this procession of people; instead they both went to their rooms to bathe and change into clean clothes. Once rested and fully attired they set off to the monastery to check on their women. The Baile Atha Cliath monastery was only a few miles away, but for these two tired men the ride was an exhausting one. They arrived to find good news and bad news. Aud Unn had blossomed; carrying a child suited her well. She was over her morning sickness and her hearty appetite had returned with a vengeance, but Yngvild Unn, on the other hand, had declined greatly. Ketill did not recognize his beautiful wife; all he saw was a frail old woman lying in her bed. "My dear wife, what has happened to you?"

"Ketill, beloved husband of mine, I am relieved and happy you have returned before my *fylgia* begins its journey to the realm of the dead. My body's *hugr* has already started its journey as you can see. Brother David has helped me with my physical pain—I feel none at all—but no one can help me with my emotional pain; only my goddess Unn can do that. When I take my last breath only then will my *fylgia,* who has absorbed it all for me, be free and be able to fly directly to Unn, my chosen goddess. You, Aud Unn and Jorunn must each make a sacrifice to her when I have left this world, to open a passageway so that Unn and her sisters can accept my *fylgia*."

"Of course, we will do that for you." Too emotional for any more words Ketill could only crouch beside her. He looked like a giant engulfing this tiny woman, as he laid his head on her stomach and stretched his arms across the covers as if to hug both her and the tiny bed. She began to stroke his hair like a child; this act of tenderness undid his manliness and his shoulders began to shake as he silently cried with sorrow. He loved this woman deeply and was already grieving his loss, but her touch gave him great comfort. He managed to stop his sobbing. "How will I survive without you, my love?"

"Be happy for me, my life with you was all I ever wanted. Rest assured our life together has been a good life and I will soon be going to a better place."

Olaf had joined his wife standing beside the table. They had been watching the emotional exchange between the other two; slowly he turned to his wife whose eyes were brimming with tears that threatened to unleash themselves into a torrent. Clasping her hands in his he looked into her tearful eyes with the adoration of an expectant father. "You look so full of life, Aud Unn. Being with child becomes you well, I will have to make sure that you have many children. Especially now that we know what to do."

This declaration of love from her warrior-king was more than she could handle. She buried her head into his shoulders and sobbed quietly. Finally she was able to stop herself and found her voice to answer him. "My vision when we made our union together, my warrior-king, was to create a royal dynasty and now it has finally begun. My joy is boundless, I am healthy and strong and so is this child in me. It moves and kicks my insides constantly so I know he—or she—will be strong and is very determined to leave the safety of my body, it wants to live its own life. To me this is a good omen."

"I understand that the village is free of all the illness now. Will you return to the great hall with me?"

"No, I will stay with my mother until the *fylgia* has left her body and traveled to the seas where the goddess Unn lives. Brother David tells me that she does not have much time left."

Ketill spoke up then. "No, Aud Unn, you return with your husband, you need to spend some time together. I will remain here with your mother until her spirit has left and I will let you know when she breathes her last. Then you can return to prepare the body for the burial. Olaf, can you arrange to have a small ship built for the burial and find a spot for the mound? Aud Unn, will you organize all the items she will need for her journey? Has Jorunn been here to visit her mother?"

"Yes, several times, so *mamma* has seen her grandchild, Diarmait. He is such a beautiful boy with lots of black curly hair and his mother's blue eyes. I will ask her to come again so you can meet him too but beware, as he is a very energetic young boy and it can be tiring for *mamma* and I suspect that it will be for you as well. As for the items she will need for her journey, do not worry, it will all be taken care of, *pabbi*."

The Yule celebrations came and went as Yngvild Unn continued to cling to life, much to the surprise of Brother David and to the joy of her husband and daughters. They were able to squeeze in a few more visits with their mother. Brother David theorized that the easing of her pain was what had extended her life, and wrote much about this experience for he firmly believed that such knowledge must be passed on for the benefit of future experiments. There was no doubt in his mind, however, that she would pass on. She expelled her last breath just after the Yule, a few months before her second grandchild came into this life.

The funeral celebrations were magnificent despite so few in attendence. She was laid to rest inside the small ceremonial ship along with the items she would need in the afterlife—it was a queenly burial. Jon the Priest and even Brother David attended the ceremony, but did not partake in any of the sacrificial traditions as it went against all their beliefs. Since Brother David spent much time with Ygnvild, he had come to respect and admire her; she had more knowledge of healing than he had first realized. Although the group was small and mainly family, it was a very royal send-off indeed for Ygnvild Unn. Grieving their loss was King Kjarval and his queen, her daughter Jorunn, King Olaf and his queen, her daughter Aud Unn, and Ketill, *Jarl* of the Hebrides, her bereaved husband. The mourners were part of several dynasties from both established and future lineages.

The day of her mother's funeral Aud Unn's maid, Una, gave birth to a daughter. It was days later before Olaf acknowledged and named this child. It was patently obvious to Aud Unn that he did not place a lot of value on a female child. Although thankful that Una did not have a boy, she increased her daily prayers to God, as well as made sacrifices to Unn begging her that she would be the one to produce the male child, the heir to the throne. She was so desperate for this that she also enlisted Jon to pray to his God for a male child.

Chapter 18

The rain had stopped before the morning awoke, and soon the sun was peeping over the glistening emerald-green landscape. A gentle spring breeze arrived with the sun and fluttered the newly sprouted leaves, helping them to shake off the last drops of rain that had settled on their surface. These beads of moisture looked like diamonds twinkling in the early sunlight as they fell to the earth, their final destination. A slight mist arose from all the moisture deposited during the night; meanwhile, the few clouds still present floated leisurely over the birds singing in the trees as they proclaimed it to be a beautiful day. Suddenly a lusty cry silenced the choir of birds—a child's cry announced, "I have arrived!" It was not just any child—it was the child of the King and Queen of Dubhlinn. A new dynasty was born on this magnificent Irish spring morning.

Queen Aud Unn had gone into the birthing room two days previously; her labour pains were horrendous, and the tough warrior-king could no longer handle her cries of pain. Thinking that all this time it was taking to get the child out was not a good sign, he drunk himself into a stupor so that he could fall asleep and ignore his fears. The cry of the new child was different, not what his fearful mind was expecting; it was a healthy-sounding bellow that woke him up with a start. Anxious to see whether his child was the son he so desired, he jumped from his bed and hurriedly covered his naked body with a fur-lined cloak. Before rushing to the birthing room he ordered the *thrall* that was still snoring in his bed to get up and prepare a hot bath for him on his return.

Aud Unn was exhausted from the pain but she had finally delivered the child and its cry was the most welcome sound possible. Relieved, she dared to ask, "Is it a boy?"

"Yes m'lady—it is indeed a boy—a fine healthy boy and a future king for you and King Olaf."

Una held up the still-howling child for her to see. He was shaking his fists at the world for dragging him out of his warm, safe sac. She ignored his screeching and focused on the bright red hair and smiled to herself as she exclaimed. "He is a redhead and so beautiful. He was worth all this pain."

There was a commotion outside the door; it was the king himself demanding to see his child. Una had just finished cleaning him up and had wrapped him in a clean linen blanket, so she was the one who took him to the door and presented him to the king.

Aud Unn did not care at this point; exhausted, she closed her eyes and gave silent thanks to her Christian God as well as to the goddess Unn. There were no bad omens to contend with this day; this day extolled only good ones. *"Nothing can go wrong now,"* she thought to herself, *"I have given birth to a boy."* Spent and sore she could feel the moisture between her legs as she continued to bleed, then she overheard the voices of those attending her whispering amongst themselves. *"She is badly ripped, there is blood everywhere."* Exhausted but jubilant, their words did not faze her; her beautiful red-haired child was delivered safely. Her eyes closed as she slipped slowly into a deep sleep but before she could rest, she forced herself to recall the joy and fanfare from all in the room when her son arrived, ripping his way out of her body. Then darkness shut out her joy as she settled into a long, much-needed slumber.

Una feared for the worst as her lady continued to bleed, thinking that a peasant woman going through the same birth would have died from such a loss of blood, but her queen was young and healthy. Fortunately, Una remembered that Jon the Priest was nearby, waiting for the birth of this child. She searched for him and asked him what to do. "She cannot die, what can be done to help her, Jon?" He was much relieved that she had delivered a healthy son. He told her not to worry because he knew a man who had miracles up his sleeve; he assured her that this man would know exactly what to do. He rushed off to collect the monk with the healing powers.

When he returned with Brother David, he remained in the room praying for Aud Unn's recovery while the midwife and Una applied the poultice the monk had made. Brother David worked his magic; the new mother was to survive after all, but was drawn and very tired from losing so much blood. A wet nurse was sought out to feed the baby while she got some much-needed rest. Nobody was allowed into the birthing room for fear of infection, not even the king. Normally the midwife would have closed and boarded up the shutters to keep any air out, since all midwives feared the air and believed that draughts were carriers of infections and disease. Brother David stopped her from doing this; he insisted that the fresh air would be part of her healing. This experienced midwife just shook her head, aghast at what he claimed was right for her patient, but he was right once again. The fresh air greeted Aud Unn each day as she got stronger and stronger.

Olaf and Ketill had completed several journeys to Scotland before this red-haired baby had arrived, and there were many negotiations ongoing with King Constantine; the last one on the list was what to do with King Artgal. Ketill was stressed to distraction with both Olaf and Ivar; their ideas for King Artgal's demise were too cruel for him to accept and any further suggestions coming from Olaf was creating a rift between them. Olaf continued to argue for a public hanging. He even suggested the Norse spread-eagle killing to make this valuable prisoner not only an example to the people, but to also make him serve as a sacrifice to the gods. Ketill was very concerned about the appearance and political consequences of any kind of public killings. He tried hard to convince Olaf that there were many ways to rid themselves of this man; anything that would look like a natural death would be better overall. Then there was King Constantine who really did not care how he died, he just wanted him dead. His only demand, at first, was for total agreement between Olaf, Ketill and Ivar on how he would die.

Now creating a frenzy for a decision, Constantine stirred the pot by offering a concession to Ivar if he would get the job done. He offered the hand in marriage of King Artgal's queen, his own sister, to Ivar the Hated. Meanwhile, this queen remained a prisoner in Dubhlinn along with her husband Artgal, the King of Strathclyde, while Ivar remained in Dunbarton. With this generous offer Ivar envisioned a great future for himself—he really wanted this marriage to happen—provided he got the dead man's title. He mounted a campaign of pressure on both Olaf and Ketill, to make a decision about how and when to rid them all of this prisoner. Ivar firmly supported both of Olaf's suggestions. This did not go over well with Ketill. He was torn apart by these two men and could not understand why they were so blind to the consequences of such acts. Their partnership was now under a dark threat.

Several days had passed since the birth and now that Aud Unn was feeling stronger she returned to their bedroom and immediately requested the presence of her husband and father, asking if Olaf was ready to name their child. Barely speaking to each other, the two men arrived at the same time and found Aud Unn propped up in the bed with many pillows behind her; she was obviously still recuperating from the difficult birth. Una was there with the child in her arms and both men were overjoyed to see him; both held out their arms to hold him. Una, of course gave him to the father over the grandfather. In her mind she had no choice as he was not only the father but more importantly, he was their king. It seemed unfair to Ketill since Olaf had already visited his new son several times; this was his first time visiting his grandson, but he capitulated graciously like the gentleman he truly was.

Regardless of the obvious competition between them there were many oohing and aaahings from the two men, then Olaf finally handed him over to his *afi* to hold. When he turned to hand over the bundle to his father-in-law, Olaf spied the other redhead, his cousin Jon, sitting in the corner of their bedroom. Buoyant with happiness, he could not squelch the joke forming in his head and did not realize or much care about the pain this crude comment would bring to all in the room. For some reason he felt jealous that his cousin had more access to his wife then he did. "If I did not know that my cousin Jon was a eunuch, I would doubt my ability to father such a red-haired child."

Jon stood up slowly folding his arms into the sleeves of his cassock and walked towards his cousin. "Olaf, you and I share the same red-haired grandfather and both our mothers had different shades of red hair." Deeply offended, he could not stop his response. "Why would you be so insensitive on such a joyous day?"

"Do not be so quick to react dear cousin—it is just a joke! And I must warn you to be careful, not to overstep your boundaries. You cannot tell me what I should or should not do! Remember, I am your king and you are not my priestly advisor!"

Silence enveloped the room. Aud Unn was not unaware that Jon was a eunuch, but she was not impressed with her husband's treatment of him. She quickly tried to recapture the moment by ignoring his crass comment. "Dear husband of mine, do you have a name ready for our beautiful son?"

"Yes of course I do—Thorstein will be his name; it means Thor's stone. I want to name him after Thor, our God of Thunder. We all know that he is a powerful god and when he strikes his stone flames fly, red flames. Can you see why I want this name for him? His red hair makes me think of power and I predict that one day he will become a very powerful king."

With the naming, happiness returned to the room and replaced the ominous feeling of gloom that was threatening to overpower everyone. All appeared to be forgotten as everyone embraced the new name for this child. Jovial once more, Olaf ordered the wine to be poured to celebrate the naming. Even though it was the pagan way, Jon convinced himself that it was a form of baptism and one that he could accept, so he readily accepted the goblet of wine along with everyone else. Plus, he dared not raise the ire of his cousin, the warrior-king; he suspected the king begrudged his presence in their room. He decided there and then to stay away from the great hall unless he was invited but he knew he would miss Aud Unn more than he cared to admit.

Olaf raised his goblet, "*Skol* to my redhaired son—Thorstein."
They cheered and blessed the child shouting "*skol* to Thorstein the
Red!" Most people had to wait to attain a nickname, but his was set for
life on the very day of his naming ceremony!

Chapter 19

A week had passed after the naming ceremony, when both Ketill and Olaf happened to visit Aud Unn in her bedroom at the same time. The only thing they seemed to have in common these days was the mutual admiration of the healthy child, their new son and grandson, but once together their old argument came up about how to rid themselves of their prisoner. Since there was no one else present other than the three of them and the baby, Olaf brought up the subject of Artgal's demise. He was still fixated on a public killing while Ketill continued to argue against it. Aud Unn could not avoid overhearing and added her opinion, which may have angered her husband more than she thought possible.

"Remember all of our discussions in the Hebrides, Olaf, when you claimed that you believed in treating all people with fairness before the law? Artgal may be your prisoner but he is also a king and a Christian. Whether they like him or not the people of both Ireland and Scotland may take offense to a public killing and view it as cruel and unjust. Is there not some other way?"

He growled at her. "Have you converted to the Christian beliefs behind my back?"

Her heart dropped from the tone of his voice, but it also triggered her defiant nature. "No, at least not yet." It was obvious that he did not appreciate her advice but then she realized it was because she had made it in front of her father; it showed that she supported him and not her husband.

"There is no other way. He has one of his servants taste his food and wine before he eats because he is not stupid and knows we want him dead." Olaf just stared at her with cold blue eyes and Aud Unn felt a chill run through her body. At that moment he looked just like his cousin Ivar the Hated. How she wished she could take back her words of advice, or had saved it for a later date when it was just him and her. She should have known that he could be extremely stubborn when he wanted something to go his way. What could she say to bring him back to reasonable thinking? Then for some reason she thought of Artgal's wife and she suddenly realized that she couldn't stop now, she had to grab the moment to present her idea.

"What about his wife Aed; does she want him to remain king? What is her opinion of all this?"

Olaf was surprised she asked about her. "Why ask about her? She has no feelings for him, she says that he is a cruel husband and that his people are afraid of him. She wants rid of him too."

"Perfect! Make sure she is very comfortable within her quarters, then spend some time with her and talk to her, draw out her opinions and ideas. Reassure her that she will be freed but while she remains married to this man whom she dislikes so much, you cannot let her go. If anyone can lure her over it will be you; you have this gift of seduction, my lord and master, which endears you to all women." She paused but then quickly added, "Including your wife. When you are confident that she will do anything to rid herself of this man, give her the poison, so that she can tip it into his wine when he is not looking. She must have ways of distracting him; after all, she has lived with him for many years. If she does agree, you must guarantee her that with him gone she will be able to return to her home in Dunbarton and remain the queen. I am sure Ivar would agree with this plan as well; hasn't he been promised her hand in marriage? This will guarantee them the titles that they both desire."

"Hmmm—not a bad idea." At least his voice was softer this time, so she felt somewhat better about voicing her opinion.

"If she has remained married to such a cruel man and still lives, I am sure she has learned to be cunning to avoid his cruel ways." Aud

Unn could not help but think about Ivar. *"If she agrees, that poor lady will return to her home only to be married off to another cruel man. How unfair is that?"*

Ketill clapped his hands together, startling Aud Unn from her thoughts of Ivar. "It took me a few minutes to digest what you just said but I think that this is a very good idea. Aud Unn is right, Olaf, that out of the three of us only you have the charm and the ability to convince Aed to do such a deed. She must be fed up with living in captivity with a man she claims to hate."

"I will visit them today and check out the lay of the land. If I feel she is the ideal person to kill her own husband, then I will make it work. Well thought out, Aud Unn. I will have to make sure I never get on the wrong side of you, won't I?" With that comment left hanging in the air he sailed out of their room and Ketill followed right behind him. Before her father closed the door though, he winked at her trying to reassure her that all was well; but Aud Unn knew it was not, and maybe it would never be right again.

Not long after this incident Jon appeared to visit with Aud Unn to remind her of his challenge. He had heard that Olaf was at his military camp so he was confident that he would not run into him at the great hall. "Remember my challenge to you a year ago? If I could guarantee you had a child, you agreed that you would consider becoming a Christian? Look at you, you are now the mother of a future king."

"Funnily enough Jon, I have been thinking very hard on this just in the last few days and I think I just might do that. But first I must find a way to break it gently to Olaf. He may object strongly and just recently he has become rather wary of me. He no longer seems to trust me."

"Would you like me to speak with him?"

"No—no—please no—do nothing about this. I do not think he is that trusting of you either these days." Jon nodded in agreement. "Do speak about me and Thorstein as a mother and child though, and see how he reacts, and let me know if you think his reaction or words appear to be with anger or with feelings of care."

"Are there problems between you two and at such a momentous time?"

"I am not sure. He seems wary of me since I gave him some unsolicited advice in front of my father. I may have overstepped my queenly limitations. Please be patient, let me think on your challenge for a while yet. Between you and Brother David, your help and advice has been greatly appreciated; we cannot thank you enough. Both of us—even though you may never hear it from Olaf—I know he is grateful."

Time passed and still Aud Unn had not committed to Jon. It bothered her that Olaf had not returned to their bed for many days now. She took their son everywhere with her, even to the meals so his father got to visit him whenever they were in the great hall together. To shake any negative thoughts about them, Aud Unn escaped most days to visit with Jon or to just sit in his church where it was quiet and very peaceful. Una, herself a Christian, came with her and together they would talk about the church and about their children while they made small bits of clothing for them. Aud Unn had reconciled herself with the idea that Olaf's daughter would be raised with his son. When Jon was able, he would come to the church and tell them stories from the Bible. She felt such tranquillity within this sacred place that she began to think that this truly was a house of God and if she converted, she would like to be baptised here.

Sitting with just Una while the two children slept peacefully in their baskets, she asked her if she had seen or been with Olaf lately. "No mistress, he has not requested my presence for some time now, not since long before our child was born. He only appeared for the naming ceremony and as you know he did give her the name of his mother, Thora. I took that as an honour, but he does not even come by to see her except when we are in your presence. I fear that I have angered him somehow."

"I think not; he has probably found a new woman to be with who is more exciting than either of us right now. We are too absorbed with our children. For some reason I think he is not happy to be around me either and since I keep you as my maid, he may have transferred some of his weariness of me onto you. I could find another maid, if you prefer?"

"To be honest, I like being your maid, so this is fine with me if he does not come to me again. I just want him to be as pleased with our child as he is with yours. After all they are brother and sister—well, half-brother and half-sister."

"That is true." Aud Unn suddenly felt a kinship with her maid and realized that they truly were a family. Recalling her mother's words of wisdom, she resolved there and then to put more effort into cementing their friendship, and not just for the sake of the children.

Several months later Olaf showed up in their room after a long period of time spent in Scotland. Apparently Artgal had died unexpectedly while they were away, and nobody knew what had caused him to die. No fingers, including Kjarval's, could be pointed at any of the three men, Olaf, Ketill or Ivar, as they were out of the country. Now Artgal's wife was a free woman and she would accompany both Olaf and Ketill on their next voyage back to Scotland. He had come to ask a favour of Aud Unn. "Good day my queen, I trust you and Thorstein are keeping well?"

"Yes, my lord, we are both very pleased to see you have returned and that you remain in good health."

"Good heath? You are sure you want me to remain healthy?"

"Of course, you are my king, my husband, the father of our child. I am not like Aed who disliked her husband. How could I, I have too much respect and admiration for you as a just and true leader, and care deeply for you."

"I know wife, you are a wise woman and I have been unfair in my judgement of you recently. Your advice was sound, and we acted on it. As you have heard, it has been successfully carried out."

"Olaf, you have made me a very happy woman. Can I expect you to return to our bed soon? You do know that you will be greatly welcomed; I have missed you."

"This very night, my queen. Now the favour I ask of you is to welcome Aed, the queen of Strathclyde, into our household. Have Una find a room for her so she can be treated like a guest and not as a prisoner. Soon she will return to her homeland where she will remain the queen of Strathclyde. Ivar patiently awaits her return."

She did not know whether to be happy for her or not. *"Ivar? I will soon get to know this woman and will then know if they deserve each other or whether I should be sorry for her."* She thought to herself,

"Olaf seems like his old self; now may be the best time to approach him about my conversion to Christianity." "Husband, we have much to be thankful for towards Jon and Brother David. I firmly believe that because of Jon's prayers and my introduction to Brother David and his knowledge, we were able to have a child together and will again. Lately I have spent much time in Jon's church and truly feel a peace I have never known or experienced before. Without any coercion from Jon I have decided to be baptised as a Christian—with your approval, of course."

"You are a queen and can decide for yourself. You say it brings you peace? What of our gods?"

"Yes, a peace like nothing I have experienced before, but I do not think that I will totally give up on all my pagan beliefs either. This feeling of tranquility may only be a result of motherhood, but I will proceed and give up the Unn in my name when I am baptised—for now! Jon plans to teach me the catechism, which is the basic teachings of Christianity. He also hopes to escalate my reading lessons, which may prove to be more difficult than he thinks as I do not have much interest for that. He has won the battle but not the war for my soul—if I later find it to be impossible to follow, I will add Unn back to my name and follow her once more."

"I ask that you do not pass on any of your Christian ways to Thorstein. It will be mine or his decision who to follow. Also, there is to be no public celebration of your baptism. I am not opposed to you converting as we are surrounded by Christians here, and it may even be to my advantage to admit that my wife is a Christian when dealing with the Irish. I do believe that it will make Kjarval happier with our partnership as well. As for reading, that may also be another advantage, as I was already planning to ask Jon to teach Thorstein when he became old enough. If you could read, you could help him with his lessons."

"Agreed—that is only fair. *Takk.* As I said before, nothing may come of it and I may return to Unn's fold. Although reading may not work for me; I may be too old to learn now!"

"Nonsense, you are the smartest woman I know!"

Aud Unn took great pleasure in his spontaneous praise; things might be better between them than she first thought.

Chapter 20

Aud's life was going through changes and not just because she was a new mother. Over the next couple of years Scotland became the focus for Olaf and Ketill; rarely were either of them in Dubhlinn, and then not for long. Meanwhile both Kjarval and Ivar had slid into the background. The partnership appeared to be no longer as important to Kjarval since he had received the crown and was now the High King of Tara. As for Ivar, although he was very much a voice in their partnership, he remained in Dunbarton since he had married Aed and had received the coveted title of King of Strathclyde. This suited Aud just fine; she did not miss Aed at all and especially did not miss Ivar or the menacing looks he would always throw her way. Once she had gotten to know this woman better, she felt Ivar and Aed were well-matched; they were both cruel and selfish. It came as no surprise when Olaf claimed that they had fallen in love with each other.

When in Dubhlinn, which was rare, Olaf seldom appeared in their room to sleep. He had made it clear that he did not care for this new person she had become, and on several occasions told her as much. According to him she had become a contradiction; too pious and self-righteous on one hand, and on the other hand had become too focused on past sins. Aud could not see this new side of herself as he tried to convince her to return to her pagan gods and goddesses. His comments were generally the same, "Following the Goddess Unn would return you to your passionate nature. This selfish Christian God has robbed me of my wife."

To her his comment was cruel and unfounded, but this new opinion of her no longer fazed her; his blatant disregard of her and his womanizing was slowly turning her heart cold towards her warrior-king. She took to kneeling at the altar of Jon's church or in front of her altar in her room; this way she could concentrate and think more clearly when they discussed the catechism or while she listened to one of his Bible stories. What she did not know was that Jon began to think of her as Aud the Deep-Minded.

Artgal's murder continued to haunt her dreams. Little did she know just how capable of murder that woman Aed was, when she first suggested her game plan to get rid of him. In Aud's mind Artgal ap Dyfnwal, the King of Strathclyde, had become the better person in that marriage. She even suspected that Aed had convinced her brother that he was the cruel king who frightened the people, when in fact it was most likely her who fit that description. Even though Artgal was better off living with God in heaven and at peace, this did not stop Aud from asking for God's forgiveness for her part in his death, and now that she had found the Lord, she had become remorseful and guilt-ridden.

Although somewhat convinced that the Christian church thrived on guilt, it did not stop her from developing a profound faith in their doctrine. She found herself in Jon's church daily, on her knees at the altar praying for forgiveness for her past sins. Since Ivar was out of the country, she did not fear the walk to the church on her own. Una was often too busy but always willing to keep the children with her, thus allowing Aud unlimited freedom. She began to spend much time alone with Jon, which she valued, but their closeness began to confuse her as well. There was an attraction there that she could no longer deny, but it seemed to be one-sided. He only ever appeared to be her friend and tutor.

Meanwhile the uprisings in Scotland were constant. Constantine and his brothers waged war against the English; they fought hard to keep them from invading Scotland despite their internal turmoil. This continued to keep both Olaf and Ketill away from Dubhlinn, fighting their many battles for these Scottish rulers. Ketill was putting his sword *Fotbitr* to good use and claimed it had saved his life many times. Aud prayed for her father's life constantly and even though Olaf was no longer the centre of her life she prayed for his safety as well. Nevertheless, she saw but little of either man.

Thorstein was becoming a sturdy little boy who thought he was his mother's protector now that his father was always away. Aud was very proud of him. Una's daughter, Thora, and Thorstein grew up together as brother and sister; they were very close, Thorstein thought he was her protector as well. Besides Jon, Una became Aud's only other friend and constant companion. Since she had so much free time to pray as Una gladly looked after the children, pray she did, constantly. She could not understand why her soul was tortured with guilt about her role in Artgal's death. Jon talked much about confession and how it cleansed the mind and the soul but Aud was unable to admit such a feat to her mentor and best friend.

She could not bear it if he thought ill of her; she loved being near him and she was slowly realizing it was not just because he was her priest. These new sensations she was experiencing confused and tortured her sense of right and wrong. *"He is a priest and a eunuch—married to his church! Why am I thinking like this? The goddess Unn must be trying to seduce me back into her arms. Stop this nonsense!"* With so much time available to her and spending the greater part of it with Jon, she began to realize that she was fighting a losing battle with her desires. This battle between her new god and her old beliefs tore her emotions apart. The goddess Unn's seductive pull on her old beliefs ran amok in her head, but thankfully Jon displayed no desire for her. Knowing it was not reciprocated kept her emotions contained.

He read much of the Bible out loud, which she absorbed with a hunger he thought was impossible for a woman. Little did he realize that she was using her constant questions to divert all those desires that threatened to overpower her, and little did she realize that with all her questions he began to feel incapable of answering them. He was starting to be threatened by her intelligence, and she by her growing attraction to him. "Aud, you are much more intelligent than me. I watch you on your knees every day praying, but I think you are really thinking up all these questions just to challenge my knowledge. You have become a formidable debater, more so even than Brother David. Lately I think of you as Aud the Deep-Minded; now I do believe I will call you that to your face."

"Funny you say that; once long ago, so did Olaf, but he called me a *deep thinker.*"

"Aaah—so he recognized your intelligence before any of us did, so the nickname was well chosen then."

"Why is it that all you Northmen need to have a nickname for everyone? I must confess that this new journey you have started me on is very fulfilling, Jon. I never dreamt that I would embrace your faith with such a passion. It has filled the gap of loneliness and rejection I used to experience when Olaf would not come to me at night, and now I no longer care if he ever returns to our bed, although I do miss him and our heated discussions. Does that make me a bad wife, a bad queen?" She walked up to him to look into his eyes.

"The Lord will be the judge of that—not me, Aud." He leaned backwards and held his hands up as if to keep his distance from her. This startled Aud, as she was almost in his face when Una rushed in at that very moment. Mortified, she realized that subconsciously she may have been pushing Jon into a corner, hoping for a different reaction, by admitting to her loneliness. Her maid's untimely interruption may have saved her from a great embarrassment, but this did not stop her sharp tongue from lashing out at her.

"Yes Una, what is it? Is it Thorstein?" Her questions were short and sharp.

Bowing her head with her curtsy, "Excuse my interruption my lady, your father has arrived back from Scotland and wants to speak with you immediately." Una appeared agitated, "your father looks worried." Grateful for an escape from this awkward situation, she hastily excused herself from Jon's presence. Off they went back to the great hall to meet with her father; when she saw him, she ran to embrace him.

"Aud, I have some news to bring to you. As you know the English regions of Wessex and Mercia have been trying to extend their power into Scotland for two years now, with the help of other Viking forces. The bad news is that Constantine has met his death in the latest battle at Inverdorat, the Black Cove. He was buried at the Iona Abbey and laid to rest beside his father; his younger brother Donald was crowned King Donald II."

"Where is Olaf? Is he safe?"

"He is safe and remains in Scotland with the new king, who has made him an offer to solidify their agreement, an offer that you may find offensive."

Aud could see that her father was very sad as he struggled to tell her the about this offer. She rubbed his arm softly, "Pray continue, *pabbi*."

"Donald has offered his daughter's hand in marriage to Olaf."

"What!" Shocked by such an offer, "He is already married—to me! I am the Queen of Dubhlinn! How is that possible? What is her name? Does he want to divorce me?"

"Remember, Aud, Olaf is not a Christian and he does not think it is wrong to have more than one wife; her name is Ceana and she is quite young. And no—he does not want to divorce you."

Aud had to sit down; this was shocking news indeed. "Ceana? I have never heard that one before. Pour us some wine *pabbi*, I need to think this over. This has come as a great shock to me. I know Olaf has many other women and I have learned to live with it, but to marry another? Does that make her his queen too? I don't understand how this could work."

"Olaf assures me that you and you alone are the Queen of Dubhlinn. He needs me and my men to remain with his forces, otherwise he will have no power within the Scottish realms. If he needs me, he needs you, it is that simple. But he not only needs you because of me, he needs you to come with me to Scotland to show your acceptance of this marriage. King Donald has requested this, not Olaf. He heard that you were a Christian and because he is too, he wants to hear it from you personally, that you agree. Donald also knows that the two of you were not married within the church, but by a pagan. Therefore, he does not see anything wrong with Olaf marrying his daughter. In his eyes you are not legally married."

"Never!"

"Aud, think about it. King Donald needs to be assured of Olaf's support and in turn Olaf needs mine and yours. Wessex and Mercia are gaining strength with the help of many mercenary Vikings, and Scotland wants to keep those English influences out of its country. Their country is more Gaelic in nature; that makes Ireland a natural friend, while England is seen as an enemy. He needs us all, including Kjarval. As you can see, I was given two directives. Before returning to Scotland I will go see him, and I need you to come with me. You need to stay married to Olaf so Thorstein remains his heir. Pagan marriage or not, it is important that you show support for Olaf. You know in your heart that this is the wise thing to do, right, *elskamin*?"

Aud put her elbows on the table and rested her chin in the palms of her hands and just stared straight ahead as if in deep thought. Ketill knew better than to distract his daughter from her concentration and poured himself another mug of wine. Finally she spoke, "You are right as usual, *pabbi*. Thorstein must remain his first choice for his heir to Dubhlinn, therefore I will come with you as requested."

Chapter 21

King Kjarval readily agreed to send men to aid the Scots, since they were of the same culture and understood each other—even if they could not always get along with one another. It would take only a few days to gather all the men and weapons required, leaving Aud no choice but to return to Dubhlinn with her father to await the readied ships. Soon after they left for Scotland with many ships, men, and weapons; a virtual armada. She stood at the helm with her father for much of the journey but gladly went to her tent to rest and to pray for understanding. *"Why is Olaf's request torturing me so? Pabbi has assured me that he does not want a divorce. We have not been husband and wife for so long now—my fear is that he does want to divorce me. I fear for Thorstein—where does he fit in with this new marriage? Too many unknowns here."*

Aud arrived in Scotland for the first time ever, but for some inexplicable reason she felt as if she was coming home. As much as she did not want to be there in the first place, the land was calling to her. *"It feels like home, I have never been to such a treeless place other than to the Orkneys. Or is the land itself telling me I will end up here one day?"* Her mind was confused with these sensations, as well as still struggling with this marriage. She needed to keep a clear head, so she shook away all these thoughts tumbling around in her mind.

They were allotted private quarters in King Donald's castle. The main room had a large fireplace with a roaring fire. Olaf was waiting by it for her. As she approached, he appeared to be very pleased to see her, but she could see that he struggled to look her in the eye. "*Guilt-riddled*," she thought to herself. Trying not to be smug, Aud threw her first question at him as he hung his head to avoid eye contact. "How could this man, King Donald II, who claims to be a Christian, agree to marry his daughter off to you, a pagan who is already married?"

"Hah! It gets worse!" He finally looked her in the eye, "King Donald proposed this union, and he also wants me baptized. I objected at first, but can see the benefits. Many of us pagans have gone through with this ritual even though we do not believe in it. For me it is for convenience only. By appeasing him with this marriage contract, it will reassure King Donald of my support against the English."

Aud could not stem the sarcasm from her voice, "You Northmen, pragmatic as always!"

Olaf recognized it for what it was, sarcasm, and bantered back. "Yes, of course and I am glad to see that you are as defiant as ever." Her lips turned ever so slightly into a smile. Feeling like he had maybe opened the door to conversation, he went on to explain that Scotland embraced the same system as Ireland did for their heirs, called *tanistry*. "Literally translated, it means 'the chosen one'. The successor to the throne does not necessarily have to be the eldest son," he continued, "but will be chosen by the king during his reign. Since I have been able to produce a boy child, King Donald thought there was a good chance that I could have one with his daughter. If we have a son, King Donald promises that he would choose him as his heir because his one and only son Malcom was critically injured in the same battle that killed his brother, King Constantine II. He does not think Malcolm will survive or ever be able to have a child himself. Even if he does live longer, he will never be healthy enough to become the king. I could not resist this offer; I may very well have a son who could become the King of Scotland and I know that your dreams closely match mine, to create a dynasty of kings." After much discussion together, she finally gave in to his request.

"You have always understood my ambition, to create a dynasty of kings. I knew you would understand better than anyone, given the opportunity to explain it all to you in person, why I cannot resist or refuse this offer, Aud. Your goals have always been in line with mine and I value the support you have just given me." Olaf hesitated a moment. "Remember your promise at our marriage union—to obey me always? I could have ordered your obedience, but as you will soon see, I prefer to have your support willingly as my queen." He pulled out a scroll hidden inside his cloak. "I promise you that you will always be the Queen of Dubhlinn. Here is a charter that I had drawn up that names you as the rightful queen and it gives you the right to rule in my place. My people will listen to you because my charter condones it and the Irish will praise you as their Christian queen. You will be in a powerful position once this charter has been delivered to the council. I trust you like no other."

Although exhausted from their heated discussion, this lifted her spirits, and remembering her mother's wise advice, it was better to be friends than lovers. "I am honoured my lord, and accept this charter with a heavy heart. No one can replace you, but I pray that I can do it honourably. We have similar ambitions so I will back you in this decision of yours, even though it goes against everything I believe in. Even *pabbi* has encouraged me to go along with it so I would have had no one to back me up if I had chosen to say no." She fully understood now that there was no other way. There never was. This charter proclaimed her a queen who could make decisions, direct men to do business for her. She was no longer just a consort who wore a crown with no ruling power. This charter, his trust in her abilities, convinced her that she could bear this burden.

"That has never stopped you before from disagreeing with me, my queen." He held her tight and whispered into her ear. "I cannot thank you enough for your continued faith in my decisions, good or bad." She felt all those lusty emotions flow through her body; she had forgotten the hold he still had over her. *"Damn you Olaf! Damn you to hell—why can I not resist you?"* She had to walk away from him before she broke down.

Once all the negotiations were complete and all the drinking and hand-clasping had worn themselves out, Aud begged her father to take her back to Dubhlinn. Back to her throne, to her son, and to her church where Jon was waiting. Sadly, she would be returning to Dubhlinn without its proper king, but she was going home with a greater power than before, while Olaf would remain in Scotland to wed the king's daughter and work on producing that son. Aud stood at the helm of the returning ship, thankful to be returning but still astounded over the change in her life. The charter was safely wrapped in skins and stowed in her trunk, to protect the words from the salt air, but the capabilities they would give her were unprecedented. The charter declared her as the *ruling* queen with the right to stand in for her husband, the King of Dubhlinn. This charter would give her the ability to directly influence the Longphort Council. Fear suddenly gripped her heart. *"He trusts me; I must not fail my warrior-king!"*

It took almost a full year for the Scots, together with their Viking mercenaries and King Kjarval's men, to send the English and their own Viking mercenaries fleeing back to England. This war was hard won; it took many lives to erase this menace from their land but now there appeared to be no further threats on the Scottish realm. The campaign was a success; the English fled with their tails between their legs, and of equal importance, Olaf had fulfilled his promise and had produced a son for the Scottish crown. His son was named after his grandfather, Donald II, and once crowned he would become Donald III.

Scotland appeared to be at peace for the first time in many years. The Scottish victory was lauded in song and in poems, making Olaf, Ketill and Ivar the heroes along with King Donald II. It was widely acknowledged that the peace Scotland was enjoying for the first time in many years would never have been achieved without them. Hero or not, Olaf felt it was time to return to Dubhlinn; he had been gone too long. He claimed to his allies that his people needed him. In reality, he needed to show them that he was still their king and back in control, even though he had heard that Aud had proven to be a strong and fair leader. Threatened by his presence in time of peace, King Donald willingly gave him leave by throwing him a celebration party that lasted into the wee hours. There everyone drank themselves into a stupor while they sang songs that heralded their heroic deeds during the many bloody battles that had finally rid them of their menace, the English.

When Olaf arrived back with his guests, the first thing on his agenda was to call a *Þing*, to hear what disputes his people had and to administer to them with his queen by his side. More importantly to Aud was that he planned to spend time with his first son, Thor, who was now four years old and full of questions for his father, whom he barely knew. Ketill came too, and sadly so did Ivar along with his queen, but Olaf's second wife and child stayed behind. There was much feasting where they retold their stories of battles won and lost. Aud tried to be gracious with the unexpected guests but found it to be very difficult.

During each feast night she made sure that they were seated on Olaf's side and her father was on her side, along with Jon whenever he was invited, just to avoid having to talk to either of them. She often found Aed staring directly at her as if she could read her guilty conscience. This sent shivers of fear up her back; this hateful woman sensed her unease. Aud smiled bravely at her but was forced to quickly avert her eyes. This fear of her evil looks prompted Aud to slip away early after each meal leaving them to drink away the night. Every time she would whisper her apologies to her father or to Jon if he was present. To her father only she admitted, *"Pabbi,* I need to leave, as you know I cannot tolerate Ivar or his wife, but I look forward to our conversation in the morning. Please help Olaf amuse them, I cannot spend another minute in their company."

To further elude their unwelcomed company, she made her escape to Jon's church directly after the morning meal, taking Una and the children with her. Now that Ivar was in town she dared not go anywhere alone; plus, their company would be a buffer between her and Jon if he was there. Her catechism classes were put on hold for the time being so he was often not even around. Only her father seemed to miss her presence, but he knew where to find her and sought her out at the church each day where they could enjoy each other's company—uninterrupted by any guests.

Ketill valued his short time with his grandson. Unfortunately, her father could not stay in Dubhlinn for long, as he too needed to return to his seat of power. Like Olaf, he wanted to show his people that he was still their leader. After he left, she prayed hard that the other visitors would soon be gone, leaving only Olaf here with her. God finally answered her prayers.

The day before they were to leave, Aud, along with her maid Una and the children, made their daily walk after the *dagmal* towards the church. To their surprise Ivar and his queen Aed were standing in front of the little church. It appeared to Aud as if they were waiting for them; she had no choice but to nod and greet them. "Good morning. Are you waiting for your cousin Jon?"

Ivar gave her a knowing look, "No, I was just showing Queen Aed around and ended up here. However, since I was here, I did look for him. He appears to be away at present. How about you, are you here to see Jon?"

"Normally if he is here, he gives me a lesson on the catechism." Telling a little lie to Ivar gave her no feelings of guilt but Thorstein started to say something. She squeezed his hand and continued, "Since he appears to be away we will return to the great hall."

"In that case," Ivar responded, "we will join you. It always appears to be raining and I sense the threat of more to come. My lady claims to have seen enough of this famous Longphort; it brings back too many bad memories."

Aed quickly walked to join Aud and linked her arm. Aud had to struggle with herself not to shake off her touch; thankfully Una took Thorstein's hand in hers, forcing him to walk behind his mother. Ivar joined Una and the children, stopping her to ask a question about a building which Aud was sure he knew all about. When there was some distance between them and the troop walking behind, Aed broke the silence between them. "We appreciate your hospitality but we both look forward to returning to Strathclyde on the morrow."

"Nobody looks forward to your leaving more than I," thought Aud but told a lie to cover this fear she felt of this woman. "You are always welcome here, as you know."

"Thank you, that is good to hear since we are sisters in death."

Aud's heart froze*! "Sisters in death! She knows! She knows that it was my idea to use her to poison Artgal—how will I ever forgive myself for suggesting such a thing?"* She simply stared straight ahead as they walked, Aud in silence praying for their quick return to the hall, while Aed went on about her exile in Dubhlinn and how she was looking forward to returning to Scotland. Fortunately, the distance was short; the walk was only a few minutes but it felt like an eternity. She quickly excused herself saying, "Thorstein has a reading lesson I must attend to. Please send Una and the children directly to me when they return. *Takk*." They weren't far behind them; Aud couldn't get away fast enough, but felt it was only polite to say something more. "I will see you both at the farewell feast tonight. Have a pleasant day." She left Aed staring at her receding back with an arrogant sneer, knowing full well she had sunk her knife in deep. She had sent Aud to hell—knowing that this Christian guilt she had recently embraced would only create more nightmares to haunt her dreams. Aed, a Christian herself, understood this guilt many of them embraced. She laughed and joked about this Christian infliction often with Ivar. They left at first light, with only Olaf to see them off.

At the *dagmal* Olaf brought up Ivar and Aed. "I thank you for being so gracious with our guests. I do know that you find it difficult to be in their company. What do you think of Ivar now? He has changed greatly and seems quite content with his life, don't you think? Love can change a man."

"Hmmm—yes he does appear to be happy with her. They are very much alike, don't you think?" To herself, she thought "*I almost convinced myself that I could suffer the man until yesterday. They planned our meeting just so Aed could send night terrors my way. 'Sisters in death' indeed. They are both cruel and evil—why did she have to go out of her way to remind me of my part in Artgal's death? Only Ivar could have told her. Worse yet—only Olaf could have told Ivar! Silly woman—of course Ivar had to know. I must stop this emotional self-abuse.*"

Meals were the only time they had together to discuss things since Olaf's return; they were not sharing their normal room. She had another prepared for him, explaining that it would be better this way, what with all the company, and also that they needed to have their own space until they worked out what was right for them. He readily agreed and although she felt it was the correct move, she was hurt that he had agreed so quickly. Now that they were alone and discussing Ivar's life without getting angry with each other, she felt brave enough to ask him how his second marriage had worked out.

"I have to confess to you that Ceana is not someone I would have married, other than the fact her father promised that he would make our child, if a son, the next king of Scotland. As a woman, I find her to be very spiteful and mean, although I must admit she does adore our son. As a child herself, her father completely spoiled her because she had no mother. Did I not tell you that she died when Ceana was born? This lack of discipline did not help her in any way. To this day, no one in their household can handle her tantrums, not even me it seems, so I freely admit that it feels wonderful to be back home living in a sane house. I intend to stay a while and get to know my son and hopefully renew our affections, if you will allow me?"

"Olaf, my king and mentor, I must admit to missing you greatly, but I still need time to think about this. As a Christian, it would be sinful to consummate our relationship. Maybe if we could renew our vows somehow within the umbrella of the church there would be no question. I have missed you more than you will ever know. The church can be very strict in many ways; I really do not know how to make this work. We must speak with Jon. Are you a patient man?"

"For you I will be, but enough about Ceana, for now I want to erase her from my mind. Since all our guests have left us, Aud, do you not find it too quiet here?"

"A bit, but I must admit I like quiet."

"We should invite your sister and King Kjarval to a feast and bring back some merriment to this great house and fill it with our children and theirs, who are many now. They seem to be producing a new child each year. It is important that Thorstein spend time with his cousins, don't you think?"

Although she knew that King Kjarval and Olaf had not really seen eye-to-eye with each other for many years, she readily agreed. This may be an opportunity to mend some fences because neither man was looking for political support, just friendship. It turned out to be the one and only feast they would have together while Olaf was there. The two men appeared to have reconciled their differences and the children had a glorious time together.

The best part of Olaf's time in Dubhlinn was that they spent several happy months with only their son Thorstein, his daughter Thora and on occasion, Jon the Priest, when he was invited to join them. On one of those evenings that Jon was there, after the *nattmal* the family cozied up to the fire to tell stories. He was the instigator of the story asking Olaf to tell them once again about the siege of Dunbarton. After repeating the same story for the hundredth time and talking about Ketill Flat-Nose, young Thorstein suddenly felt brave enough to interrupt his father and ask why his *afi* was nicknamed Flat-Nose.

Olaf looked over towards Aud, nodded his head and put his open palm forward to show that he acknowledged her as the one to answer their son's question. She cleared her throat first before responding. "Well my dear child, I am very happy you have asked. The story your *afi* told me as a young child was this. He said that when he was a young man, he was one of the strongest amongst his young companions; they even used to refer to him as Ketill the Strong. They would wrestle with each other almost every day to prove their strength. One day a cousin of one of his friends was visiting from Hordaland, where the king of that region lived. I think this friend and his cousin had some connection to King Halfdan the Black, who was on the throne at that time."

"Even though he was several years older than them he wasn't as big or as strong-looking as your *afi* was. This young man's name was Bjorn and he made fun of them saying 'Is this all you do, is wrestle? There is more to fighting a battle than this. Don't you listen to any elder's wise stories? You can learn much from them.' Well—your *afi* took offense to this statement because he was the strongest and the daily wrestling was so very important to him. He challenged the other man to a fight; he was ready to punch Bjorn in the face and prove he was the strongest and the wisest. He wanted to show off to his friends but before your *afi* knew what had happened, this boy had punched him and laid him flat on his back."

135

"All he said was, 'Now that I have flattened your nose, you will not be so arrogant with other people who probably know more about fighting than all of you put together.' Fortunately, your *afi* was a wise young man. He just stood up and wiped the dirt off himself, laughing, telling Bjorn that he was right. 'There has to be more to fighting if you can lay me flat on my back with one punch.' He shook Bjorn's hand and asked him if he would train him and his companions in the art of battle while he was visiting. His companions soon started calling him Ketill Flat-Nose and this nickname stuck with him all his life."

"The best part was that Bjorn and your *afi* became the best of friends and that is why your *afi* named his first son Bjorn, after this wise young man. This man, Bjorn, also convinced your *afi* that women should be trained in self-defence. Hence my sisters and I can shoot a bow and arrow with some skill and have our own shields with our own personal sabres."

Thorstein looked puzzled. "My hair is red and that is why my nickname is Thorstein the Red and papa's hair is so fair, he is called Olaf the White. But *afi*'s nose is not really flat."

"*Jæja*, you are right! He got the name because Bjorn stated in front of all *afi*'s companions that he had 'flattened his nose'. After that, they no longer referred to him as Ketill the Strong. Also, I think Bjorn may have broken *afi*'s nose and that is why it is slightly crooked. You must ask him the next time he is here."

"Okay—but why don't you have a nickname, *mamma*?"

"I used to be called Aud Unn because I once worshipped the goddess Unn of the frothing waves. Since I became a Christian, I dropped the Unn from my name. I do not allow anyone to call me that anymore."

Jon cleared his throat before speaking. "Well, I have a nickname for your mamma, and lately got up the nerve to say it to her face. To me she is Aud the Deep-Minded."

Olaf cut in laughing. "I once called her something similar—I think it was 'deep thinker'. Why do you call her that?"

"We both know that she is an intelligent woman, and when I was teaching her about the Christian religion, she had questions—and more questions—she never ran out of them, but soon I was running out of answers. I always found her kneeling in front of the altar supposedly praying, but I truly think she was busy thinking up another question to stump me. Her constant questions were turning me into a *berserker*!"

Pretending to be a *berserker*, he got up and acted all crazy, running after Thor and tickling him, making him laugh hysterically. For Aud, these few months together as a family were the best. Gradually Aud and Olaf reconciled their differences, and despite the church she finally allowed him to return to their marriage bed; like before, she was unable to resist his advances. After several nights together he hinted that it was time to produce another child, and said that it was time to talk to Father David. They had renewed their friendship; now even the passion had returned to them. Olaf even commented on this. "Your Goddess Unn has returned to you, my queen. Please keep her in your heart." Aud was more content then she had ever been; he claimed that she was all the woman he wanted. Not long after they were reunited, the future with Olaf began to look even more promising than she had envisioned, since now he wanted to renew their vows under the umbrella of the church. "Why?" she demanded to know.

"It is only fair to you that you be a wife and queen accepted by the church. You have proven yourself to be a great leader and for that I am eternally grateful. Ceana has not, so first I plan to ask the church for an annulment, which by the way was always part of that marriage plan. That will never change my status as the father of her child, but it will simply mean that she is no longer my wife. That alone will make me very happy. Then we can proceed to renew our vows but this time in a church and blessed by a priest, once the other one is annulled. I am confident that my cousin Jon would then perform the ceremony."

"I just don't see, though—how can the church make it work?" She doubted the ability of the church to annul his marriage to Princess Ceana, but she would be forever thankful because he so strongly desired to make it right between them. After all this positive chatter her dreams should have been blissful that night, but for some inexplicable reason her nightmares suddenly returned. *"Sisters in death!"* Those words and all those bad omens from their wedding day came back to haunt her dreams, warning her that this idyllic time was too good to be true. Her nightmares foretold trouble! They were right—it did not last! All it took was several ships from Scotland with a desperate message from Ivar to take Olaf away from her.

King Donald II's daughter Ceana and her son Donald III had been kidnapped. This left him no choice but to run to their rescue. The courier explained the situation to them both, according to Ivar. This group of powerful Scottish families had gathered in revenge against them, for the Dunbarton siege and the taking of slaves from these important families. They promised to release them only if Olaf removed Ivar and his wife from the throne. This group was accusing both Ivar and Aed, as well as Olaf and Ketill, of killing King Artgal. Ivar demanded a public hearing where they would be given a voice to claim their innocence. Aud feared for Olaf's life. She couldn't understand why he needed to run to help Ivar every time, although she thoroughly understood his need to rescue his son. "Why can't Ivar work this out himself? They have nothing on any of you. None of you were even in the country at the time; it is Aed they really want. Do you honestly think your son is in danger? Surely King Donald will not allow them to hurt the Scottish heir?"

"This is all Ceana's doing; she is a spoiled, wicked woman. My son and her are no more kidnapped than you or I are. You know my weakness for beautiful, lusty woman, and she is all of that. It was she who seduced me, and when she became pregnant, I was forced to marry her. Her father will do anything she wants, but it was she who demanded I marry her. Her father would have found another King, Duke, or whoever to prevent her child from being born out of wedlock. I kept this from you, but you must have worked it all out, realized that I had no choice; why else would you have supported me? My only condition was that when the child was born, I would be released from this marriage contract. She agreed to it, but I see now that she was lying. One good thing is that she loves her son and will make sure he is not in any danger. Of that I am sure. I will take my men and go to Ivar first; he will join me, and together we will find where they are holding them and get them both released. Even if it means a ransom must be paid."

"Somehow this does not surprise me. You are right! I did suspect that she was already with child and in all honesty, I disliked her on first sight. Her eyes had that deviously hard look to them and I realized immediately that she had tricked you. My father always says the eyes tell the truth so look deep into your opponent's eyes before judging. God go with you and hurry back to us. Never forget that we need you too."

"There are many different types of battles and now it seems that the war in Scotland is not over after all. I know you do not care for Ivar, but he is my blood cousin; I cannot leave him on his own. We all want to be remembered, to have our story passed on to our children, then our children's children and so on. Our ancestors were the same and we continue to tell their stories, so they still live on. I do not want to be remembered as the warrior-king who chose not to support his own cousin, or worse yet, as a man who did not rescue his son—even if I truly believe that he is in no danger. If I was to remain here and do nothing that is all people will remember and my other deeds would soon be forgotten."

Olaf left her once more without asking for support from Kjarval, knowing none would be forthcoming since it was only an internal problem. There appeared to be no threat from England. But Olaf made a solemn promise to return to her, to renew their vows and that Princess Ceana was no longer his wife nor would ever be again.

Chapter 22

Ivar slipped into Dubhlinn, badly injured. He brought the sad news that Olaf had been killed and he claimed with much bitterness that his wife left him at the mercy of her people. In the end, Artgal's family accused only Ivar and Olaf of killing their King; apparently Aed had been relieved of any blame. This vengeful family claimed that they had to protect their queen from him, saying that she feared for her life, so they took her into their protective custody. He never got to see her or talk to her. Ivar was extremely angry and confused with it all. He was convinced that Aed and Ceana had planned it with the relatives of the powerful families of the Strathclyde people who been taken as slaves. He tried to explain what happened to Aud.

"We had to hide from these avenging people; fortunately we had some good people who were on our side. Trickles of information leaked into our compound and it appears that these families paid for the help of some Viking mercenaries that had fought for the English in the previous battle. Between them they had created a more powerful army than both of ours combined. To make matters worse Olaf convinced me that it was an internal issue only, so we decided to leave your father out of it, thinking we could handle it on our own. Olaf was in a hurry to settle this kidnapping, which he said was a hoax. It turned out to be a strategic error on our part. Possibly your father would have made all the difference; maybe he would have been more objective and seen through this ruse. I can now see that he is normally more level-headed than the two of us, Olaf and I."

"Princess Ceana, being the spoiled, selfish woman she is, simply wanted revenge on Olaf for leaving her. What a disaster! When Olaf finally discovered where Ceana was held we mustered the men and rode hard to the castle where they were being kept. Then just the two of us rode to the front gate carrying a white flag and asked to talk it through. We came in peace but there was to be no talking. It was never part of the plan. Olaf was shot on first sight with a poisoned arrow and died a painful death. Why I wasn't immediately hit with an arrow too is still confusing to me, but our soldiers immediately backed me up and we were able to reconvene to discuss our options. The only possibility for us was to return to Strathclyde and arrange for battle, but the mercenary army was waiting for us on the road back. It was a total ambush. Many were killed and that is where I got injured; it had turned into a full-scale battle. The enemy had a bigger force than we thought possible. All we could do was to try to escape."

Aud was in shock but managed to ask what happened to Olaf's body.

Ivar held his head in his hands. He looked as devastated as Aud herself. "I don't know. I suppose Ceana claimed it and hopefully she had the heart to give him a decent burial. Olaf's death and Aed's deceit is more than I can take right now. Olaf was so sure that Ceana would succumb to his demands. Who was to know that the princess had a bigger army than ours and had such anger at Olaf for leaving her? She must have hated him for coming back to you! He did tell me that he had planned to annul their marriage, you must know you were always his preferred choice for wife and queen. He had much respect for you—as do I." Ivar hung his head in silence before continuing. "Olaf dead—gone from my life! My only choice was to escape. I have lost everything because of this deceitful queen I married and the devious moves of the spoiled Princess Ceana." He looked up at Aud with a sadness she had not realized he was capable of. "All this time I thought she even loved me. What a fool I was!"

Aud had heard enough from Ivar; she excused herself, saying she had to deal with Olaf's death privately and left without saying another word. Even though Ivar claimed his wife had deceived him she could not feel any sympathy in her heart for his loss, she could only think about her own loss and that of her son. The shock of Olaf's death gripped her heart with an unknown fear. What did Ivar expect from her now, and from this crown? She did not trust him. To express her own sorrow in front of him was unthinkable; she needed to find Jon. When she found him, she choked back her tears, "Olaf is no more—God help us—our warrior-king is gone! Murdered! They were set up! Jon—what am I to do?"

Jon was clearly as upset with her news as she was. The sudden, unexpected loss of Olaf was more than she could handle and she collapsed into Jon's arms. He tried to console her with words from God but all he did in the end was rock her in his arms like a baby, and that is what eventually soothed her. When her sobs finally subsided, she was able to say a few words. She told him everything that Ivar told her and even confessed her part in Artgal's death. To her surprise Jon wasn't shocked, claiming he had already known about it as Olaf could not help himself and bragged about her clever plan. He encouraged her to be strong and to return to the great hall with him as he needed to talk to Ivar himself. "I will go talk to him and find out what his plans are, and then get back to you. I hear he has been wounded so I doubt he will be coming to you but maybe you should be prepared to leave. Remember your father's warning about Ivar outliving Olaf."

When Jon returned his news was not reassuring. Ivar was badly injured but claimed it would not stop him from taking over Olaf's crown. He said he planned to talk to the Longphort Council and seek their permission to do so as this was Olaf's wish, and he was sure that they were aware of this. He even hinted that he had need of a wife and a queen. He did not care that his wife was in Scotland and still alive. "Now that he firmly believed that his wife had deceived him, he thought it was quite convenient that a Queen of Dubhlinn already existed and that maybe she should become his queen. With you as his queen I believe he thinks the Council will be more willing to accept him as king. He knows how highly respected you are with the council members."

This frightened her into action. "You are right! It is time to make our escape plan a reality and you must join us. I do not think you will be safe once I am gone. He will know that you were the one who told me of his plans."

"I cannot leave my church, Aud, you know that; so I will take my chances with Ivar. He is my cousin. I pray he has value for our kinship, but in your case and especially for Thorstein, we must not waste any time. Una and Thora are no longer safe here either."

Aud reached for his hand. "Thank the Lord I decided to hide my trunk in your church. You were the only one I could ever trust, Jon. You were right, it would be impossible to leave this place lugging such a load."

Aud searched for Una and together with Jon they organized all the items of value that they could carry in cloth bags. Then they gathered the children together and Una left the great hall with Jon and the children. Jon distracted the guard while the rest slipped out behind his back. They made their way to his church, but Jon planned to return after the *nattmal* to collect Aud. She sent a maid to make her excuses to Ivar, stating that she was still too devastated about Olaf to attend him, but would show up for the morning meal to fill him in with whatever news he would need to know about Dubhlinn. She remained in her room in case he decided to check on her to enquire about her well-being after he received her message. He did not show up, much to her relief; he must have been too injured or too tired to make the walk to her room. Better still, perhaps, he believed her.

Jon gained entrance to the great hall later that night by claiming that Queen Aud had requested his presence to pray with her for Olaf's soul. No one thought anything of this and when he knocked softly on her door, she was ready to leave. They left quietly and waited around the corner until the guard fell asleep in his chair. Jon had given him a small skin filled with drugged wine when he first entered. He claimed that it would not take long for the drug to work, but that it would not last long either; they had to be ready to slip out. It worked like a charm and the guard woke up none the wiser. As he later changed shifts, he did not know when Jon had left. Jon and Aud arrived at the church to find an unknown Irishman, who assured them that he was sent by Brother David and that a messenger had been sent ahead to King Kjarval.

Jon went to get Aud's trunk, which was full of valuables that he had hidden for her. Once the cart was loaded, with Una and the children each hiding under a crate covered by a large woolen tarp, this strange-looking man with a hump encouraged Aud to leave immediately. Unsure of this stranger she hesitated, claiming to Jon that she did not know this man. He assured her that they were safe with him, that it would be better and safer for all if the cart was driven by a local going off to the harbour at this time of night. Supposedly his cart was full of smelly empty crates that needed to be loaded onto the fishermen's wharf, ready to be filled with the morning's catch when the boats returned. If stopped, all he would have to do is lift the end of the tarp for any inspector to see that all he had were empty boxes, except for the ones in the middle where they would be hidden. The driver assured her that he had never been stopped before and did not expect any trouble tonight.

Before Aud climbed under her designated crate she checked on the children hiding under their crate together. They assured her that they were fine and that this was all a big adventure to them. Then she spoke to Una, who also calmed her fears, before she could finally say her farewells to Jon—not before pleading with him once again to leave as soon as possible. "I will be fine, Aud, please do not worry; and be assured that this man has no love for Ivar, so he will see you safely onto that fishing boat."

They made it to their ship safely with no incident, just as the man had promised. Aud breathed a sigh of relief and thanked God for looking over them and for the strange, silent man who helped them and their belongings into yet another smelly but much larger crate embedded in the belly of the fishing boat. This one was where the catch of the day would normally be stored and later brought to the harbour, to be unloaded into all those empty ones from the cart that would be neatly piled and waiting in a designated area on the harbourfront. Only it would not be this ship that would bring in the catch of the day to fill those boxes. The man with the humped back covered their hiding place with its lid, and quietly wished them well, assuring them that God would be looking over the righteous and would keep them safe. At least they were all together in this big box; even if they could not see each other in the dark, they could hold hands. They waited patiently and quietly; the children, exhausted from all the fear and excitement, soon fell asleep despite the strong fish smell. Aud and Una were too anxious to sleep. Finally, they felt movement as the boat slipped away from the harbour and heard all the greetings from the others as it blended in with the other boats. There was a slight tapping on the lid of their hiding place, acknowledging that the person knew that they were there. Aud grasped Una's hand to reassure her and whispered, "God is with us always. Trust in his love and protection."

Fortunately for the escapees, the daily routines of life were taken for granted in Dubhlinn town. Every day a small fishing fleet went out long before the sun rose in the sky. On this day, it went out as usual, but this time there was an extra ship. The harbourmaster, so used to seeing them all go out, had long ago given up counting them. They returned as usual with their catch and as usual the harbourmaster welcomed them home, once again without counting them. Unknown to him, one of them had not returned. He would pay dearly for his mistake.

That extra ship did not go fishing, but made its way to King Kjarval's castle where a much larger longship manned by some of his warriors transferred Aud, Thorstein, Una and Thora along with their belongings from the fishing boat. Aud's belongings included a large trunk filled with her wealth and several small satchels filled with clothing and some jewels, some of which she had hastily jammed into this trunk to reduce the noise of the gold and silver moving about while on the fishing boat. It was enough to muffle the jingling. Once they had arrived, Kjarval saw to it that two much larger trunks they had been keeping for her were brought on board as well. One was filled with priceless treasures—more gold, silver and many valuable stones. She was leaving a very wealthy woman. The other trunk contained more clothes for them all.

Kjarval and Olaf had not agreed on many issues recently, except to keep Scotland Gaelic and a second pact to see to the safety of Aud, Thorstein, Una and Thora. Aud wasted no time and ordered the captain to set sail immediately for the Hebrides. Thorstein complained that he smelled like rotten fish, but Aud just laughed. "That is just part of your adventure, son, now you have a great story to tell *afi* and your new friends. Relax, once we are at sea the salt air will cleanse any smell from our bodies. Besides, you see that tent on that ship? Well, that is where we will sleep and change clothes. Do not worry, we not only have a change of fresh clothing to survive this journey, but warmer cloaks as well. There is water onboard and we can wash ourselves before changing into clean clothes. I have some nice herbs to put into the water that will help us all smell better. The important thing is that we are safe and will soon see *afi*. Thora*min*, you are very quiet, are you okay?"

"Yes, *takk*. I must confess that I am scared of sailing on such a big sea, though."

Una answered her. "You are quite safe, *elskamin*. Queen Aud will see to that."

Both Jorunn, once again with child, and Kjarval were there to see them off. He readied two other ships filled with soldiers to act as escorts; they were commanded to return immediately after restocking with essential supplies. Jorunn was tearful; Aud tried to reassure her of her love. "*Systirmin*, I shall miss you more than you will ever know. Sadly, we may never see each other again, but my destiny lies elsewhere now, thanks to Ivar. The Hebrides is to become our new homeland and we will have father there to see to our welfare and our protection. King Kjarval, I cannot thank you enough for all your support."

Kjarval had these words of comfort for her. "How can I, as a Christian, allow such a man as Ivar to take you, a fellow Christian, for his wife and queen? He is an unacceptable man for the role of King of Dubhlinn. I find it difficult to believe that Olaf has left it for him. If the Council does agree to let him have the crown, I will see to it that he does not have it for long. Ireland has just declared war on this evil man and I will make sure the Longphort Council knows all about him and his past deeds. We send our regards to your father; safe travels, Queen Aud. Once my men have rested and restocked their ships, please send them back to us."

The sisters cried as they said their final farewells. Aud's tears were also for Thorstein. Still in shock over Olaf's death, she was devastated that her son was not to have the crown of Dubhlinn. She tried to be positive; they were safe and on their way to her father in the Hebrides. She vowed that she would never give up on her dynastic plans for him, once safe with her *pabbi*. Together they would find another crown for Thorstein the Red.

That evening Ivar missed her at the *nattmal*, but when he received her message he chose to leave her alone, thinking to himself that there was plenty of time to discuss things with her. The next day when she did not show for the *dagmal,* he limped over to Aud's quarters to ask how she was feeling only to find that she had disappeared from Dubhlinn along with her son, her maid and the maid's child. He roared with such anger it could be heard throughout the great hall. Even though they had nothing to do with her leaving, everyone within the hall shivered with fear; they knew he would take his anger out on whoever was nearby. There would be many bruised bodies today.

Jon was soon summoned when Ivar figured out that he was the only person who could have told her about his intentions. Jon walked into the great hall to find Ivar sitting in the high seat with a beautifully carved spear in his hand, with the blade pointing towards the heavens. On his head was Olaf's crown. To him it appeared that he was using the spear as a sceptre to show that he was now his king. "She has gone, cousin and I do believe it was because you told her I planned to make her my queen. Am I correct?"

"*Why lie?*" Jon thought. "You are correct, Ivar."

With a roar he stood and banged the floor with the spear. "I should kill you here and now. You are my cousin! Why did you go behind my back?"

"Olaf was also my cousin, but I made an oath to him, not to you. I promised him that I would look after Aud. He asked me to have some form of escape ready if needed, and it was needed, as Aud would not accept your plan of making her your wife."

"Did she tell you that, or did you just assume?"

"She was quite clear, cousin. She said that she would give up her son's crown and concede it to you and give up her own crown rather than become your wife. 'No crown will ever be important enough to me that I have to become the wife of Ivar in order to maintain it.' Her words—not mine."

"You are very brave for a lowly priest. Pray tell me cousin, what ruse did you implement to get her out of here—unseen? This is not an easy place to escape from, because all must pass through the harbourmaster's purview, and they already had orders from me not to let anyone from the great hall leave without my knowledge. I must know in case there are any others who want to escape from me."

Jon felt it wasn't necessary to keep it a secret now that they had gone. "Aud sent her regrets to you last night for missing *nattmal*, saying she was not well, which was true; she was very upset over Olaf. Except her promise that she would attend the next morning's meal was a deliberate lie. Una and the children left before the evening meal and I came for Aud later, after the *nattmal*, on the premise that we were to pray for Olaf's soul together. It was not difficult to leave this place; the guards are used to me coming and going, but I must beg their forgiveness for deceiving them. Then we all met up at my church. In the middle of the night before the sun rose we readied a cart that carried them under cover to a waiting fishing vessel, where they were hidden in the hold that would have held the fish that would normally have been caught that morning. Fortunately for our escapees all fish holds have a wooden lid with gaps between the slats, and no one usually asks to see inside. When the fleet was ready to go, they sailed away without anyone stopping them. The harbourmasters have become lazy; they no longer count the boats in the fishing fleet that leaves early each morning, or even when they return. It may have been a smelly escape, but it was an effective one."

"Who were these men and where are they now?"

"They will not return here. They were Irish and will simply disappear into the countryside. I do not know their names and did not want to know, so I am unable to tell you. All I know is that they were opposed to your leadership because of your cruelty to the Irish women you raped in the past. As you remember, I warned you that no good would result from taking advantage of these women."

"You are nothing but an arrogant priest! You do not tell me what to do—ever!"

He banged his spear so hard he cracked the shaft. "As for those men that guard our door and the harbourmasters, I will put a stop to their carelessness! Guards! Seize this priest and put him in the prisoner's hold—make sure you tie his hands together, then attach the rope to the ceiling. I want him to have to stand with his arms up in the air—praying to his God." He laughed heartily at the thought, then with much sarcasm he challenged Jon. "See if your God can save you now, priest!" To the guards he said, "I will decide what to do with him later, I want him to fear the punishment that his God cannot save him from."

"Cousin—you can't do this to me! I made a solemn promise to Olaf when he was our king—I only did what he requested of me. Also, the people of this parish need me."

"Umf! Nobody needs you—least of all me— so think again! I can and will do as I please—you have become an enemy of this kingdom. Guards—do as I say!" Terrified of Ivar, the guards led Jon out by a rope that was tied around his wrists. He was never seen or heard from again!

Ivar the Hated crowned himself King of Dubhlinn with the blessings of the Longphort Council and with the knowledge that it was what Olaf had wanted. Meanwhile, the local people proclaimed that a reign of terror had begun!

Part II

Failure is a lesson learned.
Success is a lesson applied.
Anonymous

Chapter 23

About 869 AD, ten years after fleeing Dubhlinn

The wind whipped across the southernmost Outer Isles of the Hebrides while the sun shone brightly over the large estate on top of the hill called Ketill*staðir*. A great longhouse with many smaller buildings stood on that rise, overlooking the sea where a watch would warn anyone of ships entering its large bay. Several huge Celtic crosses greeted visitors on the approach from the shore up to the top. The whole area looked open and vulnerable, but that was meant to deceive. The one and only visible path to the top of this flat elevation was nestled amongst the rocks where hidden warriors could hide and attack any enemies trying to invade the estate. A well had been dug and housed next to the longhouse, where fresh water was available from an underground stream. An escape route was hidden away on the other side of the small island, where two small ships were concealed in a small inland bay. These ships were small enough to portage over the stones that prevented other ships from entering but big enough to carry off the people who needed to escape. Ketill had been part of the siege of Dunbarton and had no intention of getting caught in the same way.

His estate was located on one of the many islands known as Bjarnar-oy of Barra Head, or Bear Island. It had received that name after a sighting of a great white bear that had floated in on an iceberg from some northern region, long before his time. The bear did not survive and never again had anyone sighted another, but the name had stuck. He had chosen this area for strategic reasons. Originally he had fought for these islands as well as the Shetlands and the Isle of Man in the name of King Harold of Norway, and since this king had reneged on his promises to him, Ketill had returned and taken all the lands for himself. He soon became known as the King of the Suðreys. He ruled wisely; his people learned to respect and honour him. This island proved to be a haven not only for him, but later also for Aud and Thorstein as well as Una and Thora. Ten years had passed and no invaders from Ireland came seeking revenge. Not even King Harold's men had appeared to take back the islands. Since Ivar never showed up, they suspected that he could not get any men to back an invasion this far north. As for Harold, was it possible that this king felt some guilt for the part he played in the loss of Ketill's lands in Norway? No one knew, or questioned, or cared; they felt safe here and that was the only thing that mattered to them.

Today was an important day for all; their lives were changing once more. Aud mulled over this as she stood at the top of the path watching several longships preparing to leave the bay. Her beloved son, now fourteen years old, and his *afi*, were on the lead ship. The captain was her old friend Einar. Throughout the years he had followed Ketill into his many battles with Olaf and Ivar when they raided other lands together, and he had proven that he was a loyal soldier. He had risen through the ranks to become the lead captain. They were on their way to the Orkneys, as Jarl Sigurd was going to foster her son and teach him the ways of leadership and warfare. Ketill, his *afi*, had been a great teacher, but the Norse tradition was an honoured one and they felt a great respect for this man who had offered his mentorship.

Sigurd was older than Ketill; he had had one son, Guttorm, who lived in Norway as a powerful *hersir* for King Harold. He had gone there as young man when he was about the same age as Thorstein was now, to be fostered by his Uncle Rognvald. He never returned home, saying he preferred living there surrounded by such powerful men as his uncle and the king. He claimed that the Orkneys was just a small outpost, not worthy of him, and he expected to receive a larger holding one day in Norway. This hurt Sigurd deeply; he blamed his brother for turning his young son's heart against his home. This 'rotten' brother, as Sigurd called him, had made promises to his son of fame and fortune, and he suspected that it was he who belittled the Orkney Islands, which in turn had influenced his son's opinion. If Rognvald thought so little of the Orkneys, it was no wonder he readily gave them to his brother; this was the reason why Sigurd partnered with Olaf and Ketill. He vowed to oppose any effort Rognvald might make against any of these islands in King Harold's name. That included his island as well as the Shetlands, Hebrides, the Isle of Wight, the Isle of Man—any island within their vicinity, for that matter. His anger was such that he promised to make Thorstein his heir instead of his own son Guttorm. Both Aud and her father accepted Sigurd's offer; they saw this island as part of a much larger kingdom, since this red-haired boy would inherit his *afi*'s holdings one day too.

Neither Ketill nor Aud viewed any one of these islands as insignificant; after living there all these years they realized the strategic value of their locations. Ambition still directed Aud's decisions; power was everything. Olaf's method of having a council of men that banded together and kept his holdings safe guided her towards the same idea for these islands. Her father set up a similar system under her advice, but insisted they appoint the leaders rather than have the people vote them in, mainly because of their isolation from each other. He felt it was important that the leader was a more permanent one. He instilled fairness in everyone they chose and encouraged the local people on each island to be open with any complaint so it could be settled before it could build up into any form of resentment. It appeared to be working and they met regularly; Aud was always included.

Besides erecting many crosses, Aud had commissioned a small chapel to be built near the great hall, and that is where she headed after the ships had disappeared into the vast horizon. Occasionally Artgal's death haunted her thoughts; she may not have poured the poison into his goblet, but it was her idea for Olaf to convince Queen Aed to do the deed. Although she struggled with this Christian guilt, she often wondered whether ridding themselves of her instead of Artgal would have made things turn out differently, or if maybe they should have got rid of them both. Aed had proven to them all that she was a troublemaker, and together with her niece Ceana they were a toxic mix.

Added to these haunting thoughts of the past was her worry over Jon the Priest. Not knowing what had happened to him was more than she could bear some days. She would kneel in front of the altar to talk to God every day to ask for his comfort, in her grieving over the loss of her husband, her crown, her son's crown and the loss of her best friend Jon the Priest—a man she knew she loved more than any other. She often played the *If only* game in her head. *If only* she could have changed Olaf's stubborn attitude towards Christianity and his trust in Ivar the Hated. *If only* she could have been more convincing and gotten him to really convert, things may have turned out differently. He may have even seen this evil cousin for what he really was. *If only* Jon had listened to her and escaped with them. But that never happened and Aud knew that this game of hers was a senseless one to play after the fact; it only tortured her soul more than was necessary. But play it she did!

News had eventually reached them of Ivar and his troubles in Dubhlinn. King Kjarval finally convinced the council that their choice of leader was not the right one, and with their help they chased him out of Dubhlinn. Apparently, he was somewhere in Northumbria with his band of renegades, but even with him gone no one ever came looking for Olaf's heir to offer him the crown. Another Viking warrior called Sygtrygg put claim to Dubhlinn, and the council as well as King Kjarval fully backed him. He had assisted them to rid Dubhlinn of Ivar under condition that he get the crown. The word was that he had since proven himself to be a great king, who agreed with Olaf's method of running the council. This sat well with them all; none of them would lose their autonomy, which Ivar had been slowly eroding. Aud had known of this man, but only slightly; he was a relative newcomer before she escaped but even then, he was fast becoming one of Olaf's trusted warriors. To have turned on Ivar he must have seen him for what he really was. This crown was also part of her *if only* game. *If only* someone had come to find Thorstein and offered him the crown. Aud knew in her heart that he would have been too young and vulnerable, that there would have been too many problems and too many ambitious men vying for the same crown. His life and hers would have always been at risk if they had returned to Dubhlinn. This reasoning brought her some comfort for their loss, but she still cherished the dream of creating a royal dynasty one day.

As for Jon, several ships of men that had come into their port had similar stories to tell of the priest. They all claimed that he had escaped from the holding cell, which was wonderful news to Aud, but then was never seen or heard of again. She prayed that he was well and had got out in time, but the Vikings that brought the news about his escape claimed that it was unlikely that he survived it. Why else was he never seen again? Ivar must have found him and killed him, was all they could say. Their claims of death did not crush her belief that he could be alive; she had faith in his God to watch over him, so she continued to include him in her daily prayers.

Aud's knees were aching and her stomach was growling; it was time to return to the longhouse. Suddenly a gentle hand was on her shoulder. "*Frænkamin*, mamma is worried about you."

"Ahh Thora, *elskamin*, how kind of you to come look for me. I needed to pray because I miss Thorstein already. How about you, will you miss your young *broðir*?"

"Yes, but I will not miss his teasing."

"You are correct, he can be quite the tease. Now take my hand and lead me home, *litla* Thora*min*."

"*Frænka*, you forget, I am not so little anymore, I am almost a woman and almost as tall as you!"

"Yah! You get your height from your father—as does your young *broðir*—but you are still my special little girl, Thoramin." The young girl smiled lovingly at the woman she referred to as aunt. Aud was not a real aunt but she had insisted on being called that right from the beginning. Thora and Thorstein were brother and sister; they had the same father but different mothers, so *frænka* seemed the logical term to use. Thorstein adopted it for Una, Thora's mother, as well. Una was no longer considered just a maid to Aun or Ketill. They had all established a very close relationship over the years; the two older women became more like sisters. Even though Una continued to run the household for Aud and her father, they had become a family.

Aud and Thora held hands as they walked together to the longhouse, where Una waited for them with their *nattmal*.

Chapter 24

Several weeks went by, and for the last few days, every day, several times a day, weather permitting, Aud had walked along the ridge expecting to see the sails of her father's longships returning from the Orkneys. Thora often accompanied her. *"Maybe,"* she thought, *"I should have gone with them, but I couldn't bear leaving Thorstein there, alone. Stop this nonsense, he is not alone, Jarl Sigurd will take wonderful care of him, that I know!"* She felt like that young girl back in Norway who used to always wait for her father's expected return, but this time there was no sleeping giant to fear. *"Giant or no giant—some things never seem to change! I am always the one waiting!"*

She was in the chapel just before *nattmal* saying her daily prayers when she heard Thora's shout. *"Frænka,* they are returning. Come quick—you can see their sails on the horizon."

Aud went running, excited to be seeing her *pabbi* and her friend Einar; she had missed them both. Einar had married a woman called Ragnhild from the Shetlands and they already had three children together, so she knew he would be happy to be home. He had made a good marriage to a woman whose ancestry went back to Sigurd Hjort, King of Ringerike, Norway. She joined Thora on the ridge and slipped her hand into hers. *"Elskamin,* your hands are cold, here let me warm them for you."

"*Frænka,* there are more ships than what left here—are there not?"

"*Jæja,* so there are my child. Can you count them for me? My eyesight is not what it used to be."

"There are seven in all."

"Those extra ships will bring more men so you know what that means—we will be having guests for *nattmal.* Run along home and warn your *mamma.* The *thralls* will need to prepare more food than normal. Then you can come back and wait with me to see who they are. Hurry now—be quick!"

Some of the men on those extra ships would set up tents on the shoreline to stay close by, while a few would camp on board, but she expected her father would at least bring up the captains of the unknown ships to meet her. Einar lived in the village that lined the coastline, as did most of the sailors, so she did not expect to see him for a few days.

Thora had returned faster than she thought possible. Panting from all the exertion and excitement she clutched Aud's hand tightly, trying to calm down. Still breathless, Thora managed to ask, "where are they now, *frænka?*"

"You were very fast, Thora*min,* you must be excited to have company! You do realize that Thorstein will not be with *afi,* don't you? He is to stay with Sigurd for at least five years."

"Of course! I know that!"

"Good. It will be some time yet before anyone walks up these steps. They may look like they are close, but they have some distance to cover before they can dock their ships. Why don't we sit on the grass and watch as they sail into our harbour?"

It took a couple of hours, but although the air had a chill to it, the day was too nice to wait indoors. Thora was getting anxious when finally, they saw some men making their way towards the hill. Standing together at the top of the steps, Aud asked Thora to count how many were climbing them. "There are five men, *frænka,* with your *pabbi.* Do you recognize them?"

"No—no—*elksamin*—they are all wearing helmets and they are too busy watching where their feet should be placed so you cannot see any faces. You sound eager; are you happy that *afi* has returned?"

"Yes, *afi* always has a good story to tell and the unexpected men, I am sure, have been to some strange places—places we may not have heard about. We do not get much company and they will have stories to tell too, won't they?"

"Of that I am sure."

Thora was only a couple years old when one day after she had called him Ketill, he had picked her up and set her on his lap and explained, "Since Thorstein is your brother and I love him and I love you—so then—I must be your *afi* too!" He had won her over forever.

Ketill appeared first and Thora ran to greet him; he hugged her tightly. "You have grown up so quickly. I remember the days when I could pick you up and throw you over my shoulders like a full sack of grain, asking if you were wheat, barley, rye or oats and all the time threatening to throw you into the grain shed."

She laughed as she replied to his memory. "Then I would say, '*Afi* it's me, Thora. I am not a sack of grain—let me down.'"

Holding Thora's hand, he came up to his daughter and clasped her hand in his other. "Aud, be prepared for a big surprise."

"Did Thorstein come back with you?" That was the only thing she could think of that would surprise her.

"No." Her father stepped aside as another man approached her. He took off his leather helmet, exposing his flaming red hair.

Aud's hands flew to her mouth to stop the loud gasp that had escaped from it. "Jon! Oh, dear Lord! Is that you?" She rushed up to him and threw her arms around him, not caring what anyone thought. Through her tears of joy, she whispered into his ear. "Thank the Lord you are alive! I have been praying for this since we escaped—your God really did save you from Ivar. But how is this possible? Everyone claimed that you had to be dead! Nobody had seen or heard of you since, after he locked you away!"

"Aud—it is good to see you too!" He softly removed her arms from around his neck but continued to hold her hands in her. "I will explain it all to you. Just give me time to catch my breath; your steps are steep, and I need a drink first. Even a goblet of water will do, but I would prefer a beer."

"Oh Jon—Jon! My heart is bursting with joy! You have not changed—but no—you have changed! You are no longer a priest?"

"People now call me the warrior-priest. It is a long story."

Thora cut in. "I love stories."

"Yes—yes! We all do, Thora*min*." Aud linked her arms with Jon and Thora, then turned towards home. "This is so exciting and the best surprise imaginable. Come—come everyone, let us go to the longhouse. I do recognize each one of you, welcome back. Refreshments await you inside." Filled with an excitement she had not experienced in many years, she envisioned a new life of hope, new adventures and possibly fulfilled dreams. For some unknown reason Unn, her old goddess of the frothing waves, popped into her head.

Chapter 25

The other men with Jon were the appointed *jarls* of Ketil's other islands: the Shetlands, the Isle of Man, as well as the independent *jarl* of the Faroe Islands. They were all part of the islands' council and had been to the island several times before to meet with Ketill and his daughter. Aud in turn had traveled on many occasions to their islands. She was well respected for her intelligent input and was always included in their talks.

During the *nattmal* Jon had filled her in with some of the details of his escape, but Thora wanted to hear about it too so Jon, Aud, Una and Thora gathered around the firepit after the feast with goblets of wine or mead, where he began the enthralling saga of his escape. "Well, young lady, it was a harrowing experience. Can you imagine—my own cousin locked me up and intended to kill me! He had his guards tie my hands together with a rope and they attached the end of the rope to the roof of the shed where I was locked in. Why they locked the door I don't know because there was no way I could escape, especially with a guard sitting right by the door. My arms were held up in the air by the rope and eventually all the blood left them, whereby they went numb. My arms were tied up like that until that night, when I heard a noise."

Always the entertainer he cupped his ear as if he had indeed heard some noise, then whispered, "I thought for sure it was Ivar, my cousin, come to do his dirty deed." Then louder, "Instead, when the door opened it was two Irishmen that I had never seen before, shushing me as they dragged in the guard. They had knocked him out and after they undid my ropes, they tied him up with his arms raised to the gods as I had been, then gagged his mouth so he could not call for help. At first, I couldn't bring my arms down; they had to massage them so some feeling would return." He acted out the massaging while continuing his tale, "We had to get them back to normal before I could leave." Suddenly Jon stood up with his arms in the air. "You can imagine how strange I would have looked—I couldn't leave that building with my arms frozen upright, now could I?"

Thora was aghast! "They would have stayed up in the air?"

"Yes, because they had been held up in the air by ropes most of the day, they felt like there were frozen in that upright position. Normally we cannot hold up our arms for any length of time; you try and see how long you can last. Keep them above your head now and see if you can keep them there without any ropes to hold them up until the end of my story."

She did so, and Jon continued. Aud could see that he was thoroughly enjoying Thora's full attention; she couldn't help thinking what a wonderful father he would have made. Suddenly he was talking in such a hushed voice the women listening had to strain their ears to hear. Jon was trying to create an atmosphere, as if they were there with him trying to escape quietly into the dark. "We had to be very quiet as Ivar had guards everywhere, but my rescuers knew their way around. They rubbed dirt all over my exposed body just as they had done to themselves; this helped us disappear against the wood. The mud also kept the light from the sliver of moon that was in the night sky from reflecting on our sweaty skin and exposing us. Then we slithered along the sides of the walls of the surrounding buildings like thieves in the night. We almost got caught—twice!"

"Twice?" shouted Thora bringing down her arms in surprise.

"The story is not over, raise your arms." Thora groaned.

Jon nodded, then stood up and acted out their moves as if he was against a wall. Thora's arms started to relax once more, but he wasn't about to let her bring them down just yet. "Now—now—remember your hands are tied up and held up in the air by imaginary ropes. You must keep them up high above your head. For the effect to work!" She groaned once more but tried again to hold them above her head. Jon knew it would not last much longer, but it would make his story more dramatic to her, so he insisted at least for a few minutes more.

Shaking his arms all about, he continued with his story once again. "My arms were tingling so badly from being held up above my head for so long that I couldn't touch anything at first. I kept shaking them like this to get the blood circulating again, even while we slipped along the walls. My rescuers kept me in the middle of them so they could be prepared to fight for me; they each had an axe in their hand and a knife strapped to their waist. We crept slowly away from the town to a bluff of trees where they had hidden some horses. Eventually we ended up near the abbey where Brother David was waiting by the boat launch. I was very surprised, but very happy to see that it was him who had organized my rescue. How he knew I was taken prisoner is still a mystery to me, but there was no time for discussion. The boat was small, made of cowhide lashed together. It was a *currach*, a typical Irish boat and just big enough for the three of us. We had to squeeze our legs under each other, it was that small. Did you know that they rub butter on the laces to stop the water from entering?"

Thora pulled a face. "Butter, ugh! I hate butter! In my opinion that is a better use for it, don't you think?"

"Maybe, for you!" He pointed a finger at her, then directed the same finger at himself, "But I love butter and there can never be enough for my bread. Now back to my story. There was much grumbling from the three of us as we tried to get comfortable so we could row the little boat. Then Brother David handed me a package of butter in case it started to leak. How do you think that made me feel? IN CASE IT LEAKED!" He held his arms out as if in wonder. "Where did you find this boat and these men, I asked him? I was quite incredulous with him, but he assured me that these men were very trustworthy and experts at rowing this boat in the dark. Fortunately, there was not a full moon that night, but there was enough of a moon to make it dangerous for us. He said these men had eyes like owls; as you know owls can see in the dark and are great night hunters."

He made circles with his fingers around his eyes to emphasize big round owl eyes. Thora laughed, then dropped her arms. "I cannot keep them up any longer, Jon. It hurts so, I think I understand how much you must have hurt."

Ketill and his *jarls* were seated in the corner drinking mead where they had been discussing local politics, but they were obviously listening to the story too, as it became very quiet over there. Ketill came over first and sat down beside Thora, rubbing her arms to bring back the circulation. She smiled at him then slipped her arm through his while they waited for the other men to come over and sit down. He patted her arm and stated why they had decided to join them. "We had trouble hearing him and his story was becoming too interesting to miss."

Jon nodded to the men then continued his story. "Thora, you did very well to keep them up as long as you did. Well, back to the *currach*; it was indeed small. After we settled in, we left immediately because Brother David feared for our lives. Cramped as we were, we rowed silently away under cover of the darkness. We made our way to King Kjarval's castle, and lucky for us nobody followed the little boat—I thank God it never leaked, so I kept the butter for later." Thora pulled another face at the thought of butter, to which he laughed and replied, "Yum!" while rubbing his tummy. "When we finally got there the sun had risen; we could hardly get out of it because our legs were that sore and stiff from being cramped into such a small boat. We were safe and that was all that mattered, but I can imagine just how angry Ivar the Hated was when he found me gone. I wish I could have witnessed his astonishment and his anger."

"Why is he called 'the Hated'?"

"Because his grandfather was hated, but his grandfather's nickname was Ivar the Boneless because he really was born a cripple. You all must have heard the story about Ivar the Boneless, the crippled son?" Without waiting for any reply, he continued, he wasn't about to give up being centre stage. "His own father, the famous Ragnar Lothbrok, did not want him to face life with such a handicap, so one night he set his baby son outside in a distant field for the wolves to eat. The wolves all cried, yum, yum yum! But his mother, Princess Auslag, had been spying on Ragnar and saw what he did. She rescued her son and after that incident she never let her crippled child out of her sight, nor did she ever forgive Ragnar for doing this. Ivar was coddled for the rest of his mother's life, which was not long, as it turned out. In the short time she had left and the limited time they had together, she created a monster—a very spoiled child who grew into a very irascible and selfish man."

"Always angry at life in general he would fume and rant at the gods for creating him with legs that did not work. His mother twisted his handicap into something special and eventually convinced him that he was a god himself, and that the gods created him with boneless legs because he was special, thus persuading him his destiny was to become the greatest man that ever lived. There was no doubt about it, despite being a cripple, he was very intelligent and as we all know he did become a legend. When he was older—that is, when he became a man—he along with his brothers started to win battles using his strategies. Soon the men who fought alongside him made him their leader. One of these men was as intelligent as Ivar, but in a different way. He was a ship builder, a man called Floki, who built many wonderful vessels for him and helped win many battles for the brothers by creating devastating weapons."

"The best thing he built for Ivar, though, were wooden straps for his legs so he could stand, as well as a cart pulled by horses, where he could stand as they took him into the middle of the action. Ivar discovered the freedom of movement and became a powerful war lord; he truly considered himself a god. Thus, his mother was right—well, partly right! His legacy would not have been what she wanted for him; all anyone remembered about him was his legacy of hate and death. My cousin Ivar grew up with this knowledge of his grandfather and with a father who was also a cruel man, so he had to learn to fend for himself."

"As you know Thora*min*, young boys tend to tease whenever they can; all the boys that grew up with Ivar? Well, their fathers had told them about the awful things his father and grandfather had done, so they taunted him with it all. He did not have an easy life and for this reason he hated most people except your father, Olaf, who always fought his battles alongside him. Even with the love and care of his cousin Olaf, Ivar grew up into a cruel and selfish man, just like his father and grandfather. The apple does not fall far from the tree, right? The young boys that teased him had nicknamed him 'the Hated' and it stuck. Nowadays I am sorry to admit that he is my cousin. I did try to like him, truly I did, but he never liked me, he only ever cared about Olaf, his other cousin. Why Olaf put up with Ivar is beyond me. Thora, do you ever think of Olaf, the King of Dubhlinn—your father? Do you remember anything about him?"

Thora answered sadly. "No, not really, I just remember a tall man with very blonde hair. *Mamma* said that he was very good-looking, too."

Aud had an answer for Jon's question. "Why indeed did he put up with him? Once long ago in the beginning of our marriage we had a big discussion about Ivar. I suppose discussion is too kind a word, we argued over him and his actions. Our first and really only argument, in fact. We may have had many heated discussions, but to me there were never arguments like the one over Ivar. I asked him that very question: Why did he put up with him? He said that they grew up together in Dubhlinn, they were both born there, both spoke Gaelic and were like brothers instead of cousins. When they grew into adults they went raiding together and when fighting battles, he said that you needed to have someone you trusted that would look after your back. Olaf had saved Ivar's life more than once and after that he was even more steadfast in his loyalty, but now I understand even better why he was so loyal after listening to your tale of Ivar, Jon. Olaf claimed that Ivar had also saved his life as well several times over the years. He said that kind of allegiance was worth more than any treasure."

"That is true, but somehow Olaf inspired steadfast loyalty from Ivar, and we all know how charismatic he was. We were all loyal to Olaf because he inspired us all."

Thora was bored with all this talk of loyalty. She wanted Jon to get on with his story. "What happened to you when you arrived at the castle, Jon?"

"King Kjarval welcomed me of course, but Jorunn, your *frænka*'s sister, did not know I had arrived there. She was not to know for several years what had happened to me. She did not know whether I was dead or alive either, just like your *frænka*. Kjarval felt it was better if everyone, including Ivar, thought I was dead. I was sent to an isolated abbey, but the isolation of abbey living was not for me, so they later sent me to a military camp where I trained to become a warrior and was nicknamed 'the warrior-priest'. That was about the time that King Kjarval had raised an army to rid Dubhlinn of Ivar and his reign of terror. This army included me. We tried to capture him, but he was as slippery as an eel. He had a plan of escape along with a few trusted men, whom he took with him. We later heard that he was in Northumbria and has an army of rebels and has become very wealthy. You have all heard of the great Viking leader named Sygtrgg? He helped King Kjarval bring about Ivar's downfall and for his reward the Longphort Council handed him the crown of Dubhlinn, although there was some talk of looking for Olaf's son, Thorstein, for the crown. Believe it or not!"

With that he looked over at Aud and gave her a nod as if talking only to her. "Sygtrgg argued that Thorstein was much too young to wear the crown, that neither he nor his mother would have survived in a town full of such ambitious men. The Council obviously agreed with him, as did both Kjarval and I. Since then I have been traveling to many countries with a group of Vikings and Irish warriors under King Sygtrgg's flag. He is an honourable man. He was a very good choice for King of Dubhlinn." Looking back at Thora. "I think your *frænka* will like him very much. That is another reason why people thought I was dead; because I was never in Ireland for long. Everyone soon forgot I existed."

"*Frænka* will like him, you say? How will she get to know him? He lives far away from here." Thora never missed anything.

"This young woman is full of questions, is she not? Your *frænka* knew of this man from the time she was Queen of Dubhlinn but I am not sure that she knows him—really knows him—well."

"Yes, she is always asking questions, but it is time for us to clean up, *elskamin*, then it will be bedtime." Her mother rose and took her hand. "Come now, even a warrior-priest needs to have a good night's sleep, just as we all do. Say good night to everyone." With that order from her *mamma* Thora dutifully went around and said goodnight to everyone, then she and her mother headed for the cooking area to inspect the *thralls'* clean-up from the feast.

Aud had a question for Jon. "She may be full of questions but that was a very valid one to ask. Just how am I to get to know this honourable man, this new King of Dubhlinn, after living so many years away from Ireland? The only other place I go to these days is to *pabbi's* other islands, as well as the Orkneys and the Faroes."

Ketill intervened. "As Una said, even a warrior-priest needs rest, and I too am tired. Tomorrow your storyteller and I want to discuss something with you."

"*Pabbi*! That is just not fair! You cannot do this to me—I won't be able to sleep now."

"But I must insist; my *jarls* and I have not agreed on everything and before even I can go to bed, we have to discuss something else. Come, Jon, you are a part of this discussion too."

Aud sat there fuming as her father walked away from her but he could no longer contain himself and burst out laughing. "Come daughter of mine, I was only teasing you. Of course, you must join us, you too are part of this discussion."

"*Pabbi*! That was cruel—I see where Thorstein gets his teasing from." Aud could hear Thora snickering in the background.

Chapter 26

They sat around a table in the corner of the longhouse where there was a large stone dish with whale oil in it, and a wick that was lit. It made their area quite bright. Ketill liked to be able to see everyone's eyes when there was an important discussion; he firmly believed that the eyes were the windows to the soul and if someone was insincere their eyes usually gave them away. The men around this table he trusted with his life, but old habits were hard to change. Fortunately, none took offence; they were all used to his methods and did not feel as if they were being interrogated. Aud sat down amongst this united front with the confidence of inclusion. "My daughter is still a little angry with me so ignore that scowl on her face, it is meant for me only. Aud, as you know we have all been together in the Orkneys so you must be told before we begin that *Jarl* Sigurd is with us in our plans."

"I am not surprised, *pabbi,* but now I am anxious to learn what your plans are. Thankfully I do not have to wait until tomorrow to hear them—so you are forgiven—for now!"

All the men had a silent chuckle at their leader's expense. "Hmmmm! Right—let us begin. As you know Aud, Scotland has been falling apart for years now from a lack of leadership—that bit of information is not new to any of us here. King Donald II is weak and unable to control all the clans, his daughter Ceana and her aunt Aed do not help things as they cause more problems than he can solve. Plus, it doesn't help that the Picts are running amok, terrorizing everyone. A number of the clan kings and chieftains, mostly from the northern part of Scotland, have asked for our help to stop them. They cannot get all the kings and chieftains together in safety to discuss unification because of the Picts."

"First we have to decide if this venture is worth getting involved in, but the Picts have to be stopped. As you know, King Kjarval has made it clear that internal issues in Scotland are not of his concern but I think he should be very concerned. If someone does not stop the Picts and take some leadership to get the clans united, the English could just walk through the gates of Hadrian's Wall and take over. I am convinced, as are the other Scottish leaders, that they are just sitting on the sidelines waiting for the right moment to invade. It wasn't easy to rid Scotland of this English curse years ago. Back then, the Scots were a much stronger, more cohesive unit and even then, they would not have succeeded without the assistance from the Irish or from Olaf."

"Somehow, we must convince Kjarval that he is needed once more, before another English invasion occurs. I truly believe that you, Aud, with the support and guidance of Jon, are the only ones who can persuade him to join us. I and all the men here believe that his commitment is needed, not just in the future if the English invade, but now. We need men, many men and as the High King of Tara he has that commodity; he has the ear of all Ireland. He is fooling himself if he thinks this is just a Scottish internal issue. Scotland needs their Gaelic cousin to step in with men and weapons; they need a strong commitment, a promise to come to their aid."

"When do we have to leave?"

"Immediately. We all believe that this is a crisis and you must make Kjarval understand that time cannot be wasted thinking it over. We need his commitment now; no, we needed it yesterday! It is that serious!"

"Okay *pabbi*, gentlemen, I will do what I can, but you do realize that I cannot guarantee anything. I know you think because King Kjarval is a Christian, as are both Jon and I, that it may help, but I am only a woman and most men do not like to negotiate with a woman. I do not want to hinder Jon's negotiations."

"You underestimate yourself. Olaf always bragged about your intelligent input and I know King Kjarval has a high regard for you, too. He has spoken highly of you on many occasions. Jon most likely will be addressed as the main ambassador, but you will be accepted as one also. I have no fear of your opinion been overlooked or ignored. We think it is will be more effective to have two good minds discuss this with Kjarval. Chances are that one will catch what the other forgot to mention. Our forces must remain here to be on the ready just in case England moves before we have Kjarval's answer. We have a warning system set up in case Scotland is in trouble and the system will only work if we remain here. Sadly, we haven't really committed yet to our Scottish friends either, so we may already be in a dilemma. Our spies in England tell us that there are rumours of an invasion, but so far they appear to be just that—rumours."

"Don't forget that Ivar is still in England with an army of mercenaries and is ready and willing to fight for them—especially if he can get back at both Aed and Ceana for putting the blame of Artgal's death on his shoulders. My spies tell me that he is pushing hard for the English to invade; he is offering them assistance since he knows Scotland like the back of his hand. But that was yesterday and now we are here today, and things could have easily changed. We need to be ready for any eventuality. Both you and Jon are available, and we all think you are both very able. We need your help!"

"What do you think, Jon? I am ready if you are?"

"There is no question—I am ready too. Nobody wants the English in Scotland, and we especially do not want Ivar involved; it would change everything—not just for Scotland, but for us in the north too."

Aud suddenly realized the bigger picture—where this was all going. "Ahhh—yes. I understand why now. It is all about us here in the northern islands. Of course—we need to look after each other, and I agree. My father's islands will eventually become Thorstein's, as you know, Jon—so I have a vested interest in making this plan work."

"Of course! That is why I am here too. Thorstein is my cousin, he is the only family I have left besides Ivar the Hated and we all know I would never back him in any venture, especially after he tried to kill me."

"Well, since we are all agreed let us call it a night." Ketill addressed his daughter directly. "Aud, please come with me to my room; I have a few things to send to Jorunn and her children." Ignoring both Aud and

Jon he spoke to the remaining men. "After Aud and Jon leave tomorrow the rest of us will discuss which of you men will take the risk and slip into Scotland to talk to some of our friends there, in case there is no news waiting for you on your return to the Orkneys."

Aud walked with her father, but when he entered his room Ketill made sure there was no one around before he handed his daughter a small bag. She thought it very strange. "What is it, *pabbi*?"

"Ssssh! Just a few things I found of your mother's, that you and your sister can go through. You can both choose what each of you wants to keep. I used it as a ruse, as I needed you here on your own." He claimed that he had more to confide in her; he always had other plans for his grandson and now he was finally going to reveal those dreams to his daughter. "Not only will my islands and Sigurd's become his when we die—that part you know—but if everything else goes according to our plans, Thorstein could well become king of Northern Scotland."

"Northern Scotland! That is a very ambitious plan, *pabbi*!"

"It will take a number of years to put it all in place and by then he will be ready. Sigurd and I are the only ones who have discussed this, and now you are privy to our long-range plans. Those northern lands of Scotland are just sitting there waiting for someone to take over. The king never goes there or puts men in place to control it. The chieftains of the north are very frustrated with their king's lack of support. The rivers there are teeming with fish and the wildlife herds are growing bigger every year. I truly believe the few Scottish people living in the highlands will be receptive to us Northmen; they have no time for their weak king who ignores their needs and only wants to collect their taxes. There is much unused land ready for us Northmen to settle and farm, or even to raise sheep on. The last thing we want is the English in Scotland; one day they too will realize the strategic advantage of controlling the highlands. Even if they never figure out their value and even if we do not take the northern parts for ourselves, if they eventually get into southern Scotland, they would be too close to us here in the islands. Just too close for comfort! We must have the advantage of holding northern Scotland. Do you not see what I am saying, daughter?"

Aud had always prayed for a crown for her son, but she was shocked that her father not only prayed for it but planned for it too. This was more than she could have done or have imagined for her son. A large part of Scotland was there for the taking and now she could play a part not only for her son to take over, but also be part of helping to protect all the islands north of Scotland. All these plans overwhelmed her—but only for a moment—she knew that she was now committed to it more than ever. She had a part to play, a vested interest in saving these northern islands, known as the *Suðerlys*—these lands that now belonged to her father, but which would eventually go to Thorstein. But first, they must save Scotland from itself and make sure that the collateral damage would become an advantage for her son in the very near future. Politics could be incredibly exciting and rewarding if played well—but it was a dangerous game, too. Confident in her reply, she said, *"Pabbi,* I fully understand and back your future plans."

"With all this in mind, Aud, you must listen with two separate ears and report back to us as a group; but if you hear something—anything—that may affect our long-term goals, then you only report back that part to myself or Sigurd. Do you understand?"

"Yes, *pabbi*! But what about Jon? Should he not be in on this plan? After all, he is related to Thorstein."

"Well, not yet—he may very well be included one day soon, though. From what I have seen from him so far, he is honest, very careful with his words, but honourable—maybe too honourable. He may think that since most of Scotland is a Christian country, the Highlands and the other parts of the north should remain with a Scottish leader. You will be the one to decide, when the time comes, if he should be part of our strategic planning, since you will be spending so much time with him in the future."

Her heart skipped a beat thinking about all the time they might have together. "You have much faith in me, *pabbi—takk*!"

"You will sail to the Orkneys first, just in case one of our Scottish spies has arrived. Jon is aware of this first part of your journey, in case this spy is there and has news. At this point no news would be wonderful, I am deeply concerned that we may be too late already at enlisting the Irish to aid us."

"Okay—wonderful! I will get to visit with Thorstein too. *Goða nott, pabbi*—I will do my best for you all."

"I have great faith in your abilities daughter. Now sleep well tonight, and we will say our farewells in the morning."

Chapter 27

Dubhlinn

No spy awaited them in the Orkneys. They both took hope from that, thinking all must be quiet for now in Scotland. After a quick visit with her son and the *jarl*, Jon and Aud wasted no further time and set off on their assigned journey to Ireland. They sailed towards the mouth of the Liffey with only one escort ship following theirs, which was captained by Aud's old friend Einar. Both ships flew King Kjarval's flag so there was no need to check in to Dubhlinn. There were two other flags flapping in the wind below the king's; Jon's as well as Aud's old banner, that she had used when she was the Queen of Dubhlinn. Kjarval's castle was further south, so they passed by the Liffey's estuary, then continued their way south keeping the coastline in view. Even though he was the High King of Tara, he remained in his own castle in Leinster.

"Tara itself is north of Dubhlinn in the kingdom of Meath," Jon explained. "The site is ancient and now only consists of several mounds with two enclosures, one being a ringed fort or the Royal Enclosure, where Kjarval stays when visiting there. It is known as Cormac's House and is named after the most famous High King of Tara, who in the third century was a pagan. Little has been done to it since that time; only enough to keep it standing, so the house is no longer an ideal place for a king to stay for any extended time. They would be basically camping inside of it and King Kjarval is getting older. I cannot imagine that he or his family can handle the harsh conditions for very long. Gossip has it that he seldom brings them because of the conditions. Even before Kjarval, the High Kings of Tara would only spend the necessary time it took to perform the ritual ceremonial duties, so that is not news. The others stay in tents, which are cleaner, warmer and more comfortable than the enclosure. Why Kjarval doesn't do the same I do not understand, because I guarantee that King Kjarval returns as soon as possible to his own castle, which is much more agreeable to his needs and has more room for his growing family."

"The hill itself still exists and the only other enclosure near the hill is ancient, and is no longer used. It is called the Mound of Hostages and was claimed to hold the cremated remains of many bodies, the names of people that sadly no one can recall. This mound is still revered during the ceremonies held when the High King of Tara is present. People claim that there used to be a large banqueting hall as well, where great feasts were held in pagan times, but the land has reclaimed that hall and most of what was once a vibrant community. Everyone who comes for the ceremonies all say that they can feel the power, the energy, from the ghosts of the past. They affirm that it is a spiritual experience like no other. I have been there myself and can vouch for the mystic power generated by this ancient site. Now the Christians have adopted this divine experience in the name of God." Jon was very knowledgeable about the Hill of Tara, and Aud readily absorbed all this knowledge and filed it away in her head for future use, if the need for it ever arose.

They arrived at the castle to an unexpected crowd. Because of their banners, Kjarval had been forewarned of their arrival and was waiting at the harbour for them along with Jorunn and a couple of the older children. As a royal family they went nowhere without their maids and guards, which always attracted curious onlookers. With the dockworkers going about their business attending to two other ships already docked, there was not a lot of space left for their gangplank. Aud was surprisingly excited to see her older sister; she had thought that she would never see her again, living so far north from Ireland.

Jon whispered into her ear, "Just think what an ostentatious display of pageantry we would have arrived to, if King Sygtrgg was visiting his friend the High King of Tara. For your information, they are good friends, and he is often a guest of theirs."

Aud held her hand over her mouth as she giggled. "This harbour could never accommodate two kings at once as well as a queen, albeit a former queen. If Olaf was still alive, he would have designed a new longphort for King Kjarval." Giggling aside, she was thrilled to be greeted with such fanfare; it made her feel like a queen—the queen she once was. This royal welcome reinforced her determination to convince King Kjarval to help protect his Celtic cousins. *"Scotland must never fall to the English. We need to keep that country under Scottish rule, to keep it safe for all, and especially for Thorstein!"* Aud thought to herself as she watched their crew throw the guide ropes to men on the harbour apron, to moor their ship.

The men worked quickly; the gangplank was laid across the gap of sea water and secured to the wooden planks. Aud walked as regally as possible down it, but once on the wharf the two sisters dissolved into each other's arms. There was much laughter and tears as they greeted each other. But immediately after they exchanged hugs, Queen Jorunn gathered herself together, remembering her station in life. Aud quickly took the hint, for she too was once a queen. Aud spoke formally first. "Greetings from the *Jarl* of the *Suðerlys* to your Highness *Ard-Ri hEireann* and to his Queen, his beloved daughter Jorunn. He apologizes for not being here himself but both Jon and I feel blessed to make the journey for him, and are honoured by your personal welcome party. Prince Diarmait and Princess Aillis, your *afi* sends his greetings and his love to you both. He dearly wishes that he could have been the one to come and visit all his grandchildren, but urgent business has kept him away."

"The honour is all ours, Queen Aud, and Jon, our warrior-priest of note. As you well know, both of you are always welcome here."

"Queen Aud. He still thinks of me as a queen! That is good! This is a step in the right direction, and I must thank Jon for coaching me to greet the High King of Tara in Gaelic," she thought to herself.

179

The first few days passed swiftly with much merrymaking, although they were both anxious to start the talks with King Kjarval. They had discussed this while still on the ship; both acknowledged that it would be a mistake to push him, as he could be a stubborn opponent if pushed too hard. Although the situation in Scotland could very well be in a crisis, they had decided to let him make the first move, to let him think that the talks were started through his initiative. That way it might be harder for him to find excuses not to become part of their plan.

The gifts from his father-in-law, gifts that cost a king's ransom, pleased him very much. The two special ones consisted of a carved ivory chalice for his personal chapel, to be used for communion by the royal family only, plus an ivory statue of the Madonna and Child in honour of their many children. The ivory was purchased from an Icelandic trader when Ketill happened to be in the Orkneys. Even though this trader claimed his country had many seals in the north, the cost to purchase the ivory was still outrageous. Ketill could not get him to lower his price because he claimed that he could sell it in Norway to the royal family for more than he was asking. He took the bait, hook, line and sinker. If King Harold, his nemesis, could afford it, so could he. Plus, he knew Kjarval would know and appreciate its value. Fortunately, Sigurd knew of a talented artist in the Orkneys who could carve ivory and would not charge a fortune. They both believed that such an esteemed gift was essential to sway this king to their way of thinking; he must be treated as if he was the highest king in all of the lands, not only Ireland, and would be the only one that could save Scotland from the scourge of England.

Motherhood suited Jorunn; because of all the childbearing, she had put on some weight, but being a mother had also softened her tongue. Aud had been prepared to take some sharp retorts from her sister but none came her way. She had never seen her sister so content, so loving. It was obvious that Kjarval doted on her and all the children, and for the first time in her life she was jealous of her older sister. She had not only become a higher queen than Aud herself ever would be, more importantly, she had found love and contentment.

Finally, over breakfast one morning a few days after arriving, Kjarval invited Jon and Aud to the library to discuss the reasons why they were in Ireland. He was rather abrupt. "We may as well get to the real reason why you are both here."

They gathered in the same library as before, where there was a roaring fire going in the fireplace to take the chill out of the air. It was a very cool day and the rain was coming down in buckets. *"Olaf was right about these imposing stone buildings; they may be able to build several floors upwards, but they cannot prevent the cool air from seeping through,"* Aud thought to herself. She could feel the dampness from all the heavy rain, as if that too was seeping between the stones and into her bones. She shivered as she sat down and pulled her shawl tight around her. Maybe she was too nervous and showed it, so she tried to relax and immediately loosened her shawl as if she had no cares in the world. Jon sat in the chair next to her; he looked very relaxed, as did Kjarval. *"Dear God, maybe negotiating really is for men only? Please give me strength, I am fearful that I will look a fool."*

"So, tell me'" said Kjarval, "what really brings you both here?"

Jon started as planned. "Scotland is under siege once more, the Picts are once again terrorizing the people and we—that is, myself and all the *jarls* of the Northern islands—firmly believe that Scotland is weakened by this, and the English are sitting on the sidelines waiting for the right moment to invade once again. Even the chieftains in Northern Scotland are worried that they cannot travel safely to the south because of the Picts."

"As I have said many times in the past—I will not intervene with Scottish home politics."

"Yes of course, my lord, you have said so many times in the past, but we have spies in England and now fear the worst could happen. And sooner than we thought possible!" He was trying to drive the urgency of the Scottish problem through to this man. "You have proven your support in the past for your Gaelic cousins, and they would not have been able to send the English fleeing home a few years ago without your support of men, weapons and wealth to feed and clothe all the warriors. With the Picts running amok in their own country, they have destabilized the peace and prosperity of Scotland as a whole and this opens the land up to an invasion. England has been sulking all these years over their loss; they have been patiently waiting for an opportunity to return and finish what they started. Our spies have confirmed this. They tell us that they are strengthening their forces, increasing the number of men and arms. For what, though, is the question? There is no talk of ships being built, so all this investment means it is for a land invasion, and that means Scotland!"

Aud continued their argument. "King Kjarval, my lord, as you well know, England has been trying to rid their country of the Northmen since they first arrived. They have failed miserably, and Northumbria, the land of these men, is clearly there to stay. Sadly, for us, these Northmen have integrated so well they will now fight for the English. They have become farmers, merchants, and traders; they have become more English than the English. As you well know England is a very ambitious country, and trust me, the English, with the power of Northumbria, will not stop with just Scotland. They will come after Ireland as well as the Northern Islands."

"Ahh, I see where this is going. You fear reprisals from the English because of your interference in Scotland and now you need my help. I do not want to get involved! Why would they come to Ireland? We are too strong for them to invade! We may be a country of many small kingdoms here in Ireland, but believe it or not my title as the High King of Tara is the only cohesive link. It is an ancient, well-respected title and the only real power it has is that if Ireland is ever threatened, all these kingdoms would come together. They would fight to the death to protect this land, and England understands this spiritual power."

There was silence, but then Aud had an idea. "Overall—yes—Ireland has many men, many kings, chieftains, leaders who will band together against the English, but the English are very clever. They do not need to invade all of Ireland—just your land—and I don't mean Leinster, but Tara!!"

This shocked Kjarval. "Tara—why?"

"Why!? Because, of who you are! You are the *Ard-Ri hEireann*! The High King of Tara! All they need to do to destroy the spiritual heart of Ireland, is to destroy Tara itself. You said yourself that it is the spiritual heart of Ireland that really unites all the smaller kingdoms! Tara may be just a ceremonial site, but it is the physical site that is the divine power that could be destroyed. There are never many people there; they could easily enter that area with many men and obliterate what little is left there. The element of surprise is all they would need, because it would take time for Ireland to unite and fight back. With the seat of the High King of Tara gone, vanquished into nothingness, your power could very well be demolished as well."

Aud stopped momentarily, then continued as Kjarval stared at her in shocked silence, "It would be so much easier for the English to come after Tara first, whereas, it will take time, men and wealth to conquer Scotland, or our northern islands for that matter. I am not saying that they would not come after us, but it makes strategic sense to me to conquer Ireland first. All the five main roads in this land converge at the base of the Hill of Tara, and if this historical site no longer exists, what will happen to your authority?"

To Aud, Kjarval appeared offended with her analysis when he finally snarled at her through clenched teeth, "I cannot believe that this would or could happen!"

Aud bravely replied, "As the *Ard-Ri hEireann* you have the responsibility to protect all of Ireland, not just Leinster, and most important is to protect the ancient land of Tara itself! You must also be informed that Ivar the Hated is ready to fight with the English. We have spies in Northumbria who can attest to his involvement. All here present know he is intelligent and that he knows both Ireland and Scotland well. It would take such a man with his knowledge to think of this crazy scheme I have just put forward. Revenge is a powerful motive, and we both know a man like Ivar craves vengeance; he must know it was because of your influence that he had to flee Dubhlinn. I have tried very hard to put myself into his head; he is a dangerous foe, as you know!"

Shocked to the core, the king stood up, "Ivar!"

"Yes! Ivar the Hated! I am not saying that this will happen, but if it did, you could be conquered with one simple attack and in the confusion and loss of their spiritual heart, the Irish, your people, could be easily overrun. Then England would have access to even more men to send where they want."

Sitting down carefully, he looked hard at the two ambassadors in front of him. Silence reigned as he stroked his beard, trying to calm himself down. "Well—well—" he stammered, "Queen Aud, you seem to be well-informed about Tara. I suppose I have Jon to thank for that! As for Ivar's involvement—well, that is just too distressing to hear.

Let me think on this. When I have made a decision I will call another meeting. You are a clever woman and have given a deeper meaning to my so-called responsibilities, although I do not thank you for reminding me of my duty towards Tara itself and to all of Ireland, for that matter. As difficult as it is to believe that such a plan would ever be devised, you have opened my eyes to such a possibility. Your argument has placed me in a quandary. I must think hard about what authority, if any, the *Ard-Ri hEireann* really has. Please leave me now to think over all we have discussed."

He stood up as if to dismiss them. "Ivar—hmmmmm! That really is not good news. I hear he has become quite powerful and wealthy through all his raids. I will get back to you."

Jon stood up and held his hand out to Aud to help her rise from her chair. They both bowed to the king, but only Jon spoke. "Of course, King Kjarval. If you have any questions, please call for us."

As they walked out Aud thought to herself. *"What have I done? Stop this doubting, I must remain strong because I believe Ivar maybe the key to turning King Kjavarl. I must be as evil as Ivar to think like him or Aed. Sisters in death indeed! Has Satan taken over my head? God forgive me! What must Jon think of me? He didn't see this coming, why Ivar even popped into my head is a mystery!"*

Chapter 28

O nce alone, Jon turned to Aud. "You were indeed very clever. I think you awoke his conscience; he has been far too comfortable for too long. Now he needs to think of the future risks, not just to him, but to Tara and to all of Ireland!"

Much relieved to hear he approved of her actions, Aud replied, "Oh, thank god you are not angry with me. I know we did not discuss this previously and I cannot understand why I even thought about Ivar. I am not convinced that we have won him over fully. Our spy's rumours about Ivar may have pushed him closer but we all know that Ivar is for Ivar and may not come through with his promise to help the English. Although if he does, I firmly believe him capable of this scheme I proposed. But we must be prepared with other arguments in case Kjarval rejects this one. Come to my room; I will order some mead brought in, plus there is a lovely fire going to keep us warm while we plan. This beautiful big stone castle is too cold for me. We may live on a cold northern island, but our longhouses are so much warmer and more comfortable than this big stone house."

Sipping their drinks slowly, they discussed other ideas that might convince the king to join their cause, then Jon got up to leave. Aud walked him to the door and put her hand on his arm to say something, when he turned and looked directly into her eyes. Her heart lurched and before she realized what was happening, she was in his arms, passionately kissing the very man she had just recently realized she was in love with. Jon suddenly pushed her away.

"Oh my god Aud, I am so sorry. I do not know what came over me."

"Please Jon, do not apologize! You have made my dreams come true."

"I don't understand this attraction I have for you. I am a priest as well as a eunuch! I have nothing to offer you; I am ineffectual as a man."

"How can you claim to be a priest? You have not been a practicing priest for years now; you are more of a warrior. That is not what concerns you, is it? Your manhood is—as for being a eunuch—well. that does not bother me. I have fallen in love with you because of who you are. You are a wonderful man, kind, thoughtful and I love being with you—I always have. I do believe now that that was why I became a Christian in the first place, so I could understand who you really were, as well as to spend more time with you."

They fell into each other's arms once more. The passion was too much for either of them to control. Entwined in their love for each other, somehow they ended up on Aud's bed. A few hours later they woke up under the covers—naked! Jon's arm lay across her body as they snuggled under the warm bed covers, facing the embers of an almost-dead fire. The room had cooled off considerably, but their love for each other was still burning bright. Aud turned to face the man she loved so deeply. "I did not think it possible to feel such joy; there is nothing ineffectual about you as a man, my love."

"This is a miracle, an impossible miracle! I do believe that God has sent me a message—to go forward as a man. You do know what this means, my beloved, I can offer you marriage now—if you will have a half a man—but a man who is no longer totally incapable of expressing his love."

"Of course—I will marry you! You have no idea how happy you have made me!"

"Good—we will announce this to King Kjarval and your sister as soon as possible, but first I need to talk to Brother David. He is an excellent and knowledgeable doctor, as you well know; maybe there is an explanation for this miracle? I want to keep you happy and must know that if I can make love to you once, will I be able to do so again."

Aud sat up, pulling the cover under her chin and Jon followed suit. "No matter what happens Jon—even if you are not able to physically express your love, I love you too much to lose you. It is only a *penis*—remember that—too many men have allowed it to rule their life. It was true for Olaf, he was a strong leader, yet he allowed it to make decisions for him like marrying Ceana, the Scottish princess. Because of his forced marriage and his commitment to Scottish politics, look what happened to him. He lost his life because of her insane jealousy and because of her convoluted politics."

"What do you mean by that?"

"Come now Jon, I knew that she was already carrying his child and Olaf had to make it right. She tricked Olaf into marrying her. That is why King Donald insisted I come to Scotland; he had to be sure that I would not object to Olaf marrying his daughter. He could have convinced some other lord to marry her, but she wanted only Olaf and her father would never begrudge her desires. Even though I suspected she was already with child, Olaf admitted it all to me just before she killed him."

"Nothing slips by you, my love."

"If I have your heart, your love is more important to me than all the rest. To know that I can wake up with you beside me as my husband is everything I desire. I have always desired you! Could you not see my passion and the love I had for you? Or did you just choose to ignore it?"

He took her into his arms and nuzzled her neck. "You were a married woman and I was a priest as well as a eunuch. I couldn't allow my feelings to be known. To guard myself against love, I could not allow you into my heart. I have always had such admiration and respect you, and yes, I was secretly in love with you. Only now can I admit to many nights of lustful, crazy dreams of you and me together! I wonder what Olaf would have to say about me, if he saw us together? A eunuch capable of making love, impossible! Maybe I should try his potion from brother David? I do believe that if I had remained a priest, loving God and doing his work would have sustained me through life, but now that I have fallen in love with you and know you love me back, I can never be a priest again. God has found a new destiny for me, for us both. Only the love of the right woman has control over me and it."

Smiling, he peeked over the blankets and pointed to his miracle. Aud had only one word to say, "Amen! But Jon, I truly believe that this is the wrong time to leave. We are in the middle of negotiations and Kjarval may think that you are not placing enough importance on them, so please wait until after we are married to talk with Brother David. I want to marry you regardless. I need you by my side as my husband whether you are physically capable of loving me or not."

"I would feel so much better talking this over with Brother David but, yes, you are correct. The timing is not good."

"Good, I am relieved that we are together on this."

"*Jæja*! Now I must approach King Kjarval. Your father is not here; he is your brother-in-law and he must be the one I speak to for your hand in marriage. As a widow you have every right to choose for yourself, but it is just common etiquette to ask him, as we are his guests. I would like the ceremony to happen as soon as possible, I do not want to live another night without you as my wife."

"Me either—me either!"

He requested an audience with the king the next morning and was granted one that very afternoon. Aud asked to join him, so they both went to speak with him.

"The northern ambassadors have arrived and are anxious, I see, for an answer."

"Not at all, King Kjarval; we have a separate request to make of you, more important to us both than even Scotland."

"Really? Here I was ready with an answer for you about Scotland."

Jon asked if they could be seated in his presence. "Of course—how rude of me—please sit. You have made me curious now, with this new request."

"King Kjarval, I have been your warrior for some years now as well as Sygtrgg's. I have not practised my vocation for many years, so I have come to tell you that I do not plan to ever return to the priesthood. Instead I plan to marry and have come to ask your permission to marry the widow of my deceased cousin, King Olaf of Dubhlinn. I ask for the hand of none other than Queen Aud herself. As her brother-in-law you have the right to refuse her permission to marry, but I beg of you to sanction our union."

"Queen Aud, I see you are here with this man, so I gather you have accepted this proposal? You do realize, once you are married to him you will lose your title of Queen?"

"Yes, my lord, I do, but I fully accept Jon as my husband and ask that we can marry as soon as possible, and in your private chapel since we are both Christians. It is very important to me that the church sanctions my marriage this time."

"I see! Your sister may want to make it into a celebration, and may want some time to organize."

"That won't be necessary as neither of us want a big party. The only people that need to be there are yourself and your family, as well as my good friend Einar. He is the captain of our escort ship, and staying in an inn nearby."

"Really, then you must bring Einar here to stay as our guest if he is such a good friend. I have one request, that King Sygtrygg of Dubhlinn and his lovely wife be invited. They will both be overjoyed to hear that now there will only be one Queen of Dubhlinn to contend with."

"Of course." Aud was too happy and in love to refuse him anything.

"Do you honestly think that nobody could see the love between you two? Jorunn commented on it shortly after your arrival, saying that you had eyes only for each other. So yes—of course—you have my permission. Neither of us are surprised, though."

They thanked him in unison.

King Kjarval laughed as he remarked, "And your request for an audience was most propitious—I was just about to request your immediate attendance. I have thought long and hard over your request. Aud, I must say you were the most convincing. With Ivar in league with the English an attack on Tara is feasible. The English would never think of Tara, but Ivar would; he is clever and nasty enough to think in that direction, and as the reigning *Ard-Ri hEireann* I must never allow that to happen, must I? The threat of Ivar's involvement in any attack is a dangerous possibility, especially since it was me that instigated the attack on him. He would love to destroy my power in Ireland and we both agree that he is devious enough to think of attacking Tara itself. How very clever of you to think of that, Aud."

Jon looked at her and smiled, he bowed to her, giving her permission to be the one to speak. "Thank you, *Ard-Ri hEireann*, you have made a wise decision. The history of Tara is very fascinating, and you were correct, it was Jon who educated me on it. Although I must be the one with the more devious mind, like Ivar, to even think of it!" She giggled, then shook her finger at both men. "Don't answer that one, either of you! Now what happens?"

"Well, it will take some time to organize men and ships, so you must remain here until then. I think your northern partners would approve of this, because I am sure they will want you both here to make sure that I go forward with my promise. You can send your friend Captain Einar back with the good news of my agreement, and also of your marriage; then he can sail back here with any orders your father and his partners have for you both."

Chapter 29

The day of their wedding arrived with the sun shining brighter than on any day since coming to Ireland, with no rain threatening to put a damper on their union. It was just like the day Thorstein was born; to Aud this was a good omen. She could not help but think back to her first wedding in the Orkneys. Such bad weather had prevailed that it had shrouded her joy with the ominous feeling of bad luck to come. Although she would never regret her marriage to Olaf, she knew that he had never loved her fully, not as Jon did. She had been prepared to accept an arranged marriage, especially if it meant a crown. At that time she was but a young woman and had been delighted to accept the handsome warrior-king as her husband and was happy most of the time. He had a gift, a charisma that had bewitched her in the beginning and had awoken desires she didn't realize she was capable of feeling. Giving birth to a beautiful, healthy son was her happiest day, but Olaf's constant affairs were heartbreaking for her. She would have endured anything if he could have been true to her in public, at least. Only just before his death did it look like there was a possibility that he might become the husband she desired. But deep down, she knew that he would have eventually strayed again; it was just who he was.

Through her marriage to Olaf she was able to meet the love of her life, Jon the Priest, even though she did not realize it at the time. Today she gave thanks to God for such a man, a man she knew in her heart would remain true to her always. Every day since their discovery of each other's passion, she was grateful for his love. Now she understood Jorunn's contentment—it wasn't about a crown—it was all about being well-loved. However, this did not prevent her from dreaming of a crown for her son, and now she must convince Jon that this dream of hers should become his as well. King of the northern islands for sure, and the possibility of northern Scotland! There was much to dream about, and Jon was soon to learn that there would be no hope of fighting a mother's ambitious plans for her son. Not even a deep, abiding love from such an honourable man would be able to stop her determination.

King Kjarval walked Aud into his private chapel to her waiting lover. Beautiful in her sister's borrowed tiara and white fur-lined cloak, she glowed with contentment. The cloak, embroidered with gold threads, covered a gold silk dress which was also her sister's. The amber beads and the linen underclothes were the only items that were her own; soon, the ring Jon would put on her finger would also belong to her. It was the Christian custom for a woman to wear a bridal ring; it showed she belonged to someone. As Jon slipped the intricately carved gold ring onto her finger, newly blessed by the priest, Aud did not think about being owned by a man, only of being loved by one very special one. They made their vows to each other, promising to honour and obey each other, as well as promising faithfulness. Aud made sure that they both made this commitment to each other, and Jon had no issue with it. Once the vows were over, they took communion in the gift of the ivory chalice. They were the first to use the beautiful vessel. After sharing the blood and the body of Christ they knelt in front of the altar while the priest prayed for their union to be happy and blessed by many children. Both knew that would not be possible but Aud could not help herself. *"We have already experienced a miracle, could there not be another?"*

They walked out with Aud's arm entwined with Jon's, beaming at the few guests in attendance. Once outside the chapel they stood together as husband and wife and greeted the guests as they came out.

them both; he had to save face, even though that wife had ceased to be one of his favorites and was no longer summoned to his bedroom. They lost their heads, but they had found happiness together and had gotten away with their love affair for many years."

"I agree, that is a sad story but a happy one as well. For two people in love, to have even a short time together is a gift to be cherished; it is a risk well worth taking. Don't you agree, dear heart?" asked Aud as she laid her hand on top of Jon's, which was fiddling with a stone he had picked up on their latest walk. Her touch had a calming effect on him; he laid it aside on the table in front of them and gave her his usual broad smile.

"Yes, of course I agree with you. I just cannot get over this miracle, God's miracle; he works in mysterious ways, does he not?"

Their short stay at the monastery was idyllic, but it was time to move on. One thing they were thankful for was that Brother David had finally told them who the man was that contacted him about Jon's arrest. It was none other the innkeeper of the Black Swan. They discussed this together and decided to give him a big reward the next time they would be in Dubhlinn to discuss strategies with Sygtrygg. For now, however, Tara was to be their next destination. Jon had promised to show her that ancient seat of power, and during their journey Jon explained further about its long history.

Once there they set up their tent, as did the two guards that accompanied them. Aud and Jon travelled back and forth over the ancient site, picking wild mushrooms and other wild foods whenever they came across any. Meanwhile, the two guards hunted for meat or tried their hand at fishing. Aud could feel the power and the magic of this primeval place and felt truly blessed to be able to experience it. More than anything though, she was thrilled to have Jon all to herself for those few hours a day and during the nights. Too soon, she would have to return home to the Hebrides, while Jon would be off fighting for Scotland. She would be left on her own once again to stand guard on the edge of the hill at Ketillstaðir and await their returning ships. This time she had a beloved partner's return to look forward to. Knowing Thora, she would not be alone. She was confident that her niece would be her companion during her watch, as she had been when Thorstein moved to the Orkneys.

Chapter 30

Orkneys

ud and her beloved Jon returned to the Orkneys as heroes; there was much fanfare when they stepped off the ship. Thorstein was there to greet his mother, along with his *afi;* to Aud's astonishment, so was her brother Bjorn from Iceland. *Jarl* Sigurd held a great feast for them that very evening. During the feast Aud sat with her brother; she was anxious to hear all his news. "Pray tell me, brother what are you doing here in the Orkneys?"

"Many of us new settlers have heard good things from other Icelandic traders about the Orkneys being a good place to trade our goods, so I too have come here to trade some of my ivory and cloth for silver. I was also hoping for news of my family. You can imagine my surprise when I heard that father would soon be here and that you were expected to arrive any day. Also, that you had married again—and to an ex-priest!"

"From here I will sail to Norway to complete my trading for some grains and other essential items. Some grains we can grow in protected parts of Iceland as you can on these islands, but we cannot grow enough to sustain our needs. I suspect that is the same for you here. We have need of many things; I must feed and clothe my family and all my workers. I have built up a great estate in Iceland and have named it

Bjarnarhofn after the great harbour I have built there. People come from Norway, Greenland, the Faroe Islands—even from these islands, the Orkneys and Hebrides. They are all starting to come to my small but great harbour. I have built warehouses too. It will never become as famous as Olaf's Dubhlinn, but for our small nation it has created quite a stir. From this harbour I plan to continue my travels in the summer with other groups of Vikings, as I need much wealth and many slaves to run such a large estate. It takes many people to run such a great farm as well as a harbour. Obviously, I need not explain that to you, as I hear you have much knowledge of Olaf's Longphort.

"Tell me about our brother Helgi, and our sister Thorunn and her husband Helgi the Lean. Do you see much of them?"

"Nay, not much. Brother Helgi, as you know, did not have a lot of wealth like I did, so it took him a while to establish himself. A few years ago, he married an Icelandic woman whose father has a large estate, which he will inherit when his father-in-law passes on. His wife is an only child. Her two older brothers were both killed during Viking raids, so Helgi has found a good woman with established wealth and lineage. Even though he does not live that far from me it is too difficult to see much of each other as he is as busy as I am. Also, since his wife and her father are both Christians, Helgi has become more involved in their belief system. He no longer tells me that it is a religion of convenience; he is truly a convert now. As brothers we argue too much over our differences, hence it is better to see less of each other. It is safer that way. I would never want to fall out with my young brother—or with you, for that matter."

Aud chuckled at that comment.

"Shortly after establishing my farm in Iceland, I too married a woman who had settled in Iceland before me. Although Irish, she is well born; her name is Gjaflaug, daughter of Kjallak the Old. We have been together for many years now, and have two sons and two daughters: Ottar, Kjallak, Ygnvild, and the youngest, Sigridur. Ottar, known as 'the Wise', is the oldest and will soon be ready for marriage."

Aud nodded as she pondered over the names. "Why did you nickname him 'the Wise'?"

"Because he is just that. He never speaks without having thought things out, and usually he makes good sense. I really should have named

our first born after my father-in-law, as he reminds me of him. My second son is named after his grandfather, but he is rash and hot-tempered. Where he gets that from is a mystery to me. As for Ottar, I feel very fortunate to have such a smart son who is so capable of looking after the estate with his mother while I am away. You asked about our sister Thorunn and Helgi the Lean? They live very far in the north of the country in Eyjafjarðarsysla, but them, I do see occasionally as I sometimes travel to the north to hunt the walrus for their ivory. These animals only exist in the far north, but soon there will be none left at the rate the greedy hunters are killing them; it will be such a loss to us, as their tusks bring in much wealth. I may need to go raiding more often in the future if this happens, as I depend on them for the great wealth they bring. The problem in Iceland is that we settlers are so few and so spread out over the country. We all desire the value from their ivory. Unfortunately, it is very difficult to control the abuse of others. We are trying to set up a yearly assembly at a place called *Þingvellir*; we are slowly getting elected leaders to represent all the areas and then they will convene there to discuss and make common laws for all the regions. I am the *goði* for my area; if Helgi would only become the *goði* for his area then I would see him more often, at least once a year. My goal this year is to try and get all the leaders to agree to a law that limits the amount of walrus that we can kill. Sadly, law or no law, I do realize that the people who hunt them will just do as they please. Any law will be very difficult to enforce."

"I do not understand. You plan to limit others, but do you actually limit yourself? Do you not hunt the amount you want? You are here with your ivory to trade, why can't the others do so? Fair is fair, is it not?"

"You have not changed, Aud! But yes, you are partly right, fair is fair! Our problem is that hunters come all the way, not only from Norway, but from other northern countries to hunt the valuable walrus. They kill too many at a time, whereas I truly believe that we settlers do try to limit our kills. We make sure the bull leader at least, and all the females and their calves, are not touched so that they can continue to reproduce. The men from Norway and those other countries go into a hunting frenzy, they do not care what they kill—bulls, females or even the calves if they get in their way. Afterwards they just search out the

carcasses that have tusks, then cut off their heads and fill their ships with only the heads, to harvest the ivory on their way home. They leave all the dead carcasses to rot on our land. While cutting out the tusks from the heads on their ships, they throw all that is left over into the ocean. The sea often sends them home where they end up on our shores to rot. A true farmer would not create such waste. Now, sister, do you think that is fair?"

"No, obviously I do not. That sounds very unproductive to me, too."

"Good! I am pleased that you agree with me. Now enough about the ivory. I must tell you that you have a very fine son. Thorstein will become a great leader with the help of his *afi* and *Jarl* Sigurd; they are the two most powerful men in these parts, and I can see that they both have great plans for him."

"Yes, I agree, but first I must find him a good wife and it is not easy to find one in these parts that have a legendary ancestry. At present there is no one here or the other islands good enough for my son."

"Hmmmm—I may have a good suggestion for you. Helgi the Lean married our sister Thorunn, as you well know, but did you realize that Helgi's father married a much younger woman many years after Helgi's mother passed away giving birth to him? He found his second wife while living in Ireland, and she was an Irish princess!"

"Of course, I know about his second wife; he married Rafarta, the daughter of King Kjarval. I just never think of them, they live so far away. Do they have any children—specifically, any daughters?"

"Yes, they do—three daughters, no sons, and the oldest is not much younger than Thorstein. Her name is Thuriður and she is a beautiful and intelligent girl, soon to become a woman. Many Icelandic fathers will be after her for their sons to marry, and very soon—time is closing in on her! Her ancestry is well-regarded, especially since her mother did not come to our land as a slave but as a willing settler with Helgi's father. Who, by the way, also has an impressive lineage. Sad that Rafarta died so suddenly, though."

"Dear God! I did not know this, and I am sure that Kjarval does not know either. Please give me the details and I will try to get a message through to him. As for their daughter, thank you brother; I will discuss

this with Jon and *pabbi* and let you know what we think tomorrow. I am so pleased that you are here."

"I am also looking for a union, one for my eldest son. Do you know of a good woman who has an ancestry that is well regarded?"

"Oh my god—I do! My *litla* Thoramin."

"You have a daughter?"

"No, but my Olaf did with my maid, Una. Thora is very dear to me and regardless of who her mother is, I would have matched her with Thorstein except that they are half-brother and half-sister, whereas your son and Thora have no connection. It is perfect, and she is such a lovely girl, soon to become a woman. What do you think?"

"A maid's daughter—but would she have the skills to manage a large estate, once my son takes over?"

"She might have been born a maid's daughter, but she is also Olaf's daughter—a king's daughter—and we both know his ancestry is honorable and legendary. Her mother manages our estate in the Hebrides. I have not considered Una as a maid for many years now, and have given her great responsibility. She has become my good friend—despite her having a child with my first husband! *Pabbi* and I travel between the islands, and as you can see from my latest journey, he considers my advice worth taking, so I am away much of the time and have need of a good manager, one that I can trust. Una, I trust with my life, and Thora works right beside her mother and has learned many valuable things about managing a large estate. So yes, I truly believe she will make an excellent wife for any man now—and especially for your son."

"Well dear sister, we may be able to help each other. I too am pleased you are here. Freya continues to move our destinies in the right path, a path that continues to bring us much honour. Don't you think?"

"I know you realize that I have become a Christian so you can believe in Freya if you like and I will believe the Lord has chosen the right path for my family. I do not want to debate over our beliefs and fall out with you either, Bjorn."

Giggling as she clasped his hand in hers, she said, "Either way, we have a great destiny ahead of us—all of Ketill's children. Do you not agree, brother?"

"I agree, *litla systirmin,* and see that you are as witty as always."

Chapter 31

Four years later, mid-summer

Bjorn sailed into the Hebrides with his *knarr* laden with gifts. A *knarr* is wider than a longship, and is used by merchants because it can carry more cargo, while a longship is more narrow, longer and shallow, making it faster and easier to manoeuvre on sea or on inland rivers and making it ideal for invasions. No invasions would be fought here, though; onboard was a young woman named Thuriður, Thorstein's bride-to-be, including her extensive dowry. Also sailing with Bjorn, son of Ketill, was his oldest son, Ottar, who was coming to claim his new bride, Thora. Ketill and Aud saw to it that she had a large dowry to offer. Marrriage contracts had been agreed between Bjorn, Aud, and Una previously, and two marriage feasts were soon to take place at Ketillsstaðir that very summer.

Thorstein was now a man, and with the ambitious help of his *afi* Ketill and *Jarl* Sigurd, was in the throes of making plans to invade northern Scotland. Excitement for the invasion and marriage feasts overtook the whole island.

About 890 AD—Caithness, Scotland

Thorstein was now not only the king of the islands but also of Northern Scotland. Aud's dream of a crown for her son had been fulfilled. Ketill, his *afi*, had died saving his grandson's life in the biggest battle fought in their struggle to claim his part of the Scottish crown. Besides inheriting his *afi*'s islands, he now also carried his *afi's* legendary sword, *Fotbitr*. *Jarl* Sigurd was still alive, although now a very old and frail man waiting patiently for his soul to travel to Valhalla, but his mind was still clear. He remained steadfast and loyal to Thorstein's future plans for northern Scotland. Back in Caithness, Scotland, Aud, Jon and King Thorstein were in the great hall in their castle. Queen Thuriður was in seclusion; she had just lost another male child, leaving them with only one healthy male heir to date—Olafur, who was but four years old. He was the youngest child and heir to the crown for northern Scotland and the islands. He had six older sisters, Groa, Olof, Osk, Thorhildur, Vigdis, and Thorgerdur, who all loved and doted on their baby brother. They had nick named him *feilan,* for he loved to chase them around their great castle and growl at them like a wolf while they all pretended to be frightened of him. Aud, the Queen Mother, the children's *amma*, was pacing the hall. They loved to call her Queen *Amma* but all could see that she was unhappy with the loss of another boy child, so they all stayed clear of her. "Once again your wife has failed you, Thor!"

"Mother, why on earth do you rant so much about male heirs? I was not only the only son of my father, but I was an only child—and yet here I am, healthy and quite alive! Please stop this blaming, you will only upset Thuriður once again. I thought you were a Christian; why can't you be kinder to her and wish her well instead of always finding fault?"

"She has given you many children, I will give her that, but you need more sons because you are becoming a great king of many lands and will need sons to take the crown of each of your lands. King Kjarval once told me that his family was cursed to have only girls and he seems to have been right! The king's daughter, Princess Rafarta, Thuriður's mother, had all daughters. Your wife seems to have been cursed with the same luck! Even Kjarval himself has had only one son with my sister. The rest are all girls! Need I say more?"

"There is Olaf, and he is a healthy son! Jon, please talk to my mother! She is mad at times with this dream of hers to create a dynasty. And this crazy idea of curses is simply too unrealistic to be believable!"

"Trust me, I have tried—many times. She is too stubborn even to listen to my wise advice."

Aud shot Jon a look that would have diminished most men, but he simply stared back at her lovingly with his usual broad smile.

"Speaking of your wise advice—I still disagree with you and Thor's plan to meet with King Donald III."

Then she aimed her anger back at her son. "King Donald III may be your half-brother, Thor, but I do not trust him! He is a weak king with a conniving mother. Ceana cannot be trusted—and that much I am sure of! But this plan of yours to marry off your oldest daughter to his son is a ludicrous idea—your worst idea yet! For God's sake—they are first cousins! Nothing good can come of that close a connection!"

"Half-cousins, mother! They are only half-cousins! And with royal families you know quite well that it is common to marry cousins—even first cousins."

Exasperated with it all, she flared back at her husband. "And you Jon, supporting it against my wishes is insane. How can you do this to me?"

Thorstein had had it with his mother's displeasure, and threw his arms in the air. "Mother, I have had enough of you telling me what to do all the time. I am a grown man and a king, and I know what is right for us all. Besides, both Jon and *Jarl* Sigurd approve of this plan that you call ludicrous! I order you to stop this senseless talk! Now! Jon, we must be off; Einar and all the men are waiting on us."

Without saying farewell to either his mother or his wife, Thor flew out of the great hall in a rage. Jon followed, but not before quickly hugging his wife. "Why can't you let him be, Aud? He respects you so much, as I do; you push too hard."

"I know, my love, and I always regret it but this time I know I am right." They both left her standing alone in the great hall to ponder over her harsh words. Aud was unable to shake off the ominous feeling she had about this plan to meet with King Donald, Thorstein's bastard half-brother. In her mind he was 'the bastard', but she knew the Christian

Scots called Thor the bastard half-brother and not Donald, their king. In their eyes Olaf and Ceana, Donald's mother, were married with God's blessing, while Aud's marriage was only a ritual pagan ceremony. The Christian Church could not and would never recognize her pagan union. *"If only Olaf had converted and re-married me in the church, before marrying that Scottish wench! It still breaks my heart that he converted for her! Even if it was not a true conversion to him! The witch!"* Aud was playing her mind game once again, and it did nothing to make her feel any better. It only served to torture her soul more than necessary.

Shortly after the two men had left, her loyal friend and servant Hord entered and found her sitting at the head of the table, with her head in her hands. "Are you all right, my lady?"

She slowly laid down her hands and looked up at him through bleary eyes. "Yes, I will be, Hord. I am happy to see you have returned. Now did you do as I asked?"

"Yes, my lady, I have a group of men sworn to secrecy and they have set up a camp not far from here, and have already started building the ship you have requested. You did say it has to be big enough to carry fifty people, did you not?"

"Yes—that is correct. God forgive me, I feel like a traitor for doing this behind my son's back, but I cannot fight this horrible feeling that disaster awaits us. I can only see that awful woman, Princess Ceana, in the background and I know she is trouble. How long will it take to complete?"

"Not too much longer—they are working on the planks as we speak and are almost finished. The forest where they are hiding does not have a large selection of oak trees, and remember, they use only axes to cut and shape these planks, so they need to constantly stop to sharpen them. The *knarr* will be clinker-built, which means that they need to overlay the timbers then nail them together. The blacksmiths are also working around the clock to make all the nails they require; one of them even has his own son, who is just learning the trade, working with them, so the output of nails is miraculous. Once they have the shape of the ship made, then they can search for the right oak tree to make the frame. This could prove difficult, with our time limit and so few trees to choose from. We must pray for the Lord's guidance to find the right one. These men may not be expert builders, but they are loyal to you and that is the most important thing. They will get it done, I promise."

"*Takk*; you will not go unrewarded."

"All I ask, my lady, if disaster does strike us, please take me with you. I may be Scottish and of royal blood, but my life will not be worth anything to the Scots since I have been loyal to you Northmen. They have long memories, as you know."

"Yes, I know. We will make room for you and your family, I promise."

Chapter 32

Previously about 888 AD—somewhere in Northumbria

"**I**var, there is a priest here asking to see you privately. He says he has letters for your eyes only."

"Did you search his body for weapons?"

"Of course I did, and he is clean. All he has on him is a packet of bound letters."

"Who are they from?"

"He will not say, sire."

"Very well; show him in, but stand guard at the door with your sword drawn."

A very scruffy-looking man in a priest's habit slipped through the flap in Ivar's tent. He immediately got down on his knees to show his respect. "You are the rightful King of Strathclyde, m'lord. I have come as an emissary from Queen Aed herself. No one knows that I am here except her, and now you. You may not remember me, but I am Father Fingal. I was Queen Aed's confessor, if you can remember?"

"Of course, yes, I do remember you. I could never understand her need to confess her sins to such a man as you! Did she confess that she deceived me? I know she did—so why should I listen to you or read any letters?"

"She swears on the Bible that she had nothing to do with ousting you from Dunbarton. She made a point of doing this in front of me—her confessor. Although I do realize she is capable of deceiving someone she dislikes, you were different. I know she loved you like no other. Her niece Ceana and her friend Duncan the Maormor, along with Artgal's kinsmen, concocted the kidnapping to lure Olaf back from Ireland. Ceana wanted revenge on Olaf—and only revenge. If she could not have him, she did not want Aud to have him either. Duncan, as well as Artgal's family, tricked Ceana as well as Queen Aed. Ceana would never have had you removed from your kingdom because she knew her aunt would not have wanted that. They have always been close and have always understood each other. I do know that they played political games, but these games were only ever for their own benefit. They were both spoiled women with too much power and could never understand the collateral damage they created. Duncan lured Queen Aed away so it would look as if she agreed with their plans. Neither of these women understood or even realized what these men really wanted was to put one of their own back on the throne of Strathclyde. Aed explains it all in her letters to you."

He hands the packet over to Ivar. "Why now? Why did she not look for me before?"

"Ahhh—but sire—she has been looking for you for a very long time! You kept disappearing so I have been on the road for many years. I have returned to Scotland several times without finding you. Each letter is dated; she started writing them right after you fled. Please read them. Meanwhile, can I impose on your kind hospitality? A clean bed and some food would be greatly appreciated. Tomorrow I must journey back to Scotland to let her know that her letters have finally been received. And she is expecting a reply, sire. Only then will I get my reward."

"And just what is your reward Fingal?"

"Forgiveness from the church itself. Queen Aed convinced the abbot that I must do penance for a crime I did not commit. So, trust me—I do know what she is capable of. She is a very unhappy woman and hates the new king of Strathclyde; her brother gave her no choice but to marry this man. He did the same thing with Artgal, although he was a much nicer person than this new king of Strathclyde, his cousin. As her confessor, she always claimed to me that you were and still are the love of her life. Somehow, she satisfied the abbot of my crime and he will only return my priestly duties to me in Dunbarton if I succeed in the mission Queen Aed assigned to me—this mission. You can be sure of one thing sire—the abbot is unaware of what my true purpose is—to find you. He would never have approved."

"Guard! Take this man to the food hall and find him a bed for now. His life—which may prove to be short—is in my hands." Ivar spent the rest of the evening reading those letters, all the while sipping on wine. On completion he stood up and threw his goblet at the tent wall, spilling wine everywhere. Then he sat at his table with his head cradled in his hands; his shoulders appeared to be shaking. Could the devil himself be crying?

The next day the shaggy priest was seen walking away from the camp with a small sack full of goods, which contained some food and a clean under-tunic. A clean bedroll hung from his shoulder, but the letter to his salvation was cleverly hidden between the layers of fabric in his robe. He told everyone he met on the road that he was a priest bound for home, back to Scotland, claiming his pilgrimage to see one of St. Cuthbert's relics located here in Northumbria had been accomplished. '*Glory be to God*' was all he would tell them, since he could not describe a relic he never saw. Because he was a priest he was met with kindness and hospitality wherever he went.

Chapter 33

J on and Thorstein sat on their horses, abreast of each other, and slowly rode off together with all the men on foot marching behind them. Einar and his archers rode on horseback in the rear. Since most of the men were on foot, it was an easy five days of marching to the meeting spot selected by the negotiating team. It was on the border of their lands, with a hill on either side of a valley where they would meet. Both kings were planning to officially divide Scotland into two, Northern Scotland and Southern Scotland. Thorstein and Jon did not want the men to arrive tired, so they took their time. The carts were full of tents and food, and trailed noisily between the marching men and Einar's archers. The archers planned to hunt and fish on the way to replenish supplies, as they could be gone for up to two weeks. This was to be a peaceful journey, so only half of the armed forces were there while the rest stayed on guard in Caithness. Both Thorstein's and Donald's right-hand men had been negotiating this meeting for several months, and the two men leading in the front were still incredulous that the plan for peace had finally come to fruition.

Although King Thorstein was optimistic about going forward with this meeting, he was terribly unhappy that he had left on such unpleasant terms with his mother. "Jon, why does mother do this to me? I hate that I left so angry with her, but she seems to put me in a foul mood more than normal these days. I never even said farewell to Thuriður; she will be down-hearted, maybe even angry with me. I don't think I will want to face either one of them when we get back. This marriage contract must work out, or we will not hear the end of it."

"This has only started since our negotiations began with your half-brother, and you know that she does not like your plan to unite Princess Groa with his son, King Donald IV. She has done everything she could possibly think of to stop it because she hates your brother's mother, Princess Ceana, like no other. It terrifies her to have to send Groa to what she calls 'a hornet's nest'. She really distrusts Princess Ceana, so even if all is agreed I don't think she will ever stop badgering you over this decision. As you know, her grandchildren are very precious to her."

"I really thought that she would have approved of this union since their son, if they have one, will become king of the South and my son Olaf will be king of the North. They will rule together and then maybe, just maybe, we can have a lasting peace in this country. This way we are creating a dynasty, which has always been her dream as well as mine. Creating a dynasty of kings has been drilled into my head since the day I was born, but she only wants either me or her grandson to be the king of all Scotland. I just don't see it happening. It has taken us years to get this far and we need peace for a while to mend this country, to bring it together again. You understand my motives; why can't she?

Jon took a deep breath. "This country has been in turmoil for far too long; you are right, it does need peace. Aaaah! Can you not smell that heather—the air is so fresh! Your mother and I love it here. She once told me that when she first came to Scotland to meet with King Donald II to give her approval of your father's marriage to Princess Ceana, she felt that this country was to be her destiny. She does have this gift of intuition and it bothers me that I sometimes think she may be right. On occasion, the thought that King Donald III or his mother is not to be trusted slips into my head, but during all this time I have not seen or heard of anything to make me think she is right. My spies consistently told me that he wants peace as much as you do, and his mother has been very pliable to it all. She is the one I have worried about the most, and there has been no hint of any trouble from her. Hmm—on second thought, maybe that is why we should be worried?"

Thorstein responded, "You know there has been no indication of problems from them, whatsoever."

Jon reached over and put his hand on his. "Yes, you are correct! But now is my opportunity to inform you that your mother has taken precautions. She has ordered a ship built—in secrecy! She doesn't know that I know, so I let her get on with it just to divert her attentions from nagging you about this marriage contract."

Thorstein was astonished. "WHAT! And you did not tell me of this?! I would have stopped her! I have plenty of ships, as you both know."

"Exactly! Then she would have gone into a rage and you would have retaliated with anger as well. I couldn't take the chance that the two of you would stop speaking to each other; also, your wife was ready to give birth and we all had such hope that it would be another healthy son. That would have made your mother so happy she may have let up on torturing you over this marriage contract. The only reason she wants her own ship is because of Ivar. His showing up from nowhere is her biggest fear, I know she has had many nightmares of him chasing either you, or her and the family."

Thorstein stopped his horse and leaned over, then let out a roar of laughter. "What a woman she is, is she not? How can I remain angry with such a stubborn woman who knows her own mind on what is right and what is wrong? Even though this time I am convinced she is wrong, and I am right. I will be relieved to return home with the news that all went well, and that peace has returned to Scotland. Then she will be asking for my forgiveness."

"Don't count on it, but at least we will all have some peace."

Five days later they arrived at the hilltop above the valley where the two half-brothers would meet; they stopped and made camp. The morning of the next day was the agreed time and day for this historic meeting, and Thorstein the Red was ready to make a lasting peace with his half-brother Donald III, the one son who really resembled their father Olaf the White. Later that night, they could see Donald's troops make camp on the opposite hilltop above the same valley. Everything looked peaceful. The next morning, Thorstein and his right-hand man, Jon, readied themselves on their steeds while ten men, five on each side, marched down the hill with them, with Jon carrying the flag with their colours. King Donald and his right-hand man did the same on the other side. They came down the opposite hill in unison with Thorstein and Jon. When they met at the bottom each king nodded their head in greeting.

Suddenly—all hell broke loose! An army of men rode down the hilltop from the left, crashing out from the only forest in sight, yelling and screaming. They attacked only Thorstein and Jon and their ten men. An archer shot an arrow at Thorstein, which struck him in the arm and bounced off. *"Hellavitas*! What is happening?" Thorstein shouted out to the Scottish king.

King Donald shouted out, "Damn you, mother!" They all seemed to be too surprised to get into battle mode. None of them—not Thorstein, Jon or Donald—understood what was happening, but as warriors they automatically drew their swords and made ready to fight. It was obviously an ambush. Jon's first thought was that Aud had been right all along—King Donald III was not to be trusted. Thorstein raised his sword *Fotbitr*, ready to fight for his life. He lurched forward to fight his half-brother, but Donald shouted, "I know nothing of this attack, this has to be something my mother planned!!" Both men pulled up their horses, trying to turn away from each other. Donald fled back to his hilltop, while an arrow flying through the air found a target—Thorstein's throat—killing him instantly. Astonished at what was happening all around him, Jon had no choice but to turn his steed around and flee back up to their hilltop. Meanwhile the ten men that accompanied them down the hill tried to run for their lives. They were quickly mowed down and slaughtered like animals.

Einar and his men were in battle mode, and came flying down the hill with bows ready, but the attacking army was already locking their shields together, building a defense while the rest of Donald's army came downhill to defend the men that had ambushed Thorstein. It appeared to Jon that the whole Scottish army was in this together. Jon slowed his horse, shouting at Einar. "Turn around! We must re-organize ourselves and make ready for battle!"

Einar acknowledged and ordered his men to retreat. Turning so sharply was hard on their horses, but turn around they did, and once they gathered on their hilltop Jon came towards him. "The man that shot the arrow and killed Thorstein was with Ivar! Ivar the Hated led that group of killers down that hill! King Donald also shouted to us that it was his mother's doings! How did we not know she was up to no good? How did we not know that Ivar and his mercenaries were in Scotland? How did they keep this a secret from all my spies? We must make ready to do battle—we cannot let him get away with this murder. God almighy—how could I let this happen? God forgive me—because of me Thorstein is dead! See that the troop makes ready to do battle. Look over there, Einar, to the east; some of their soldiers are fleeing already. Wait! They look to be Ivar and his men. What is happening? King Donald looks as confused as we are and he is shouting for his men to retreat! At first it looked as if Donald's men were protecting the ambushers? What in the hell is going on here?"

Einar got his men ready to move back down the hill; they could see that Ivar and his mercenaries were not fleeing, they were waiting to do battle. They had returned to where they had attacked from, but remained just in front of the treeline. It appeared that King Donald's army was making ready to fight too. Jon and Einar knew they were outnumbered; it looked as if Princess Ceana was in more control than her own son.

Jon rode up to Einar; he had just decided what his own fate would be. "Clearly they are getting ready for battle. But you, Einar, you cannot go down that hill. You must take a few archers and ride hard back to Caithness, back to the castle, and warn Aud, because Ivar may come after her. I think he will come for her because our army has been split—especially if he has the backing of the king. I will lead the men into battle; it is the least I can do for Thorstein. I have failed both him and Aud miserably, and we both know we do not stand a chance of surviving, but we must delay Ivar from going after Aud. I have no choice, I must stay and fight him."

"I can't leave you like this, Jon."

"Yes you can, and you will—Aud must be warned! You have no choice but to leave, and to leave me with the rest of the men. Ride like the devil is behind you, because in reality he is here; we both know this to be true. First I must tell you—Aud has had a ship made in secret—she must use it now to flee. Ivar will gladly kill her and all of Thorstein's family—we both know that now. It appears Princess Ceana has her own

217

private army and she obviously supports Ivar because she hates Aud as well. So hurry, my good man! Give my undying love to my beautiful wife, Aud the Deep-Minded! Tell her we will meet again one day and sit on the right hand of God our Father."

Einar was hesitant to leave, but Jon was adamant. "You were made the *jarl* of the Hebrides, Einar, for a good reason. At this moment you have a great responsibilty: first, to save the islands and second, to protect Aud and Thorstein's family and to get them to that ship so they can sail to a safe place. Please hurry—promise me that you will go with her and protect her from anyone willing to do her harm." Einar finally succumbed to Jon's demands. He took ten archers with him and they rode off as if the devil was right on their tail.

Chapter 34

ud was in the library with Thuriður, who was still recuperating from childbirth, and the children. They were sitting by a roaring fire as the cold rain fell steadily outside, when they heard a loud commotion in the great hall. Someone was shouting for Queen Aud. She hurried towards the commotion with Thuriður and the children running behind. They were all curious to know what was going on. It had to be someone they knew; otherwise they would not have been allowed into the castle.

As they entered Einar was gasping for his breath. "In God's name Einar, what has happened?" Aud demanded.

Out of breath, the words tumbled from Einar's mouth, "Thorstein has been murdered! It was an ambush—Ivar ambushed us! We had no idea that he was even here in Scotland. Princess Ceana planned it all—her revenge against you was greater than we all thought possible!"

Shocked to the core, Aud stood like a frozen statue.

Still gasping, Einar continued, "You must realize that Jon and Thorstein went to meet Donald in good faith. King Donald would never have had the balls to ambush us or to renege on his deal with us. I truly believe he was as surprised as we were, because he shouted out *'Damn you mother!'* Only she would seek someone like Ivar—they are two of a kind. It could only have taken the devil himself to stir up this kind of trouble and there were two devils from hell there! There would have been three devils, but Aed was nowhere to be seen."

Thuriður and the children started howling with grief and fear as Aud, traumatized by the news, continued to stare into space. Einar gathered his wits about him as he realized that Aud was in shock, so he raised his voice to try and get through to her and shook her shoulders ever so slightly. "Aud—Aud!!—Listen to me!! Jon sends his undying love to you, but he will not return. He stayed to fight and to delay Ivar and Princess Ceana for as long as possible. He knows about your secret ship-building project and says now is the time to make use of it."

Aud's voice could be barely heard. "Jon knew?"

"Yes, of course he knew and now we have to gather together the people you planned to take on this ship and leave as quickly as possible."

Still she did not move. He shouted again to get her attention. "IVAR WILL COME AFTER YOU!" Then ever so softly, "You know that, don't you?"

He tightened his hold on her shoulders, trying to make her understand the danger they were all facing. She looked straight into his eyes and screamed at him. "DAMN HIM—DAMN HIM TO HELL! AND DAMN HER TO HELL! BOTH GOD AND I KNEW SHE WAS BAD NEWS!" She raised her arms in the air, heatedly questioning her God. "Ivar, of all people, has returned to haunt me once again. How could you do this to me—where are you when I need you the most!?"

Then she fell into Einar's arms and howled like a wounded animal. All Einar could do was to try and comfort her. Consoling her felt like it lasted forever, but in reality it was for a few moments only. She pulled away from him, shook her head and said. "*Jæja*! There is no time for mourning now, is there? So I was right after all. Maybe Donald could have been trusted, but he is still a weak king—and his mother! Well, that is another story! I just knew she was trouble and could not be trusted. But then there is no time to gloat either—not that I would ever want to—oh my God—how can I gloat over their mistaken judgement? I have lost them both, my only child and Jon, the loves of my life!"

Looking over at Thuriður, with a low guttural sound she lashed out. "Stop, this every one of you! Stop crying, there is no time for mourning, even though you have lost a husband." Realizing how harsh she sounded she took her daughter-in-law's hand in hers, then turned to the children and with a soft sad voice she tried to console them all. "And you my precious grandchildren—you no longer have a father. We have all lost a great man, all of us! Come everyone, Hord will take us to the secret place in the woods. There is a river there where we can launch the ship and escape northwards to one of the islands. I think we should head to the Orkneys first and inform *Jarl* Sigurd what has just come to pass. Einar, you can find a ship going to the Hebrides from there and warn them, and then sail to the other islands. You must warn everyone that Ivar is after us. He will have the might of the Scottish army behind him now, so he is a danger to us all. We must gather together all the wealth we can to take with us, so stop all this caterwauling and move quickly! Our lives may depend on our speed."

The people Aud promised to take with her consolidated what they could, then met in the courtyard where Einar and Hord organized carts to take them and the remaining family to the forest. Aud prayed that they would find a completed ship. All she could think of was saving what remained of her family, and as much of their moveable wealth as possible. With Einar's help, she was able to amass a great fortune to take with her. She ordered the remaining soldiers to close everything up and take what they could and ride to the coast where their ships were waiting. Once there, she told them to pack the ships with weapons and men, then sail to the Hebrides where Einar would meet them and decide how to divide all the force up between the islands.

To all the people Aud had promised to take to safety, she made this promise to God in front of them. "For the second time I must flee from Ivar. Why he hates me so, I do not know, but he is trying to kill me; that much I do know. He intends to destroy my dreams of glory and to obliterate everyone I hold dear. He failed the first time in Dubhlinn, but this time by killing my dear son he may have succeeded in sabotaging my dreams. I pray he fails to destroy what I have left of my family and of you, my friends. Let us bow our heads as we ask for God's help." Everyone did as she asked. "Dear God in heaven, we ask that you guide us, each and every one of us, pagan or Christian, safely to Iceland, our final destination. If you deem to do so, every year on our anniversary of landing I will erect a cross in thanks to your glory and righteousness. Amen."

Part III

Iceland

Do not be afraid; our fate cannot be taken from us; it is a gift.
Dante, 1265-1321

Part III

Iceland

Chapter 35

Orkneys

The shipload of people escaping Ivar's wrath limped into harbor in the Orkney Islands. Captain Einar had worked a miracle with a ship that was not quite ready to sail. *Jarl* Sigurd, too frail to meet them, promised them a safe haven and found them ship builders to repair the leaking ship that had been assembled in such haste. They felt safer here than in Scotland, so they planned to remain there while their ship was made more seaworthy. It needed to be made stronger and more able to fight the harsh northern waves, in order to take them on their long journey to Iceland, to the Land of Ice and Fire. To many pagans it was the land of the gods, but to Aud it was the land of safe harbour from the devil himself, Ivar the Hated. Aud prayed daily that he would not travel this far north to pursue her. As for Ceana, she had exacted a terrible revenge upon Aud's soul; her heart was torn apart from her losses. She had lost everything that mattered; even her Jon would not be able to return this time. This wicked princess had been instrumental in Olaf's death and now her involvement in Thorstein's demise appeared obvious, with the help of Ivar and some of the Scottish people. Christian or not, hatred for this woman was lodged in Aud's heart, and appeared to be set to rest there for an eternity.

Even though her heart was heavy with sadness, within days of arriving Aud saw the opportunity to arrange a marriage between Groa, her oldest granddaughter, and Thorfinn, son of *Jarl turf* Einar and the youngest grandson of Rognvald, *jarl* of both Mores and Romsdal. This man Rognvald may have been her father's old enemy, but Thorfinn, his grandson, had nothing to do with her father's animosity towards this Norwegian *jarl*. Sigurd, who knew he was not long for this world, was given the opportunity to make peace with his son Guttorm, who had recently arrived with his young cousin Thorfinn, the *jarl's* great-nephew. With this cleansing of anger against his son, Sigurd had reinstated him as his heir but made it clear that he would have to report to Thorstein, who was king of all the Islands and of northern Scotland. Guttorm had no problem with that, as he too did not expect to be long in this life. He had many injuries, some of which he realized too late that he might never recover from—injuries obtained in battles he fought with his uncle Rognvald for King Harold.

Childless, Guttorm asked that when he was gone, Thorfinn would become *jarl* after him.

Sigurd's son, Guttorm, had been there for several months, not just to heal—he had been diligently working to re-establish a father/son connection. Meanwhile, Thorfinn was learning about the Orkneys and all the other islands. Father and son had much to say to each other; Guttorm deeply regretted his harsh judgement of the Orkneys. He blamed his young age, saying that he was easily swayed by the drama that was happening in Norway during King Harold's siege of all its lands. To him it was a very exciting time, and now he saw that because of all that feverish activity, the many battles he fought in the king's name only to receive nothing much in return from him, was a serious mistake. All that action did was to shorten his life. His uncle had children and grandchildren too numerous to give him much, but he did give him a small fortune to take with him to the Orkneys, to share with his father. He also asked if he would take his grandson, Thorfinn, to foster him and hopefully find a place for him there. As a future *jarl*, Guttorm did well by his cousin.

All these agreements had taken place before the news of Thorstein's death arrived with Aud, devastating the frail *jarl*. Thorstein had been like a son to him, and his dream of making him a great king was now dead as well. Several days after the arrival of Aud, he woke early as normal, said his usual good morning in his booming voice to his slave, then promptly closed his eyes and died. It appeared life was no longer worth living for the *jarl*. During the funeral feast that followed, Aud approached Guttorm about a possible union between Thorfinn and Groa. There was no hesitation from either side. Groa was not only a beautiful woman, with a family tree of many notable people, but she had wealth as well. Aud and her mother had seen to that. Although they had known this young man for those few days only, they both liked what they saw and were confident that it would be a good match. What made it even better was that Groa seemed to be quite taken with him. It was a win-win contract; Groa was to be united with a man who would one day be a leader of the Orkneys, and for Thorfinn, well, he was soon to marry the daughter of a king.

Despite her triumph over this match, Aud felt torn between Freya's power of destiny and God's divine justice; where had this come from? With all the grief she was experiencing she was beginning to question her belief in God. Had Freya drawn a destiny of power and wealth for this young man and woman despite the hatred Ketill, Groa's grandfather, had felt towards Rognvald, Thorfinn's grandfather? Or was it God's distributive justice, where each creature gets what they need to fulfill their purpose in life? Regardless of who had the power, the pagan gods and goddesses or God himself, Thorfinn and Groa were moving forward with their lives, joined together in matrimony, and Aud had just begun her years of matchmaking.

According to Guttorm it would take a month to arrange this marriage. First, both he and Thorfinn must honour and grieve the death of *Jarl* Sigurd, and only then did he feel it would be honourable for his cousin to marry. Both women respected his wishes, especially since he had extended hospitality to them all. They felt it was necessary to stay and see it through. Shortly after the funeral, Einar left for the Hebrides to meet up with the men Aud had ordered to leave Scotland. He promised to find even more men to help protect the Orkneys and the other islands. A few days after his leaving they sighted some ships—many ships, in fact. They held their breath, hoping that they were friends and not foes.

To her utter disbelief it was Jon himself, with the men who had travelled to the meeting with him and Thorstein!! Shaking violently, she went to greet him as he walked down the gangplank, praying she would not collapse from happiness and relief. "How is this possible, Jon? For the second time in my life I thought you dead! Yet here you are!"

"Ahhh but I am quite alive, my dear and very grateful to see you still here. All will be explained and soon—very soon, I promise. First we need to speak with Sigurd."

"Sadly, my love he just passed. He simply closed his eyes and died; he was that grieved when hearing the news about Thorstein. His son Guttorm is now the new *jarl* of the Orkneys. You won't believe this, but while here I have arranged a marriage contract between Sigurd's great-nephew, Thorfinn, son of *Jarl turf* Einar, with my granddaughter Groa. They are to be married within a month and because I wanted to see it through is the only reason we are all still here. Otherwise you may have missed us."

"God is near and watching over us. Your dynastic obsession is all that can slow you down, it seems. For that I must be forever thankful."

He smiled at her lovingly. Aud could not help herself, giggling like a young girl as she slipped her arm through his. "Oh my God Jon, how could I possibly live without you or your sarcastic remarks. With my grief I was beginning to doubt God's very existence but here you are, flesh and blood. For that I am eternally grateful. Thanks be to God!"

He later explained it all to her. Apparently Donald III was not in on this attack. He even turned out to be stronger than they first thought when it came to his mother. "King Donald was furious with his mother's interference. He has put her under house arrest and sent her under guard to a convent located in the middle of nowhere, where she has been ordered to live out her days. Whether that will be carried out is another thing, but for now she is there. He has strongly advised her to pray daily for forgiveness for destroying his dream and for her part in the death of his half-brother, even though she pleaded ignorance of the intended murder. No words were needed from either of us, as we both believe she knew what was going to happen. In front of us all he publicly stripped her of her wealth, all her estates, land and jewels, and ordered her to live simply as a nun. She argued her case by claiming to be looking after his interests, firmly stating that in her mind he should rightfully be king of all Scotland. Like you, she too did not like the idea of cousins marrying each other. Her aunt Aed also played a part in the ambush. She also thought that he should not share his kingship with Thorstein, and since she was in contact with Ivar, she enlisted his help. They communicated through secret letters, no less. Can you not see now the power the written word has, Aud? A few years ago she managed to convince Ivar that she had nothing to do with him being chased out of Strathclyde or with him losing his crown there. All through letters—the written word! Apparently she claimed undying love for him and a man already in love is easy to convince, don't you think? I know I would be! And to think there was no need to talk face-to-face to develop this treacherous plan. All this time King Donald was ignorant of their renewed relationship. During our negotiations, Ceana looked like the innocent bystander. Meanwhile, with her urgings, it was her aunt working behind the scenes, in her name, under cover of the written word. Incredible that they got away with it."

"Hummrff! Incredible—I think it is unbelievable! I always knew that they were devious women and neither one of you would listen to me! They had to have had strong support within Donald's court. What do you have to say about that?"

"Not much I can say, my love—you are right once again! Once all the confusion settled and it became clear that Princess Ceana was involved, it did not take long for Duncan the Maormor to claim Caithness in his name. Remember, it belonged to his uncle before the battles fought by your father and Thorstein to gain control of that northern land. I suspect she was aware of his ambitions and had enlisted his help. There are probably others too, but I did not stay around long enough to find out. With Duncan's demands, King Donald was left in a precarious situation: to either work with this man, Duncan of Maormor, or to be fighting with a force whose power he could not fully estimate at this stage. He had no choice but to agree. Fortunately he was smart enough to concede—on condition that he become the king of all Scotland and that Duncan become his *jarl* of Caithness. He is now the one and only King of Scotland, even though he did not intend this, but we both know that it is just what his mother always wanted."

Aud's only answer was a whisper, "So Ceana won in the end! With the devil's help!"

"I can never forgive myself for your son's death, but I want you to know that I managed to bring him home to Caithness and I have buried him on a hill close by, in a mound. Donald made Duncan agree that wherever I was to bury Thorstein it would become a place of honour and would be maintained by him and by all his ancestors. Duncan did agree to that. There is to be a stone on the mound that states "Thorstein the Red, King of Northern Scotland, lies here," all engraved with the runic alphabet. I hope you will forgive me but I also had his name and date of death engraved on it in Gaelic so all the Scots would know just whose grave it is. A great man, a great warrior-king, who was like a son to me. Because of his death I will be begging your forgiveness every day of my life from now on."

"Another thing that became clear afterwards was that he, and only he, appeared to be targeted, and if he hadn't been murdered on our day of agreement it would have happened at a later date. It was going to happen no matter what we did. I suspect that this expert archer was one and the same who killed Olaf, pointing both father and son's death directly at Princess Ceana. Even though both Donald and I believe this to be true, he still protected his mother to some extent. He claims that she is mentally unstable and blames himself for not recognizing it. I have in my possession a small trunk with precious stones, as well as silver and gold for you from Donald. It is *wergild,* most likely taken from Ceana's wealth for the death of Thorstein, but it is Donald who is asking for forgiveness, not his mother. I also brought *Fotbitr* with me, which I expect will be handed down to Olaf one day."

"*Fotbitr*—yes! As for that nasty woman or her son, I don't want anything from them! I hope they both rot in hell! I pray that their dreams become only nightmares that will torture them till they die! The only godsend here is that my granddaughter Groa will not have to marry her own cousin."

"Don't be too hasty, or too nasty for that matter. This *wergild* may become a godsend; you have many other grandchildren to marry off and if you insist that they marry only wealth and power, you too will have to bring wealth to the table. Think carefully before you put a hex on them. You never have to touch this blood money, though. I will take care of it. It will be a great negotiating tool."

Aud grumbled something under her breathe. Jon ignored her comment and continued with his description of events. "Back to the battle. At first there was so much confusion, nobody knew which way to turn or who to go after, until Donald himself waved a white flag, then sent an emissary to talk to us. Once it was clear that Donald had nothing to do with the attack, with his army backing us we quickly gave chase to Ivar, but soon realized that there was no point in pursuing him; he was long gone! He was nowhere to be found. He remained by the treeline for a good reason and must have left as soon as he saw a white flag appear. Princess Ceana did not have the power over her son that she claimed, and he realized that right away. However, I am sure he thinks he has won, that with the death of your son he has destroyed you as well."

"The opportunity was just too tempting for him; why else would he have accepted this hair-brained plan? Aed was not there for the meeting, but Donald suspected that his sister had already fled and probably planned to join up with Ivar at some private location. With Ivar in charge, guaranteed there would have been a back-up plan. They are well matched, those two. I don't think she has ever forgiven her brother for forcing her to marry Artgal's cousin after Ivar was forced to flee Strathclyde. With Ivar being a pagan, their marriage was not viewed legal in the eyes of the royal family, even though they married in the church. Her brother forced her to marry Artgal's cousin again, this time with the full blessings of the church. That was the only way she could retain her title and the wealth that went with it. Her status, wealth and power was all she had to look forward to after Ivar left, so she accepted this unwelcome marriage. This cousin was an old man and did not much care for her, so I am told. I imagine she was very unhappy, what with the love of her life gone for good, or so she thought. Olaf was right about them; she had really fallen for Ivar and obviously he loved her too. Now I understand some of his intense anger when he came back to Dubhlinn. It is hard to believe that such a man could love with such intensity, only to think that this love of his had deceived him. Where was their trust in each other? What pain must he have gone through? He had to take it out on someone and obviously chose you. I truly believe that he would have gone through with marrying you and then would have slowly destroyed both you and Thorstein with his hatred of Aed. Now look at them—probably both fleeing off together somewhere! Life is constantly full of surprises, isn't it?"

"Nightmares is more like it! But I really do appreciate that you buried Thorstein, *takk,* and returned with *Fotbitr.* I had such terrible dreams, one where he was left to the ravens—horrible, horrible dreams. Now, since you think Ivar will most likely not pursue us, do we need to go all the way to Iceland as I originally planned? On the other hand, there is no good reason to return to Scotland, since Donald has given that seat away to Duncan of Maormor. Perhaps it is not worth even returning to the Hebrides. There is a good man in place there, *Jarl* Einar, who has Una running the estate for him as efficiently as before. Where should we go?"

"Let us sleep on it, and then you can tell me in the morning how you feel. You never know—you just may have a dream that tells us what we should do."

"My heart is breaking in two for the loss of my son, but at the same time soaring with joy to have you alive and well. These contrasting emotions have torn me apart; I am exhausted. Let us go to our room, I need to have a bath and rest, dear heart."

Previously she had shared a large room with some of the grandchildren, but had quickly asked for one just for them. Arm in arm they walked off to their newly appointed room, where she hoped to have a decision made as to where they should sail to. They had a good rest, so later that evening they were able to enjoy the *nattmal* with their friends and family. That night, dream she did. The past few days she had gone through so much turmoil, still grieving for her son, she was not surprised that she dreamt of a volcanic eruption. In the morning while they lay engulfed in each other's arms she told him what her decision was. "Iceland seems to have been my destiny all along, my love."

"Iceland it is, then."

Chapter 36

Iceland

Now that Groa was safely married off, they made arrangements to sail only as far as the Faroe Islands, to test the reliability of their newly repaired ship. They arrived safely; their ship had no issues, so they expected it to be a short stay only. The most prominent family there offered hospitality to Aud and Jon, which included all of their followers. They gratefully accepted. The hosts were very gracious and before anyone realized it, Aud had arranged another marriage contract. This time it was for Olof, the next oldest granddaughter. Thuriður, her mother, realized that it was a very good match, but did point out that she was still quite young. Negotiations continued; the family were anxious for their son to become connected to a family with such prestige. They offered to foster her until she became of age and promised to have a grand celebration for their union. With Jon's urgings, both Thuriður and Aud brought some of the *wergild* to the table, and all was settled quickly. Now confident their repaired ship would take them to their destination, they left the Faroe Islands expecting a smooth voyage.

They experienced no issues; the weather cooperated and after only a few days they could see Iceland in the distance. Excitement began to mount for all as the land got closer, but the island played tricks on them. Shrouded in a light mist with a strange darkness in the distance, it looked like they were almost there, yet it was still far away. Suddenly out of nowhere that darkness moved forward with a speed unlike anything they had seen before. It turned out to be black angry clouds, which began to form shapes like arms from either side of the island, threatening to beat away the arrival of their ship. Their excitement was suddenly replaced by fear. What was happening here? They were so close! Was this land of the gods telling them that they were not welcome here? These black arms suddenly mushroomed into a thick wall of clouds, which began to race towards them, threatening to engulf them. Weirdly shaped clouds appeared to be coming from all directions, with sudden furious winds that created swells that almost swamped their ship with each passing. The people began shouting to each other that they were not welcome on this island, the gods were refusing them entry. Jon, the appointed captain, shouted for the men to lower the sail and they this did just in time to see the mast snap in half. The broken part of the mast just missed sweeping young Olaf out of the ship and into the raging sea. Jon grabbed him in time and brought him to Aud, who had gathered the girls into the bow of the ship. There they quickly wrapped the rope around each other, then tied the end of it to a metal ring and huddled together with arms tightly wrapped around one another. Aud bravely whispered assurances to them, saying 'God was with them', and 'do not be afraid', but afraid they were, every one of them—even Aud herself.

"Row hard—our lives depend on it!" Jon ordered. The men set the oars out and started to row, battling the wind, cresting each wave with a determination to get to the island safely. Many began to pray loudly, shouting out to their Lord God to protect them. The swells started to increase in size. As they crested each one the men were rowing just air, then they would start their slide down into the deep troughs between each wave, which threatened to swallow them up. However, instead of disappearing into the blackness, they began to crest the next swell. They were such amateur sailors, their rowing had no effect, yet their efforts to keep their ship heading towards the shores of Iceland were nothing but heroic. With their valiant efforts, they appeared to be getting closer, but at the same time not close enough.

Suddenly a larger than normal swell lifted them higher than ever in the air. Thinking this was definitely the end, women and children began to scream with fear while the men continued to row just air. They didn't know what else to do. Suddenly any fears Aud had had before this wave left her. Smiling to herself, she felt only complete calmness because she felt the presence of Unn, the goddess of the frothing waves. "Fear not children, for it is only Unn herself. I can feel her—she is here—she will save us." The children did not hear those words, what with their screams and the roaring winds, but she was confident all would be well. Unn and her sisters were here with them, they had arrived to save them all.

The freak gale that was blowing through was forcing them into a rough landing at Virarskeid on the south shore of Iceland. The last swell that they were riding so high brought them in closer to shore than they realized, and then suddenly broke and slid back into the sea. The ship hit the sand bar just metres from the shoreline with such a force that the ship fell apart on impact. They heard the hulk of the ship crack and groan as it dug itself deep into the sandbar. Their ship was destroyed on impact, but thankfully the ship's deck was still intact—for now.

With no time to waste, Hord came up to Jon. "I will go ashore with a rope; we do not know how deep that water is between this sandbar and the shore. That way the women and children can hang onto it for safety as they come ashore."

"Good idea, Hord."

Before he scrambled overboard with the rope he tied one end to a metal ring that supported one of the oars closest to the bow of their ship. For a tall man, he still had to wade through water up to his chest to get to the shoreline, making it clear to all that it would be too deep for many. An adult would need to go with each child to keep their heads above water. This rope would not only serve as a guide rope for them; it would also give them support from the swirling waves that were breaking over the ship lodged in the sandbar, creating treacherous whirlpools between them and the shore. He fought hard to get through them and when he finally got to the shore he found a rock, secured the other end to it and returned to help with the women and children.

Aud pushed all the children towards Jon as she tried to unwrap them from the heavy sodden rope. They were soaking wet and still crying with fear and he could see that they were also all shivering with the cold, but there was nothing he could do about that just now. Jon tried to reassure Aud and the children, "This ship is clearly going nowhere—it is so deep into the sand it is here to stay. We just need to concentrate on getting ourselves ashore and finding a safe place to set up our tents and light a fire. Then we can bring our boxes and trunks inside to dry out; meanwhile they are safe enough here onboard, they are tied up tight. Trust me, we are safe now, all we need to do is hold hands and wait for our turn to leave." Soaking wet, everyone finally made it onto the shore, where many collapsed with relief and exhaustion. The men set out to build a huge fire with the timber found onshore from their broken ship, so that the women and children could dry out and warm themselves. Two of the men dragged a huge piece of driftwood close for them to sit on near the fire.

Jon, Hord, and the other men just kept moving. It took many hours to set up the tents and empty the ship, during which time the threatening clouds had disappeared as fast as they had come, allowing the bright summer sun to reappear, welcoming them all to their new homeland. This dazzling sun lifted everyone's spirits and spurred the hard-working people onwards to complete their tasks, drying their clothes as they scurried about. Steam floated off their bodies as their clothing slowly absorbed the warmth from the sun; with everyone in different positions either lifting, carrying, or kneeling, it made them look like characters from their mythological stories. The children had a glorious time naming these characters while enjoying the warmth of the fire and chewing on *hardfisku*.

A local farmer showed up with his two sons, not long after their dramatic arrival, each riding their own horse. One was carrying a keg of *skyr*, while the other two each carried a bag, one of food and the other with dried peat moss so they could light more fires. Fortunately the storm had not put out all of their fire pots, but the dry peat would definitely help build other much-needed fires. They did not bring water but told them where to find fresh water from a stream close by. Once the older children were dried off they were given the small chore of fetching fresh water.

Later that evening as the sun was starting to take its leave, Aud and Jon were walking back to their allocated spot, each carrying the last of their items to set into their newly erected tent. They stopped to survey all the work that had been accomplished in such a short time. In front of them stood a miniature village of tents, already with smoke curling out of their tops. They both set down what they were carrying and automatically made the sign of the cross. Jon spoke first. "God has delivered us safely. Glory be to God, to the Holy Ghost and to his Son our Lord and Saviour. Amen!"

Aud looked over at the man she held so dear. "God did not save us, Jon! Believe it or not, I truly felt the presence of my old goddess, Unn. That frothing wave that delivered us onto that sandbar to safety was her; I felt the presence of her sisters as well. What does that mean to me as a Christian? Am I a faithless wench?"

"Faithless? Never, my love, but I do believe you may have felt her presence, for this is a pagan land after all. Our Lord often works in mysterious ways; powerful and mighty as he is, he may have enlisted pagan help and they worked together. What do you think of that?"

"Jon, you are a wonder!" She slipped her arm through his, "the important thing is we have arrived—we are all safe—that is all that matters to me at this point. We are here in a land where people have already shown us kindness. This land is mostly filled with pagans who believe it to be the land of their gods, a land of ice and fire. I can feel the old magic and pull of my pagan beliefs here very strongly and I know that Unn is reaching out to me. We agreed that our first cross to glorify God will be erected on this very shore. This cross can be made from wood retrieved from our shattered ship, which will make it even more memorable. There is plenty of good timber available for us now, my love, so our first chore must be to retrieve what we can before the sea takes it all away from us."

Jon answered her. "Hord and I already discussed collecting what we can."

"Good, but what I want you to know, and you will not change my mind on this, is that I plan to dedicate it to both our Christian god and to Unn the Goddess of the Frothing Waves, who really carried us safely to the shore of our destination. In a way you have agreed with me when you tried to claim that the Lord may have asked for her help but I, personally, need to acknowledge her. There will be pagan symbols as well as Christian ones engraved on our first cross. What do you say to that?"

"I cannot argue with you, Aud my Deep-Minded! Our pagan neighbours must be acknowledged and we need to let them know that we are not here to change their way of life."

"*Takk*—I do believe that our destiny was always here—in Iceland."

Jon took her hands in his, kissing them both with warm lips full of love for this incredible woman.

Epilogue

ith the help of the farmer who brought them *skyr* and food she was able to locate her brother Helgi. She went to him first, because he was closer and she thought that as a fellow Christian, he would put them all up for the winter. He only offered her, Jon and seven others hospitality. Offended by his unkind offer she walked away stating, "I did not expect such stinginess from a brother Christian and a blood brother; you have disappointed me greatly, Helgi." With that said they went off to find her other brother Bjorn, who was a pagan; he greeted her with open arms and offered hospitality to all of them for the whole winter. They were treated like royalty. This pleased her and she thanked him profusely for his generosity. Aud enjoyed her stay there immensely because her Thora*min* lived there. Now a mother of four, she appeared to be content with her life in Iceland. Aud felt gratified with her matchmaking abilities, what with more grandchildren to intercede for.

In the spring she walked the land in Breidafjord and claimed the largest tract of land, more than any other settler ever had before her. Eventually she built a farm on part of it and named it Hvammur, where she lived with Jon and the remaining grandchildren. Not long after she was settledm she freed all her slaves and gave them all land. To Hord, her friend and servant of many years, she gave all of Hordadal. To all the other freed slaves she also gave land, where they all farmed and raised notable families.

Every year with Jon's help they erected a new cross somewhere on her massive tract of land in thanks to God, but Aud continued in her mission to include a pagan symbol with each one—to show her respect for her goddess Unn and respect for the peoples of this pagan land.

Aud the Deep-Minded's dream of creating a family tree with a legacy of kings and queens may have died with her son Thorstein the Red—but her dream of power and wealth did not die; that became a reality. Through her ambitious plan of marrying off all her grandchildren into prominent families only, she ended up creating a bloodline of power in the Orkneys, the Faroe Islands and in Iceland that lasted for several centuries.

One cannot help but wonder: if Aud Unn had remained faithful to her pagan gods and goddesses instead of becoming a Christian and becoming known as Aud the Deep-Minded, would those pagan gods have fulfilled her dynastic dream of kings and queens? Her Christian God seemed to have failed her. Only Unn and her sisters know for sure! Meanwhile, the frothing waves continue their relentless journey northwards, while some divert and crash into a black granite wall as they persist in their efforts to wake the sleeping troll.

The End.

Acknowledgements

I am deeply grateful to my family and friends for their unwavering support and to the ones who took the time to read my manuscript in its many forms. A special thank you to the Icelandic Roots Genealogy group; their database is a treasure trove for anyone with an interest in Iceland, its history and its sagas.

Takk fyrir

Bibliography

https://www.bbc.com/news/uk-scotland-north-east-orkney-shetland-49250718?fbclid=IwAR2PW6LHmfK5Th8bDXIrinrkGrT27z09KzAyvlGmbnImqJOs9y37YRRU3_g

http://www.hurstwic.org/history/articles/society/text/raids.htm

https://www.icelandicroots.com/

http://www.irelands-hidden-gems.com/tara.html

https://www.knowth.com/tara.htm

https://regia.org/research/ships/Ships1.htm

https://www.ranker.com/list/viking-berserker-facts/philgibbons

The Sagas of Icelanders: a selection / preface by Jane Smiley; introduction by Robert Kellogg. Viking Publishing, 2000.

https://www.scotclans.com/what-did-the-picts-really-wear/

http://www.wesleyjohnston.com/users/ireland/past/pre_norman_history/vikings.html

Author Biography

This is my second book, where I have once again borrowed characters from the ancient Icelandic manuscript, *Laxædala Saga*. I am married and live in Calgary, Alberta where I am working on my third novel. We have one son who is married with two daughters and lives in Calgary as well. I use the pen name of Alfreða Jonsdottir—why? Jonsdottir literally means that I am the daughter of Jon (John) so I do this in honour of my father Gudjon John. I hold an honours diploma from SAIT in Library and Information Management.

Author Biography

Made in the USA
Middletown, DE
23 January 2023

22878792R00146